THE HARDY BOYS

WITHDRAWN

PAPERCUTZ ™

THE HARDY BOYS GRAPHIC NOVELS FROM PAPERCUTZ

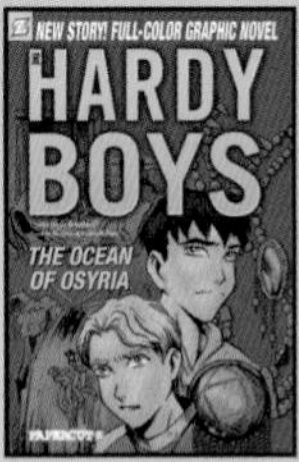
NEW STORY! FULL-COLOR GRAPHIC NOVEL
HARDY BOYS
THE OCEAN OF OSYRIA
PAPERCUTZ

#1"The Ocean of Osyria"

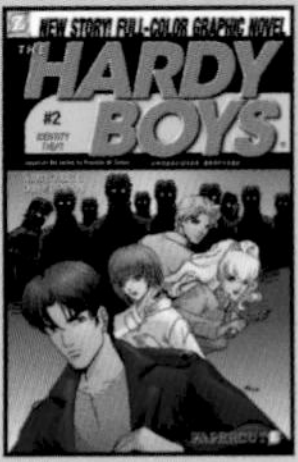
NEW STORY! FULL-COLOR GRAPHIC NOVEL
THE HARDY BOYS
#2
PAPERCUTZ

#2 "Identity Theft"

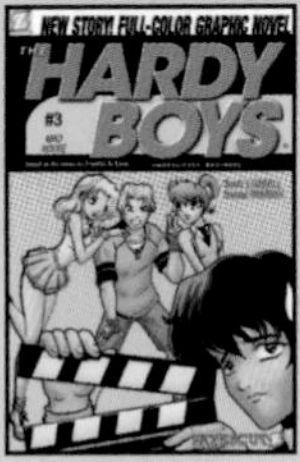
NEW STORY! FULL-COLOR GRAPHIC NOVEL
THE HARDY BOYS
#3
PAPERCUTZ

#3 "Mad House"

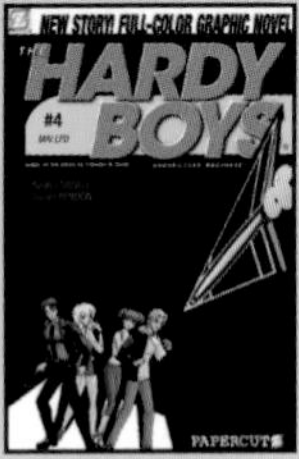
NEW STORY! FULL-COLOR GRAPHIC NOVEL
THE HARDY BOYS
#4
PAPERCUTZ

#4 "Malled"

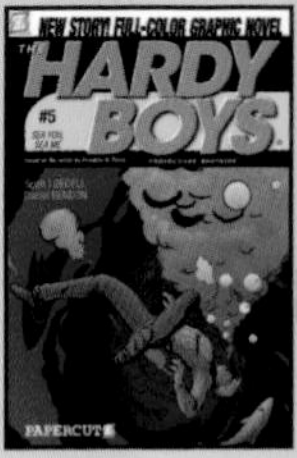
NEW STORY! FULL-COLOR GRAPHIC NOVEL
THE HARDY BOYS
#5
PAPERCUTZ

#5 "Sea You, Sea Me!"

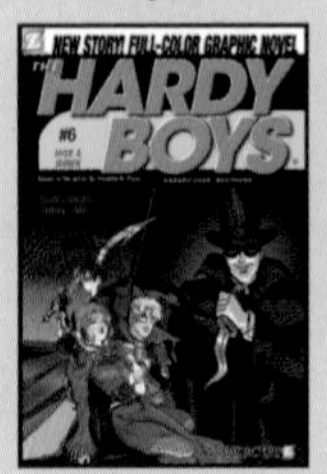
NEW STORY! FULL-COLOR GRAPHIC NOVEL
THE HARDY BOYS
#6
PAPERCUTZ

#6 "Hyde & Shriek"

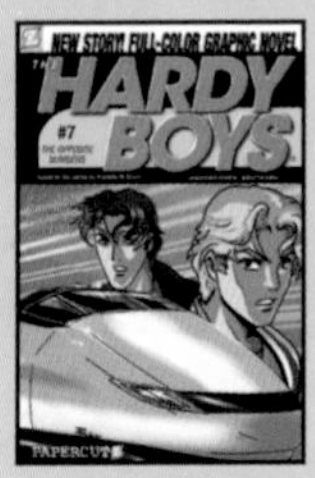
NEW STORY! FULL-COLOR GRAPHIC NOVEL
THE HARDY BOYS
#7
PAPERCUTZ

#7 "The Opposite Numbers"

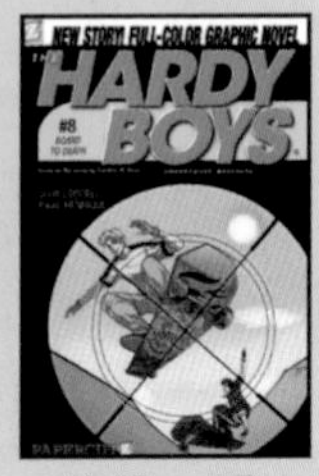
NEW STORY! FULL-COLOR GRAPHIC NOVEL
THE HARDY BOYS
#8
PAPERCUTZ

#8 "Board To Death"

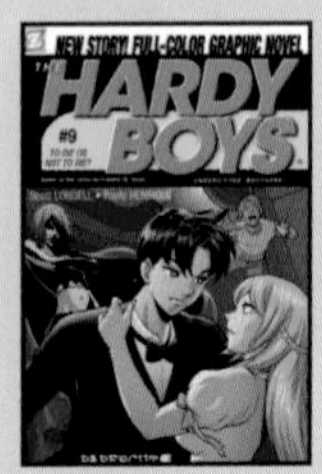
NEW STORY! FULL-COLOR GRAPHIC NOVEL
THE HARDY BOYS
#9
PAPERCUTZ

#9 "To Die Or Not To Die?"

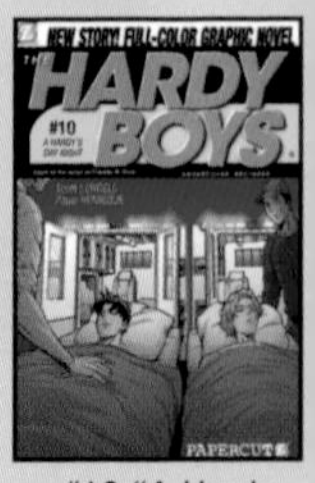
NEW STORY! FULL-COLOR GRAPHIC NOVEL
THE HARDY BOYS
#10
PAPERCUTZ

#10 "A Hardy Day's Night"

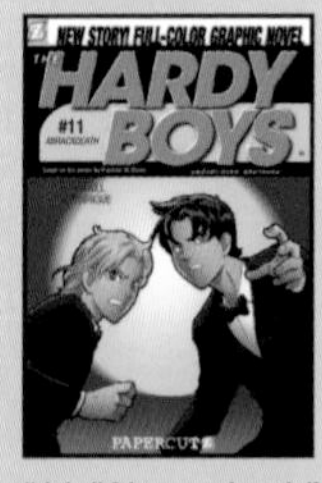
NEW STORY! FULL-COLOR GRAPHIC NOVEL
THE HARDY BOYS
#11
PAPERCUTZ

#11 "Abracadeath"

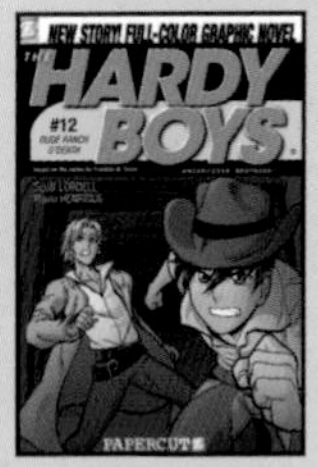
NEW STORY! FULL-COLOR GRAPHIC NOVEL
THE HARDY BOYS
#12
PAPERCUTZ

#12 "Dude Ranch O' Death!"

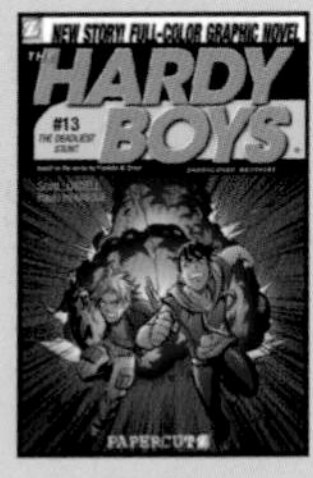
NEW STORY! FULL-COLOR GRAPHIC NOVEL
THE HARDY BOYS
#13
PAPERCUTZ

#13 "The Deadliest Stunt"

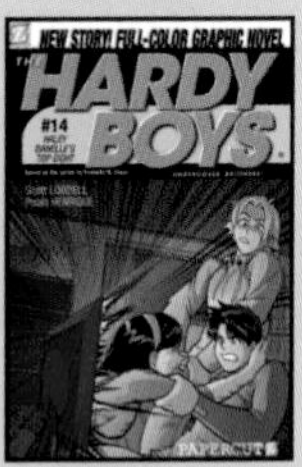
NEW STORY! FULL-COLOR GRAPHIC NOVEL
THE HARDY BOYS
#14
PAPERCUTZ

#14 "Haley Danelle's Top Eight!"

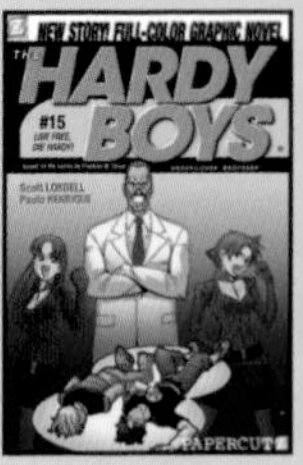
NEW STORY! FULL-COLOR GRAPHIC NOVEL
THE HARDY BOYS
#15
PAPERCUTZ

#15 "Live Free, Die Hardy!"

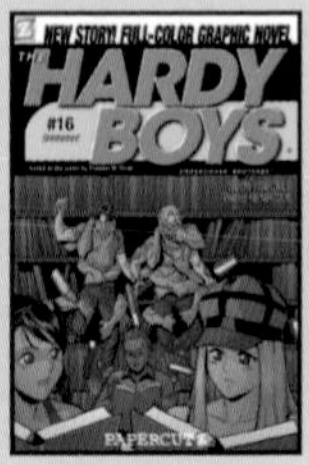
NEW STORY! FULL-COLOR GRAPHIC NOVEL
THE HARDY BOYS
#16
PAPERCUTZ

#16 "Shhhhhh!"

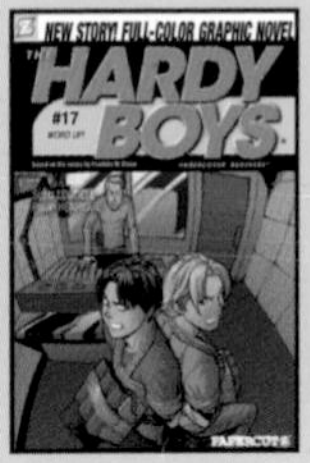
NEW STORY! FULL-COLOR GRAPHIC NOVEL
THE HARDY BOYS
#17
PAPERCUTZ

#17 "Word Up!"

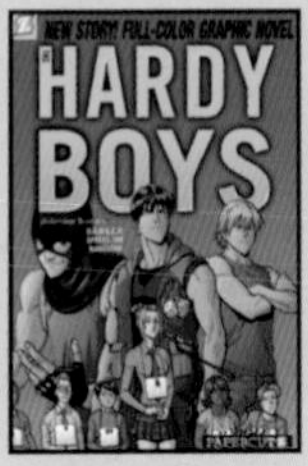
NEW STORY! FULL-COLOR GRAPHIC NOVEL
HARDY BOYS
PAPERCUTZ

#18 "D.A.N.G.E.R Spells the Hangman"

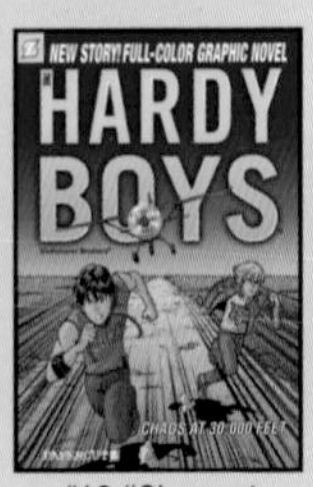
NEW STORY! FULL-COLOR GRAPHIC NOVEL
HARDY BOYS
CHAOS AT 30,000 FEET
PAPERCUTZ

#19 "Chaos at 30,000 Feet"

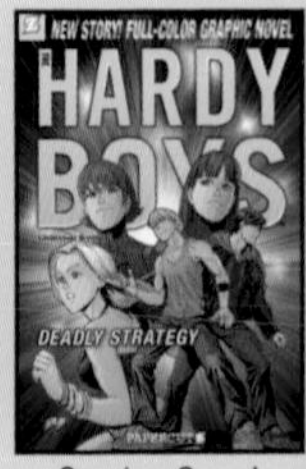
NEW STORY! FULL-COLOR GRAPHIC NOVEL
HARDY BOYS
DEADLY STRATEGY
PAPERCUTZ

Coming Soon!
#20 "Deadly Strategy"

$7.95 each in paperback, $12.95 each in hardcover except #20, $8.99pb/$13.99hc.
Please add $4.00 for postage and handling for the first book, add $1.00 for each additional book. Please make check payable to NBM Publishing. Send to: **Papercutz, 40 Exchange Place, Suite 1308, New York, NY 10005 • 1-800-886-1223 • www.papercutz.com**

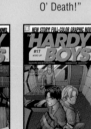

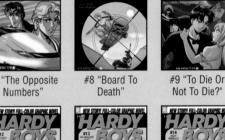

THE HARDY BOYS

Undercover Brothers®

#19 *Chaos at 30,000 Feet!*

SCOTT LOBDELL • Writer
PAULO HENRIQUE MARCONDES • Artist

Based on the series by
FRANKLIN W. DIXON

New York

Chaos at 30,000 Feet!
SCOTT LOBDELL — Writer
PAULO HENRIQUE MARCONDES — Artist
MARK LERER — Letterer
LAURIE E. SMITH — Colorist
MIKHAELA REID & MASHEKA WOOD— Production
MICHAEL PETRANEK — Editorial Assistant
JIM SALICRUP
Editor-in-Chief

ISBN: 978-1-59707-169-7 paperback edition
ISBN: 978-1-59707-170-3 hardcover edition

Published by arrangement with Aladdin Paperbacks,
an imprint of Simon & Schuster Children's Publishing Division.

Printed in Korea
December 2009 by Tara TPS
192-1 Sangjisuk-ri, Kyoha-eub,
Paju-si, Kyunggi-do
Korea 413-836

Distributed by Macmillan.

10 9 8 7 6 5 4 3 2 1

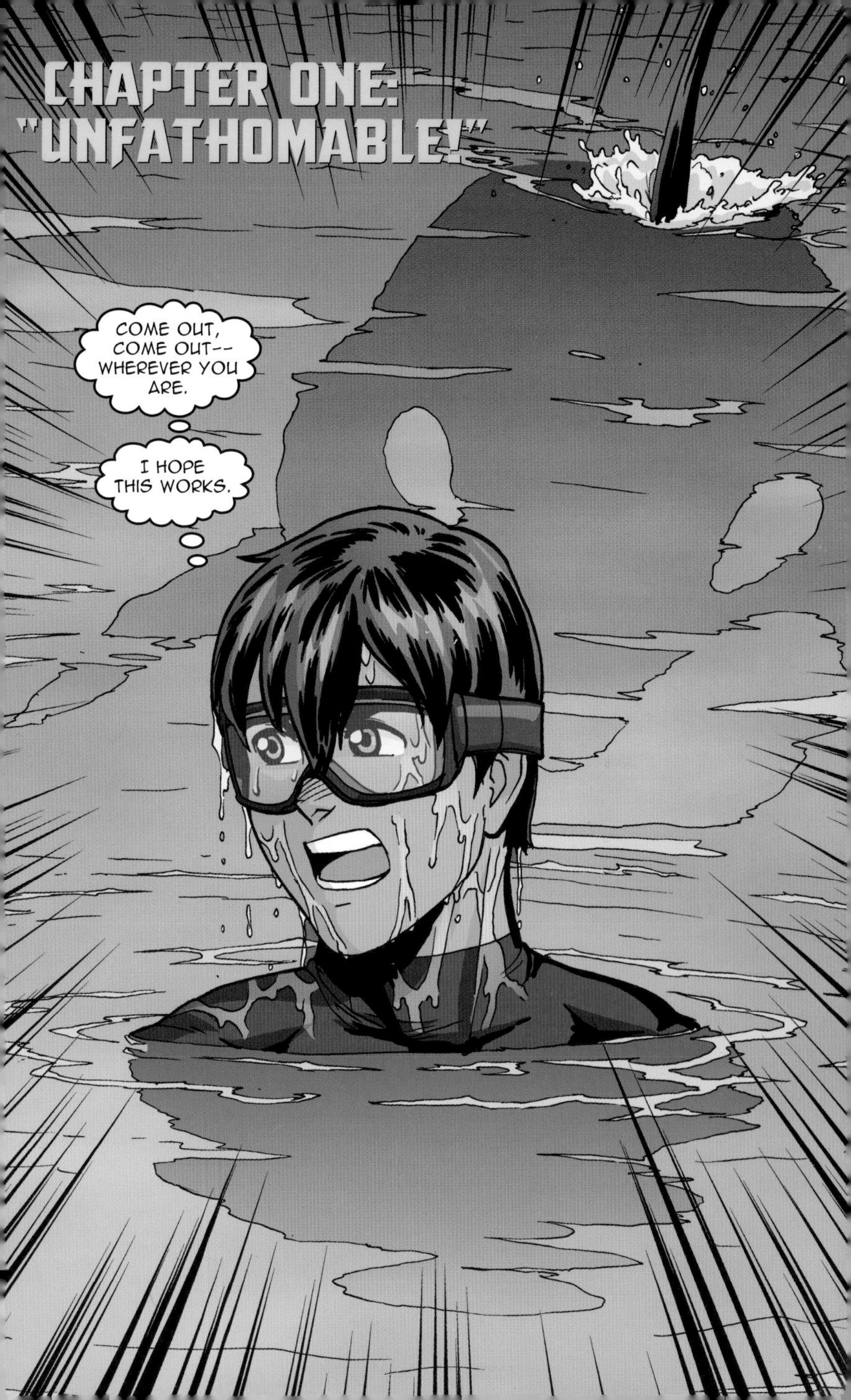
CHAPTER ONE:
"UNFATHOMABLE!"
COME OUT, COME OUT-- WHEREVER YOU ARE.
I HOPE THIS WORKS.

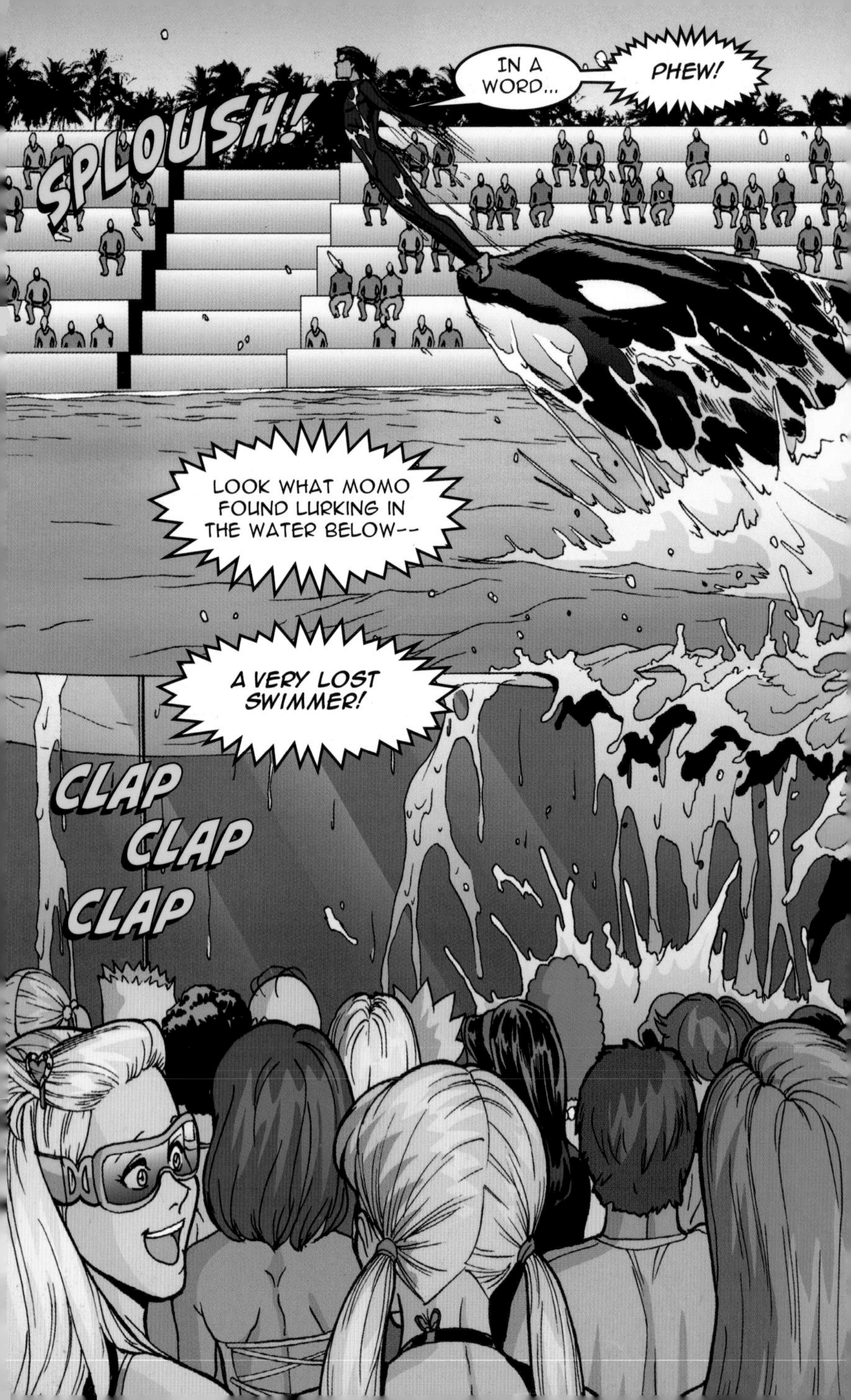
SPLOUSH!
IN A WORD...
PHEW!
LOOK WHAT MOMO FOUND LURKING IN THE WATER BELOW--
A VERY LOST SWIMMER!
CLAP
CLAP
CLAP

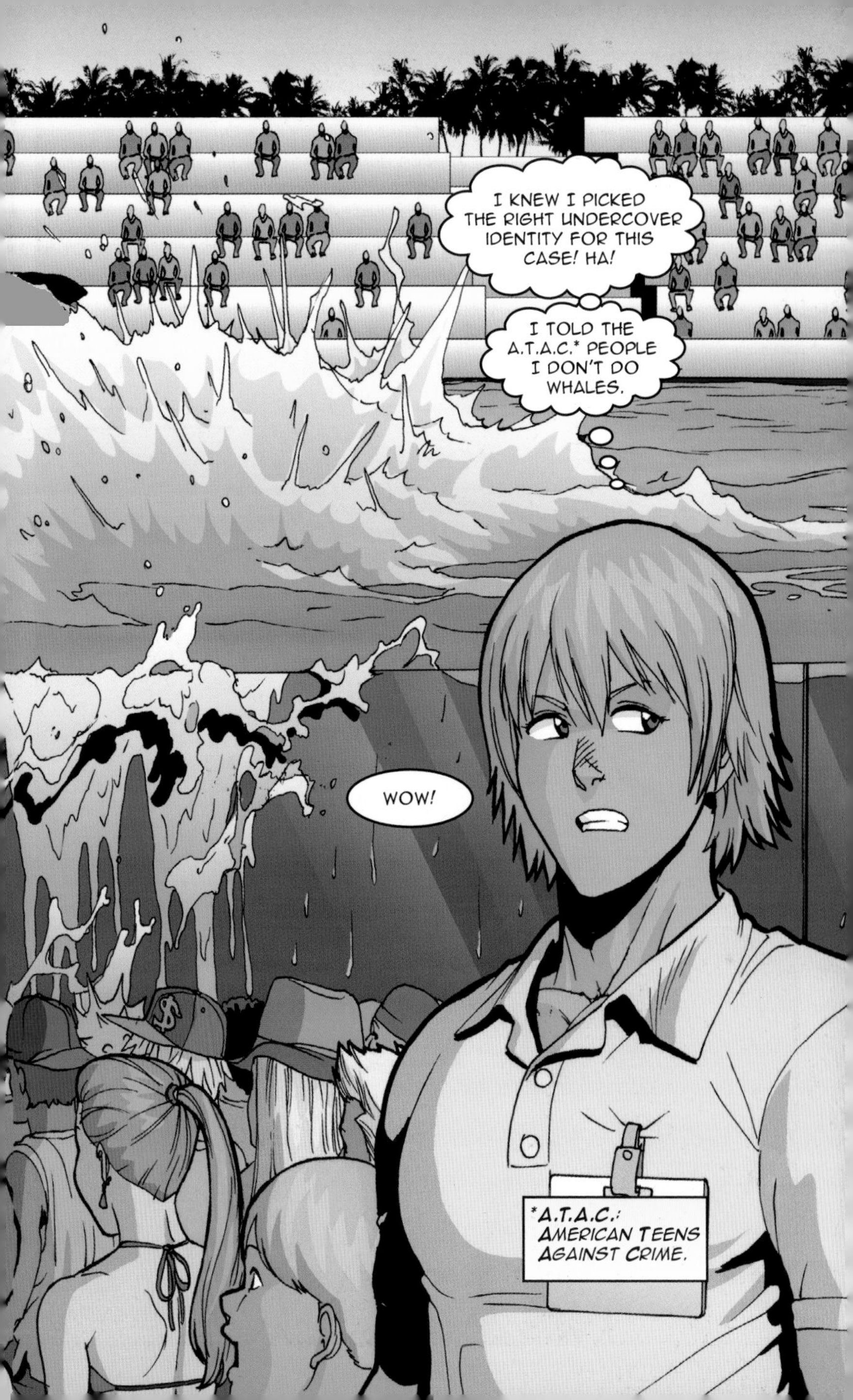
I KNEW I PICKED THE RIGHT UNDERCOVER IDENTITY FOR THIS CASE! HA!
I TOLD THE A.T.A.C.* PEOPLE I DON'T DO WHALES.
WOW!
*A.T.A.C.: AMERICAN TEENS AGAINST CRIME.

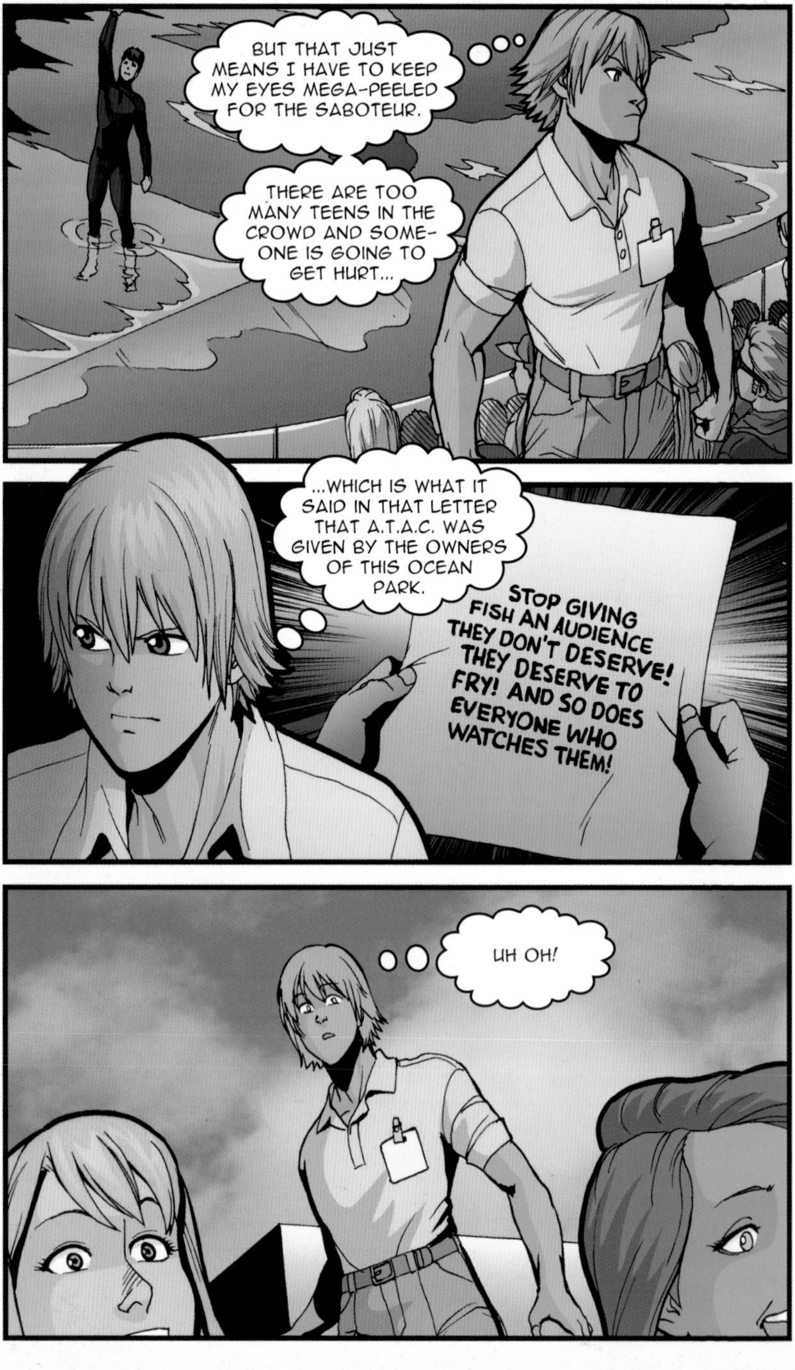
BUT THAT JUST MEANS I HAVE TO KEEP MY EYES MEGA-PEELED FOR THE SABOTEUR.
THERE ARE TOO MANY TEENS IN THE CROWD AND SOME-ONE IS GOING TO GET HURT...
...WHICH IS WHAT IT SAID IN THAT LETTER THAT A.T.A.C. WAS GIVEN BY THE OWNERS OF THIS OCEAN PARK.
STOP GIVING FISH AN AUDIENCE THEY DON'T DESERVE! THEY DESERVE TO FRY! AND SO DOES EVERYONE WHO WATCHES THEM!
UH OH!

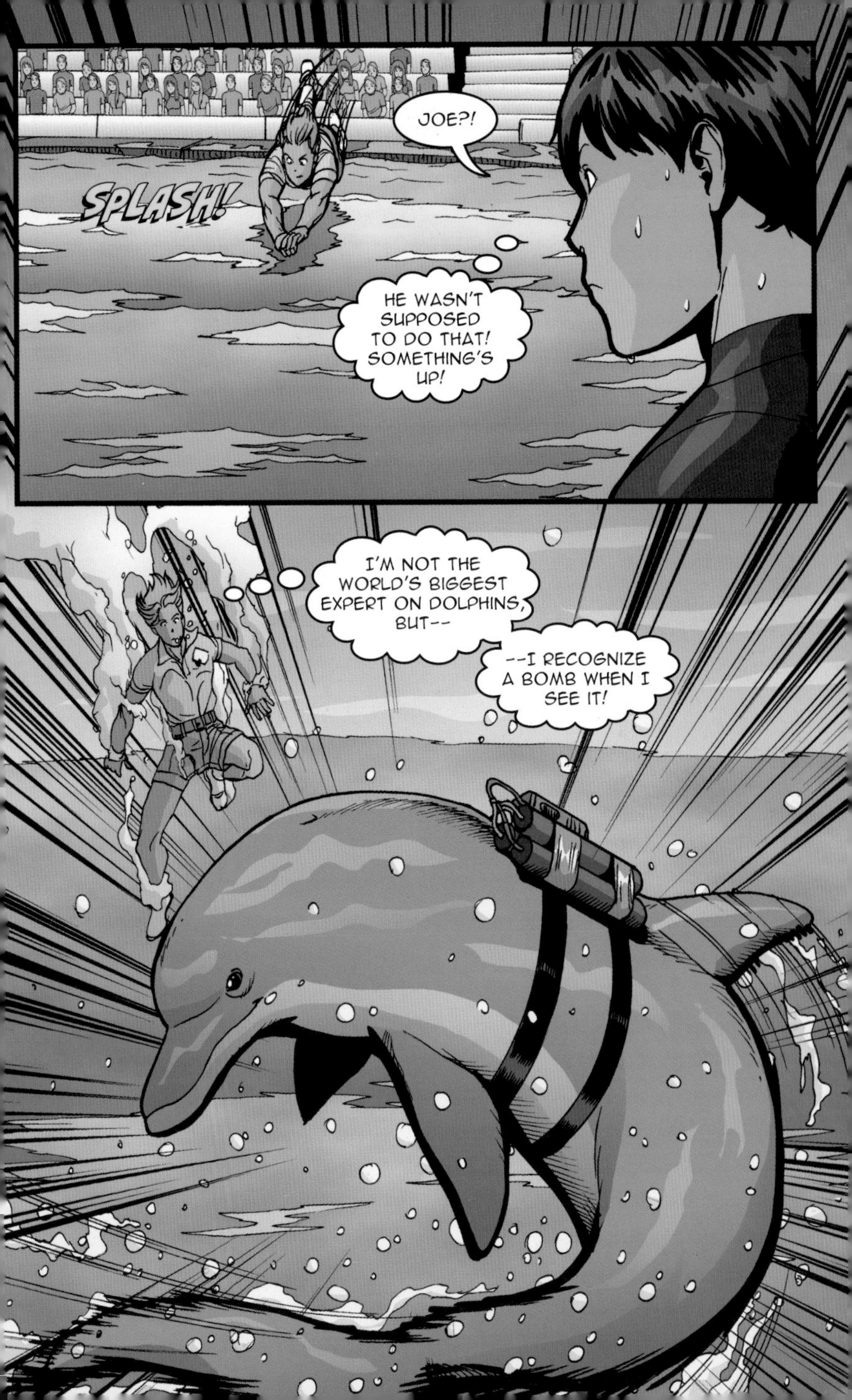
JOE?!
SPLASH!
HE WASN'T SUPPOSED TO DO THAT! SOMETHING'S UP!
I'M NOT THE WORLD'S BIGGEST EXPERT ON DOLPHINS, BUT--
--I RECOGNIZE A BOMB WHEN I SEE IT!

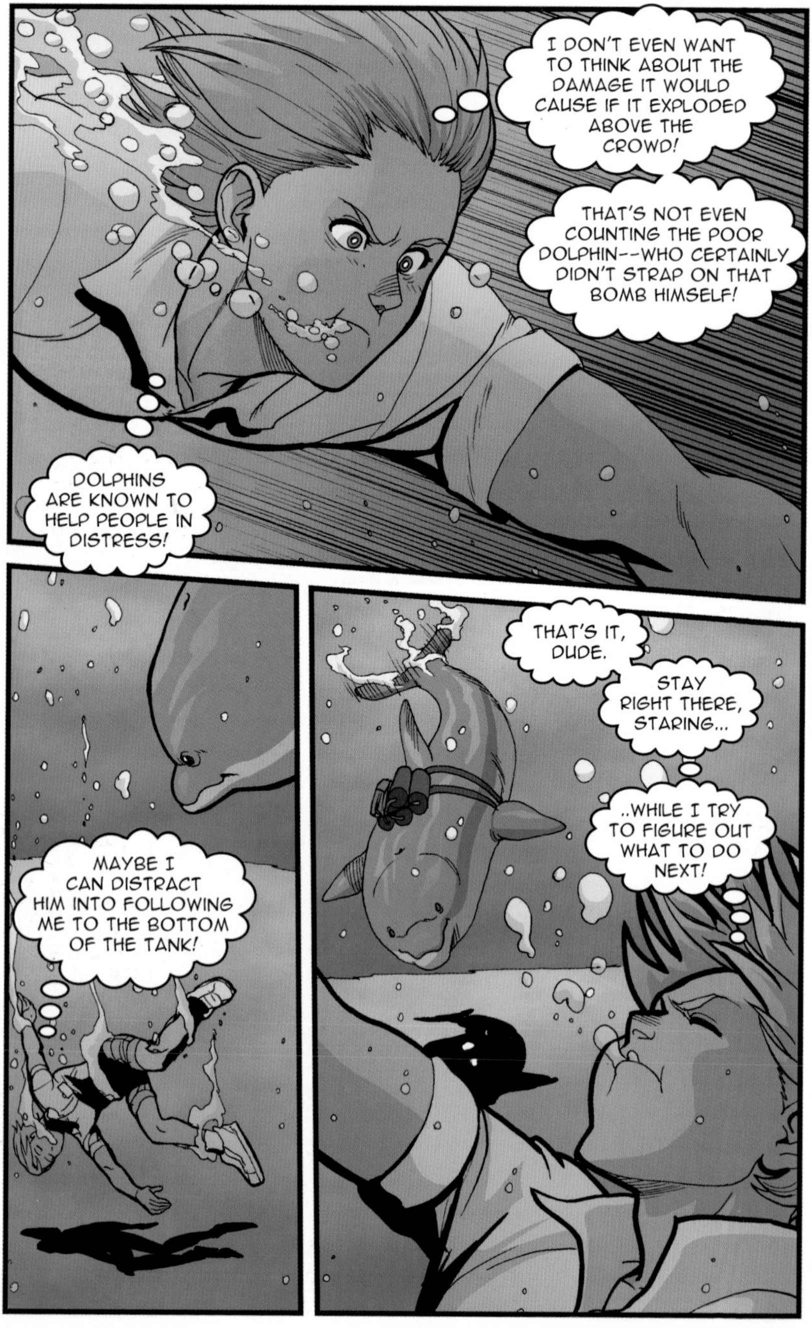
I DON'T EVEN WANT TO THINK ABOUT THE DAMAGE IT WOULD CAUSE IF IT EXPLODED ABOVE THE CROWD!
THAT'S NOT EVEN COUNTING THE POOR DOLPHIN--WHO CERTAINLY DIDN'T STRAP ON THAT BOMB HIMSELF!
DOLPHINS ARE KNOWN TO HELP PEOPLE IN DISTRESS!
MAYBE I CAN DISTRACT HIM INTO FOLLOWING ME TO THE BOTTOM OF THE TANK!
THAT'S IT, DUDE.
STAY RIGHT THERE, STARING...
..WHILE I TRY TO FIGURE OUT WHAT TO DO NEXT!

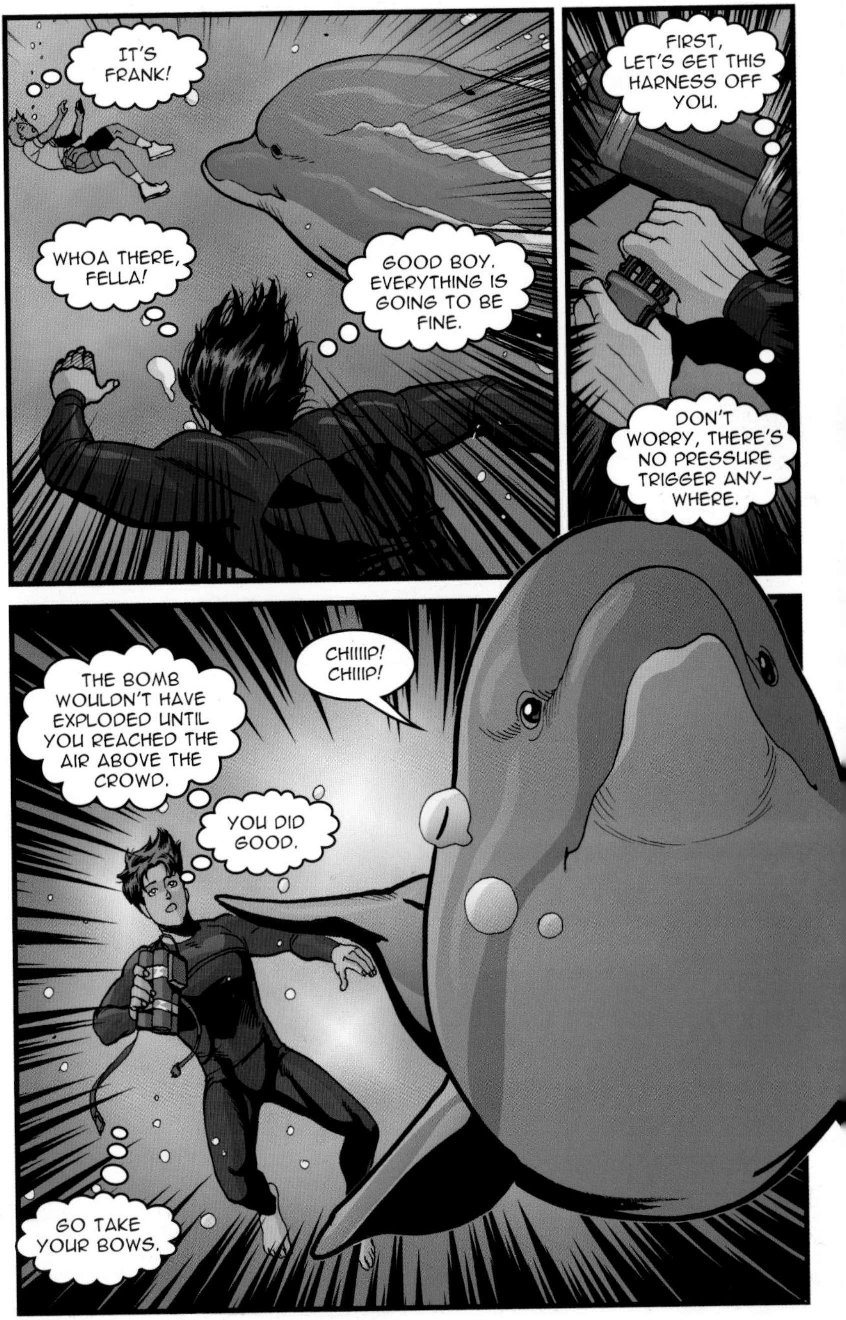
IT'S FRANK!
FIRST, LET'S GET THIS HARNESS OFF YOU.
WHOA THERE, FELLA!
GOOD BOY. EVERYTHING IS GOING TO BE FINE.
DON'T WORRY, THERE'S NO PRESSURE TRIGGER ANY-WHERE.
CHIIIIP! CHIIIP!
THE BOMB WOULDN'T HAVE EXPLODED UNTIL YOU REACHED THE AIR ABOVE THE CROWD.
YOU DID GOOD.
GO TAKE YOUR BOWS.

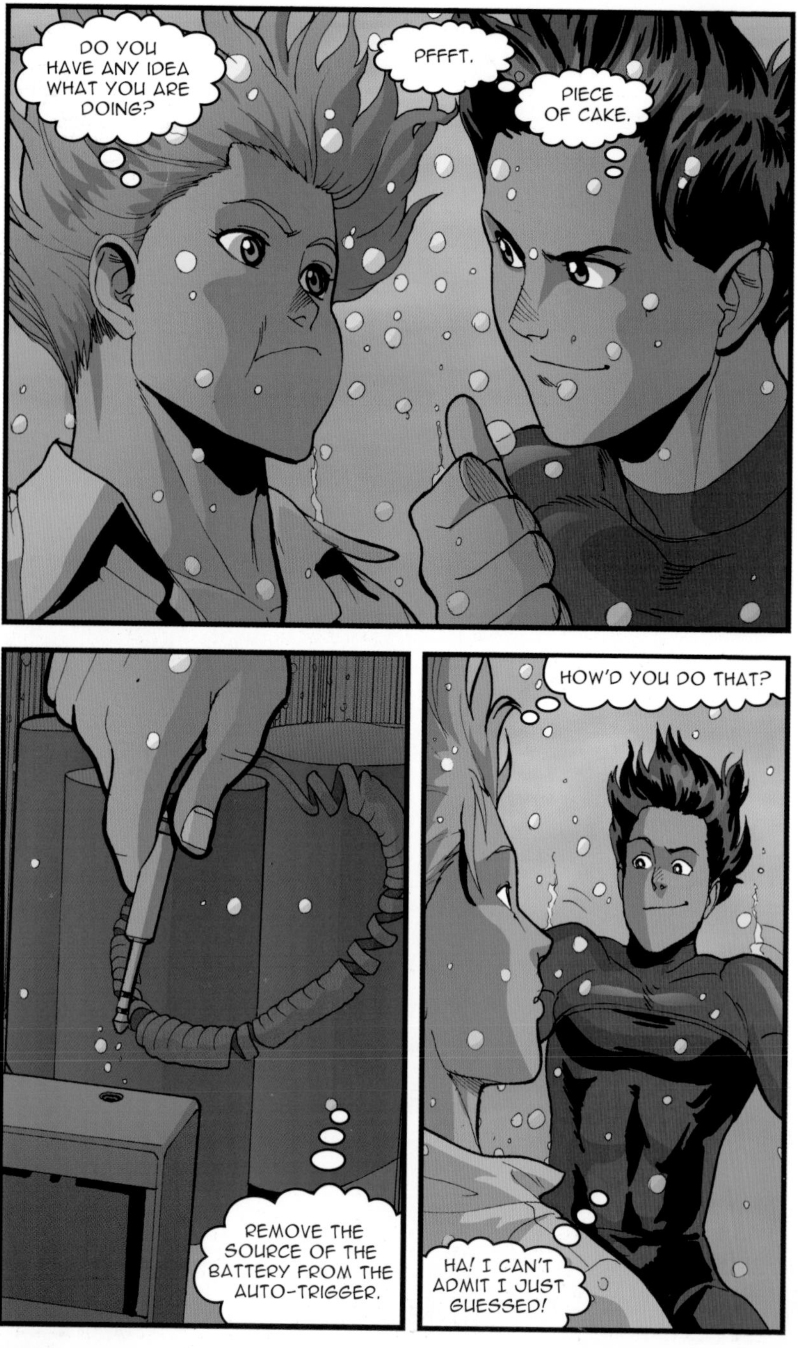
DO YOU HAVE ANY IDEA WHAT YOU ARE DOING?
PFFFT.
PIECE OF CAKE.
REMOVE THE SOURCE OF THE BATTERY FROM THE AUTO-TRIGGER.
HOW'D YOU DO THAT?
HA! I CAN'T ADMIT I JUST GUESSED!

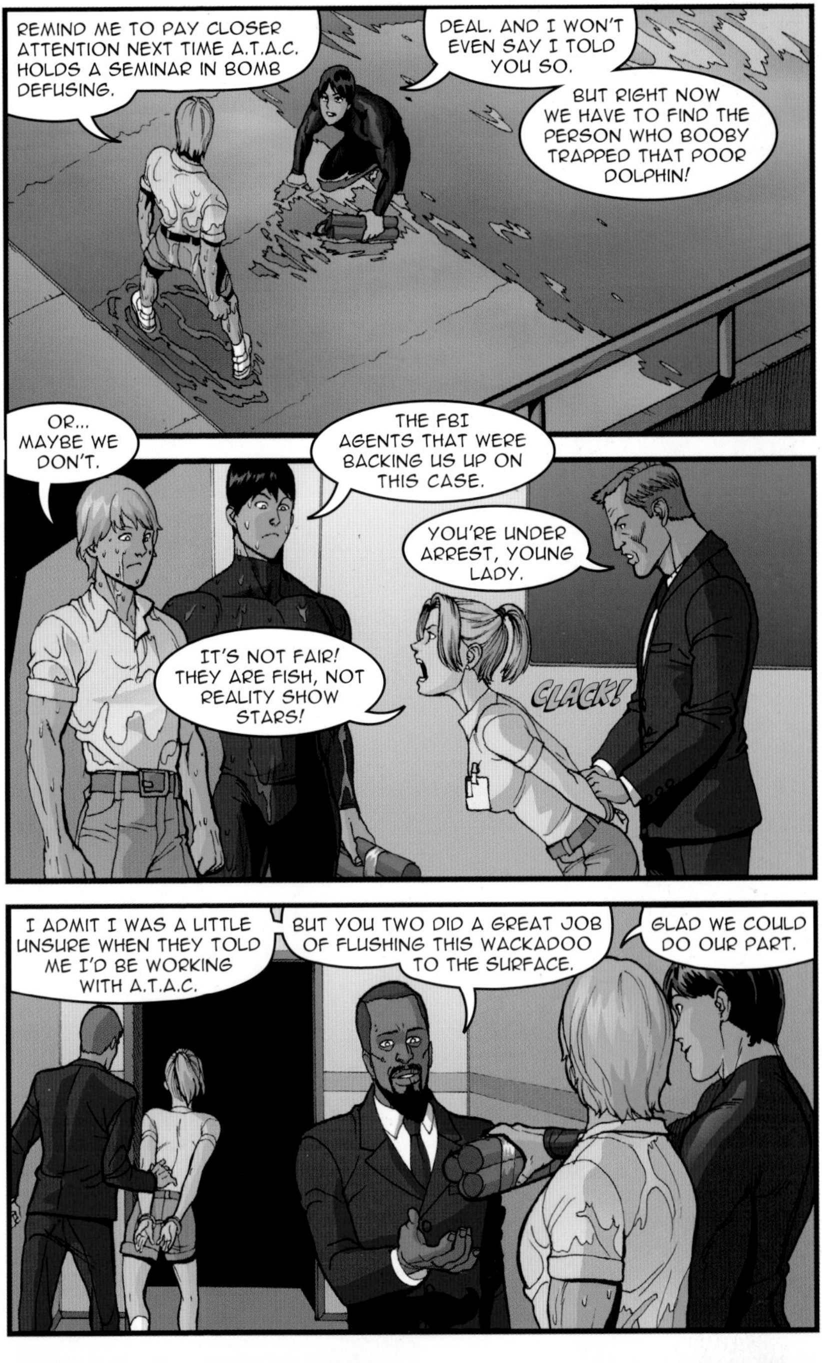
REMIND ME TO PAY CLOSER ATTENTION NEXT TIME A.T.A.C. HOLDS A SEMINAR IN BOMB DEFUSING.
DEAL. AND I WON'T EVEN SAY I TOLD YOU SO.
BUT RIGHT NOW WE HAVE TO FIND THE PERSON WHO BOOBY TRAPPED THAT POOR DOLPHIN!
OR... MAYBE WE DON'T.
THE FBI AGENTS THAT WERE BACKING US UP ON THIS CASE.
YOU'RE UNDER ARREST, YOUNG LADY.
IT'S NOT FAIR! THEY ARE FISH, NOT REALITY SHOW STARS!
CLACK!
I ADMIT I WAS A LITTLE UNSURE WHEN THEY TOLD ME I'D BE WORKING WITH A.T.A.C.
BUT YOU TWO DID A GREAT JOB OF FLUSHING THIS WACKADOO TO THE SURFACE.
GLAD WE COULD DO OUR PART.

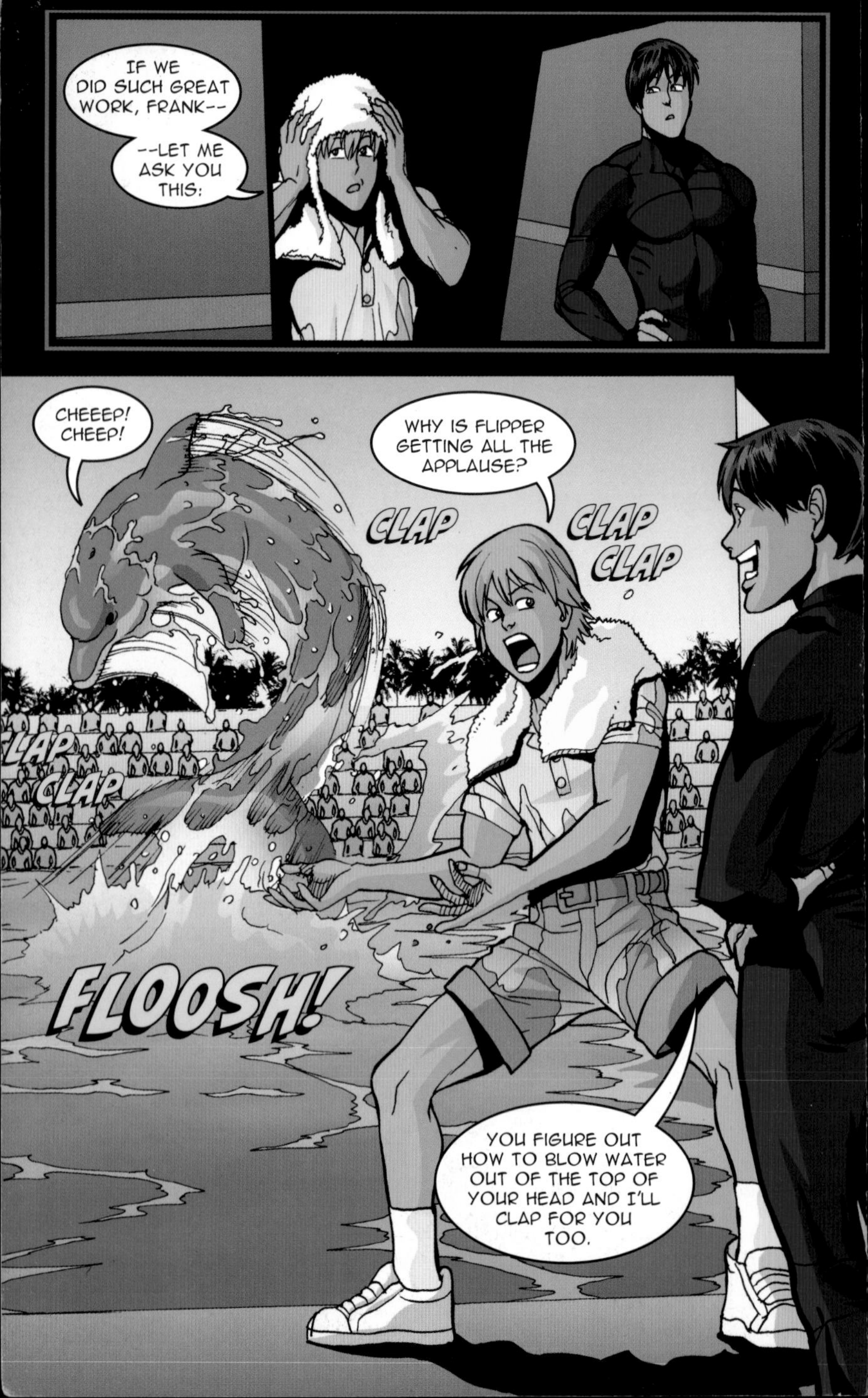
IF WE DID SUCH GREAT WORK, FRANK--
--LET ME ASK YOU THIS:
CHEEEP! CHEEP!
WHY IS FLIPPER GETTING ALL THE APPLAUSE?
CLAP
CLAP CLAP
CLAP CLAP
FLOOSH!
YOU FIGURE OUT HOW TO BLOW WATER OUT OF THE TOP OF YOUR HEAD AND I'LL CLAP FOR YOU TOO.

CHAPTER TWO: "PAST IS PRESENT...TENSE!"

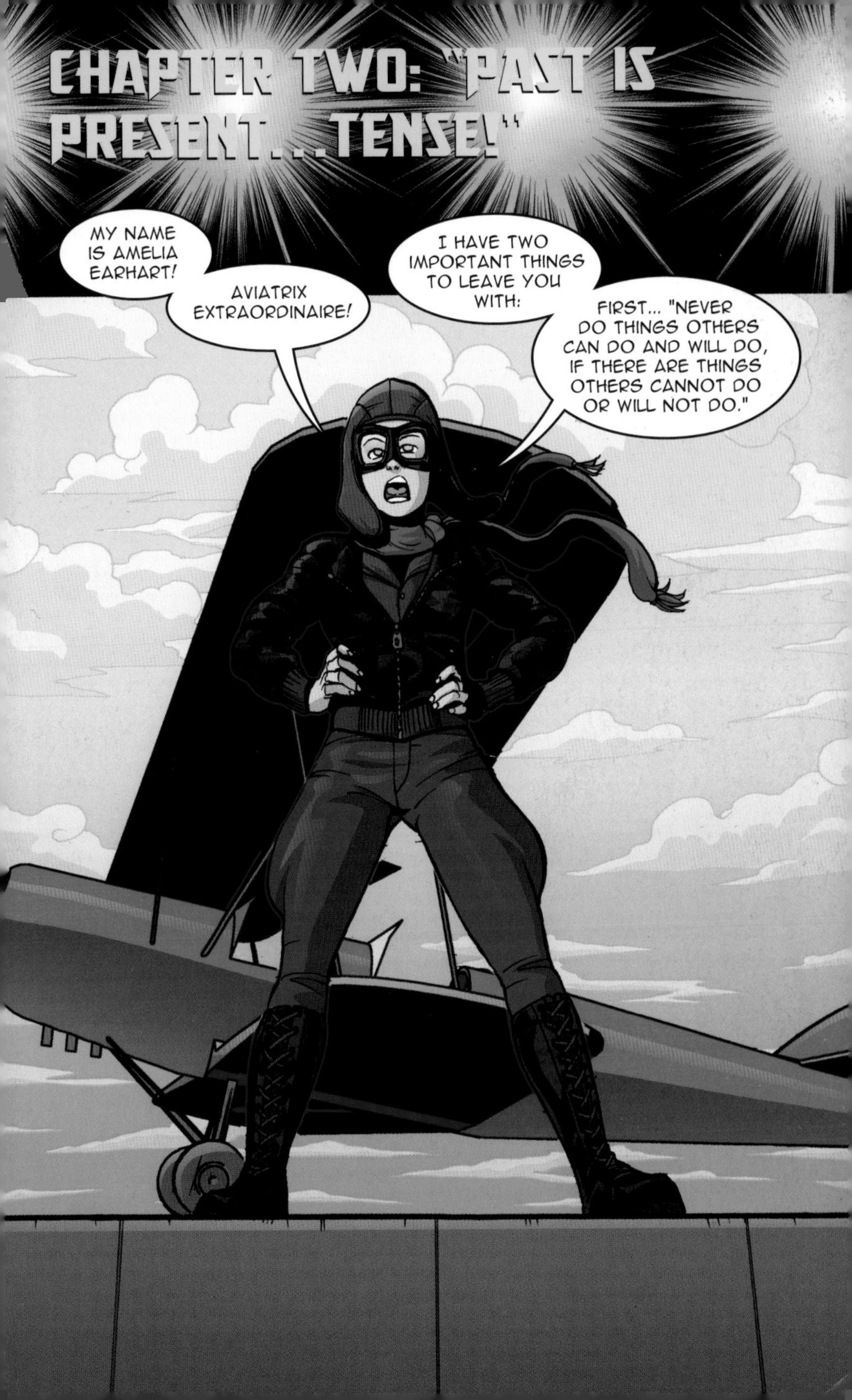
MY NAME IS AMELIA EARHART!
AVIATRIX EXTRAORDINAIRE!
I HAVE TWO IMPORTANT THINGS TO LEAVE YOU WITH:
FIRST... "NEVER DO THINGS OTHERS CAN DO AND WILL DO, IF THERE ARE THINGS OTHERS CANNOT DO OR WILL NOT DO."

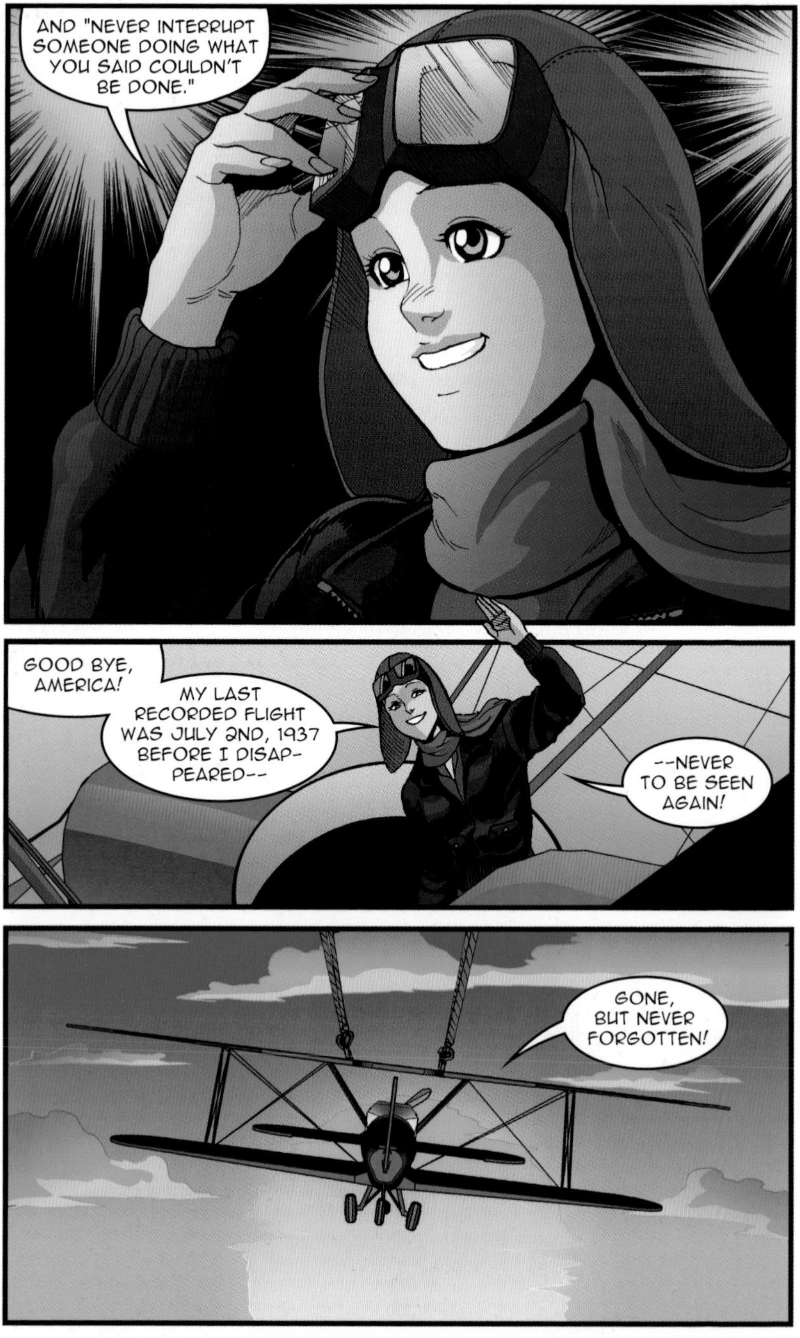
AND "NEVER INTERRUPT SOMEONE DOING WHAT YOU SAID COULDN'T BE DONE."
GOOD BYE, AMERICA!
MY LAST RECORDED FLIGHT WAS JULY 2ND, 1937 BEFORE I DISAP-PEARED--
--NEVER TO BE SEEN AGAIN!
GONE, BUT NEVER FORGOTTEN!

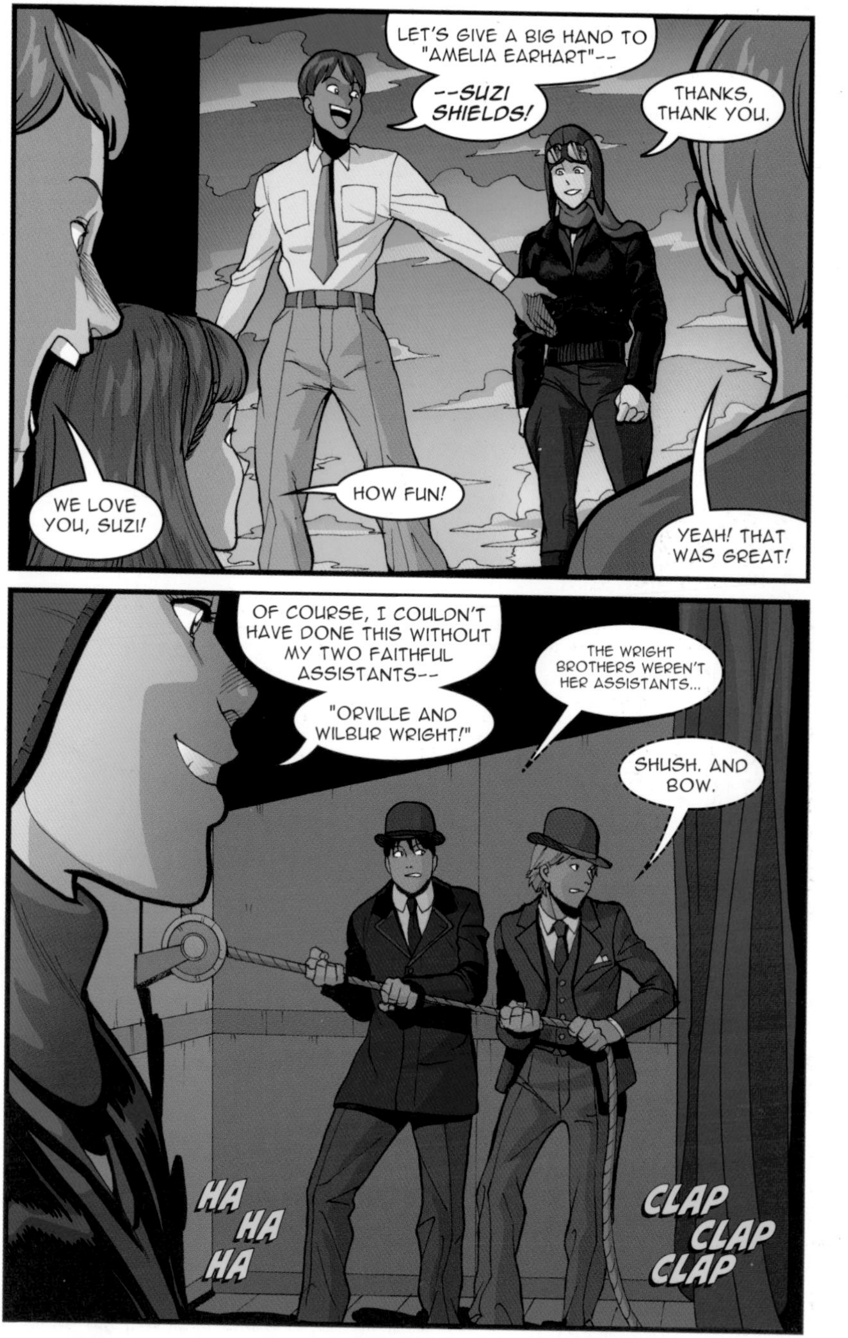
LET'S GIVE A BIG HAND TO "AMELIA EARHART"--
--SUZI SHIELDS!
THANKS, THANK YOU.
WE LOVE YOU, SUZI!
HOW FUN!
YEAH! THAT WAS GREAT!
OF COURSE, I COULDN'T HAVE DONE THIS WITHOUT MY TWO FAITHFUL ASSISTANTS--
"ORVILLE AND WILBUR WRIGHT!"
THE WRIGHT BROTHERS WEREN'T HER ASSISTANTS...
SHUSH. AND BOW.
HA HA HA
CLAP CLAP CLAP

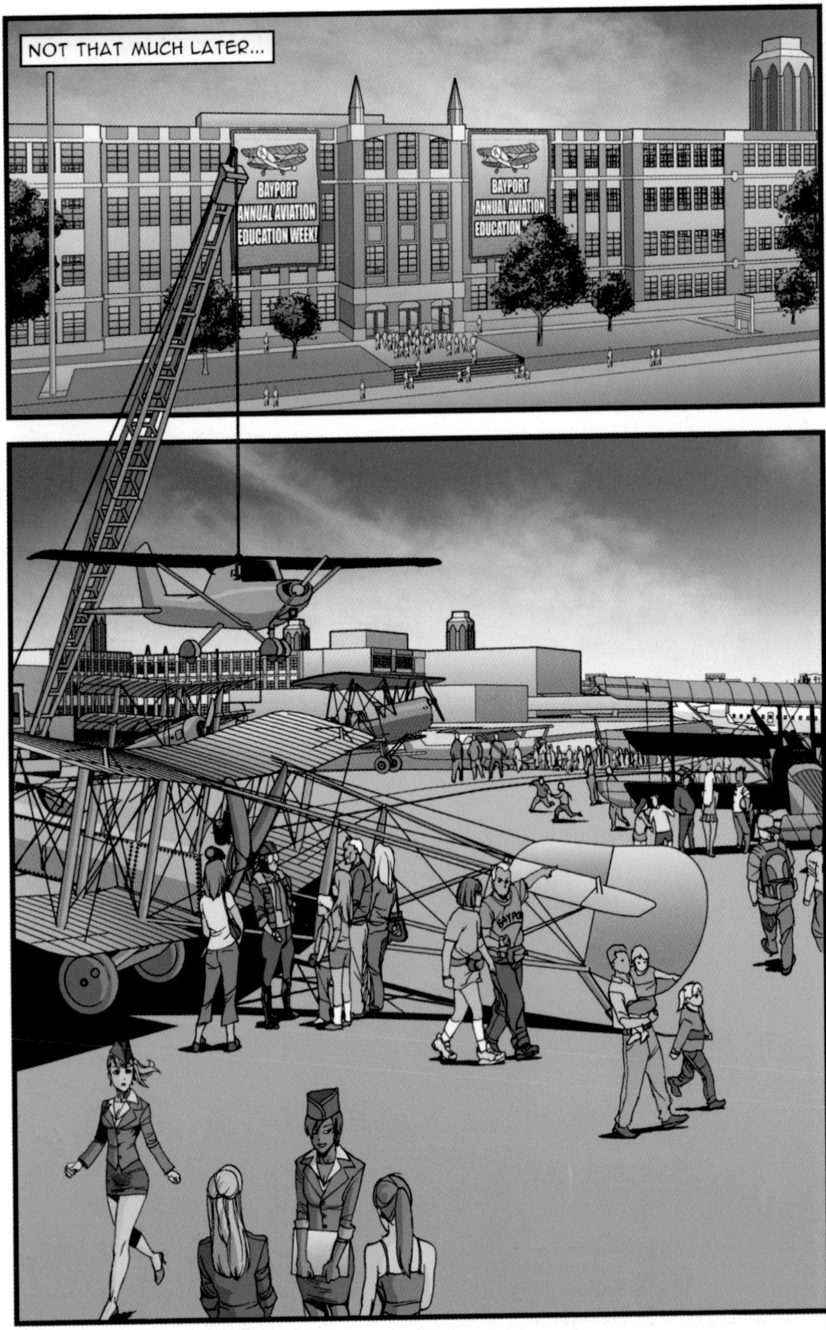
NOT THAT MUCH LATER...
BAYPORT
ANNUAL AVIATION
EDUCATION WEEK!

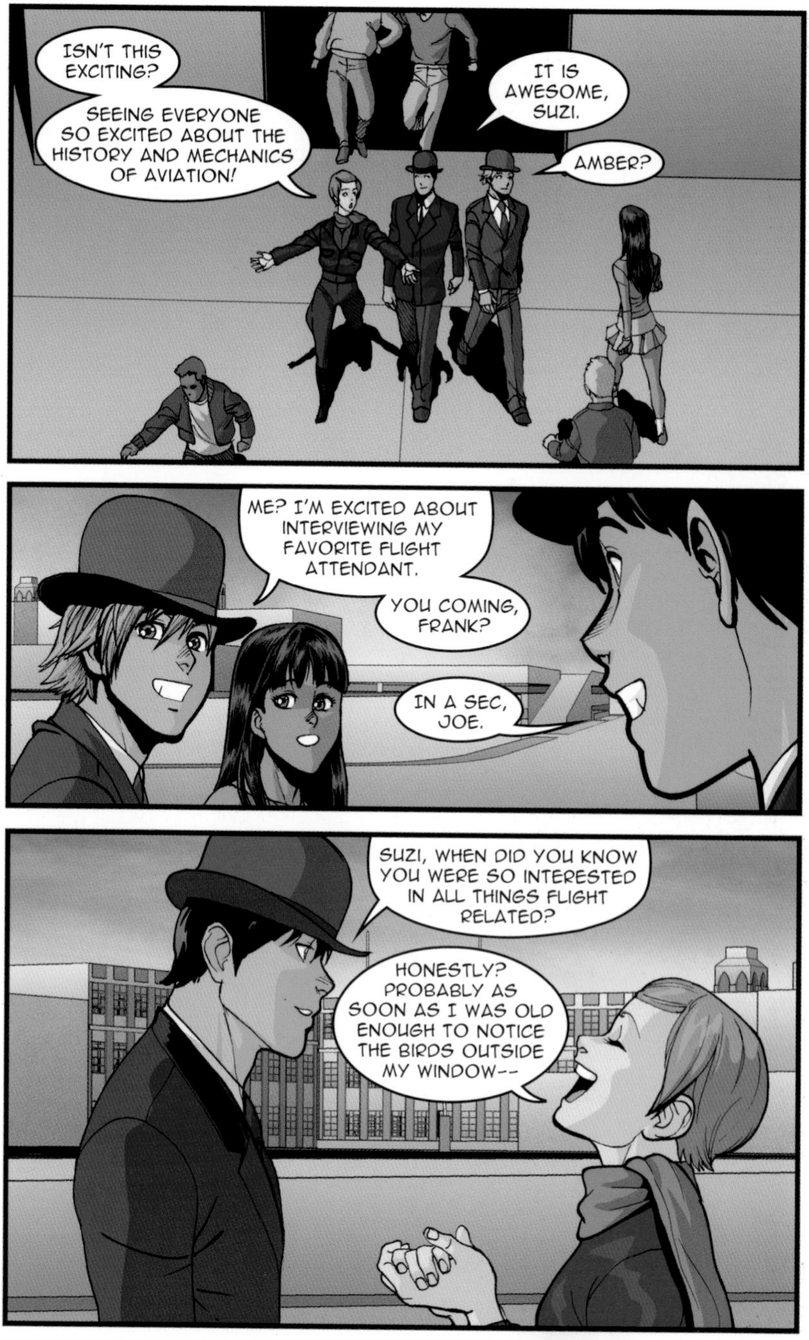
ISN'T THIS EXCITING?
SEEING EVERYONE SO EXCITED ABOUT THE HISTORY AND MECHANICS OF AVIATION!
IT IS AWESOME, SUZI.
AMBER?
ME? I'M EXCITED ABOUT INTERVIEWING MY FAVORITE FLIGHT ATTENDANT.
YOU COMING, FRANK?
IN A SEC, JOE.
SUZI, WHEN DID YOU KNOW YOU WERE SO INTERESTED IN ALL THINGS FLIGHT RELATED?
HONESTLY? PROBABLY AS SOON AS I WAS OLD ENOUGH TO NOTICE THE BIRDS OUTSIDE MY WINDOW--

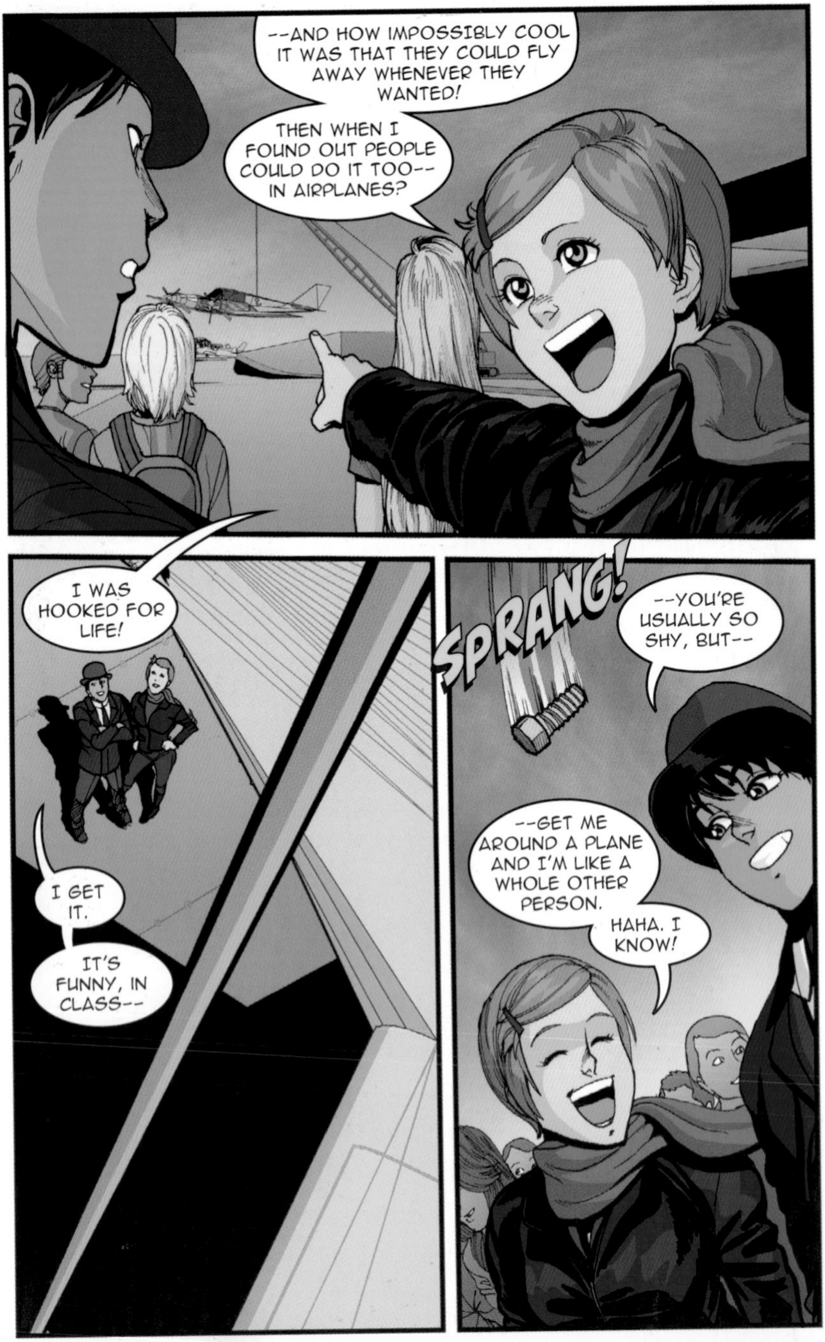
--AND HOW IMPOSSIBLY COOL IT WAS THAT THEY COULD FLY AWAY WHENEVER THEY WANTED!
THEN WHEN I FOUND OUT PEOPLE COULD DO IT TOO-- IN AIRPLANES?
I WAS HOOKED FOR LIFE!
I GET IT.
IT'S FUNNY, IN CLASS--
SPRANG!
--YOU'RE USUALLY SO SHY, BUT--
--GET ME AROUND A PLANE AND I'M LIKE A WHOLE OTHER PERSON.
HAHA. I KNOW!

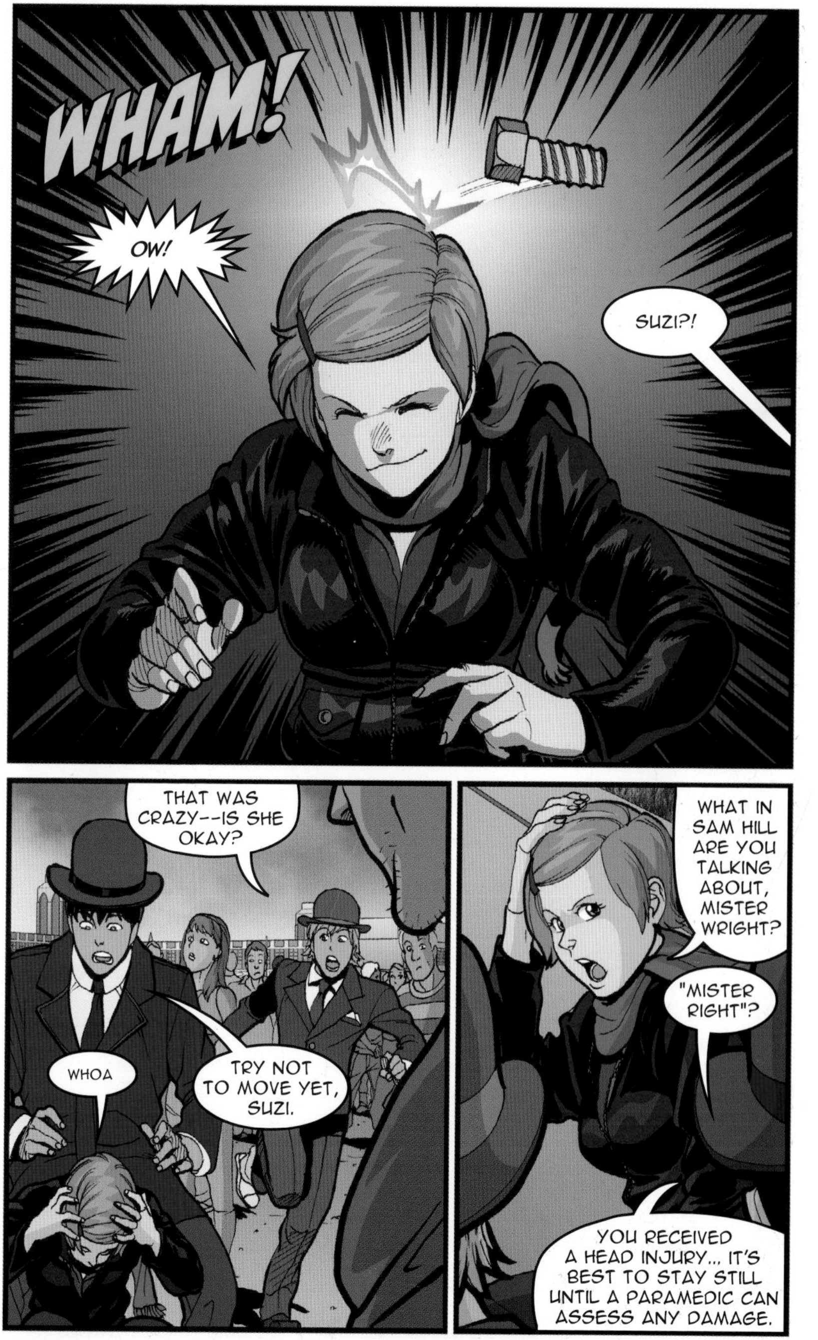
WHAM!
OW!
SUZI?!
THAT WAS CRAZY--IS SHE OKAY?
WHOA
TRY NOT TO MOVE YET, SUZI.
WHAT IN SAM HILL ARE YOU TALKING ABOUT, MISTER WRIGHT?
"MISTER RIGHT"?
YOU RECEIVED A HEAD INJURY... IT'S BEST TO STAY STILL UNTIL A PARAMEDIC CAN ASSESS ANY DAMAGE.

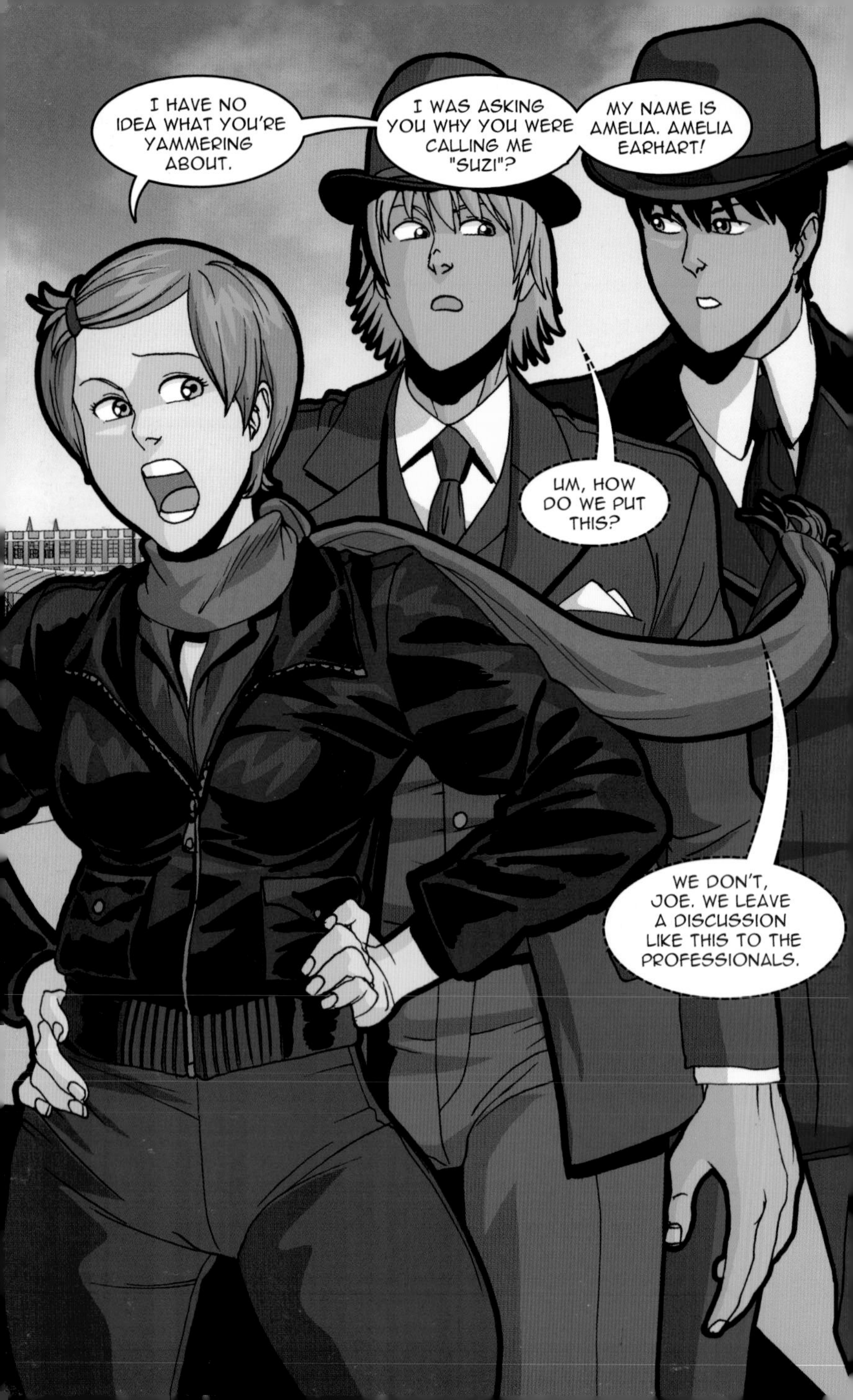
I HAVE NO IDEA WHAT YOU'RE YAMMERING ABOUT.
I WAS ASKING YOU WHY YOU WERE CALLING ME "SUZI"?
MY NAME IS AMELIA. AMELIA EARHART!
UM, HOW DO WE PUT THIS?
WE DON'T, JOE. WE LEAVE A DISCUSSION LIKE THIS TO THE PROFESSIONALS.

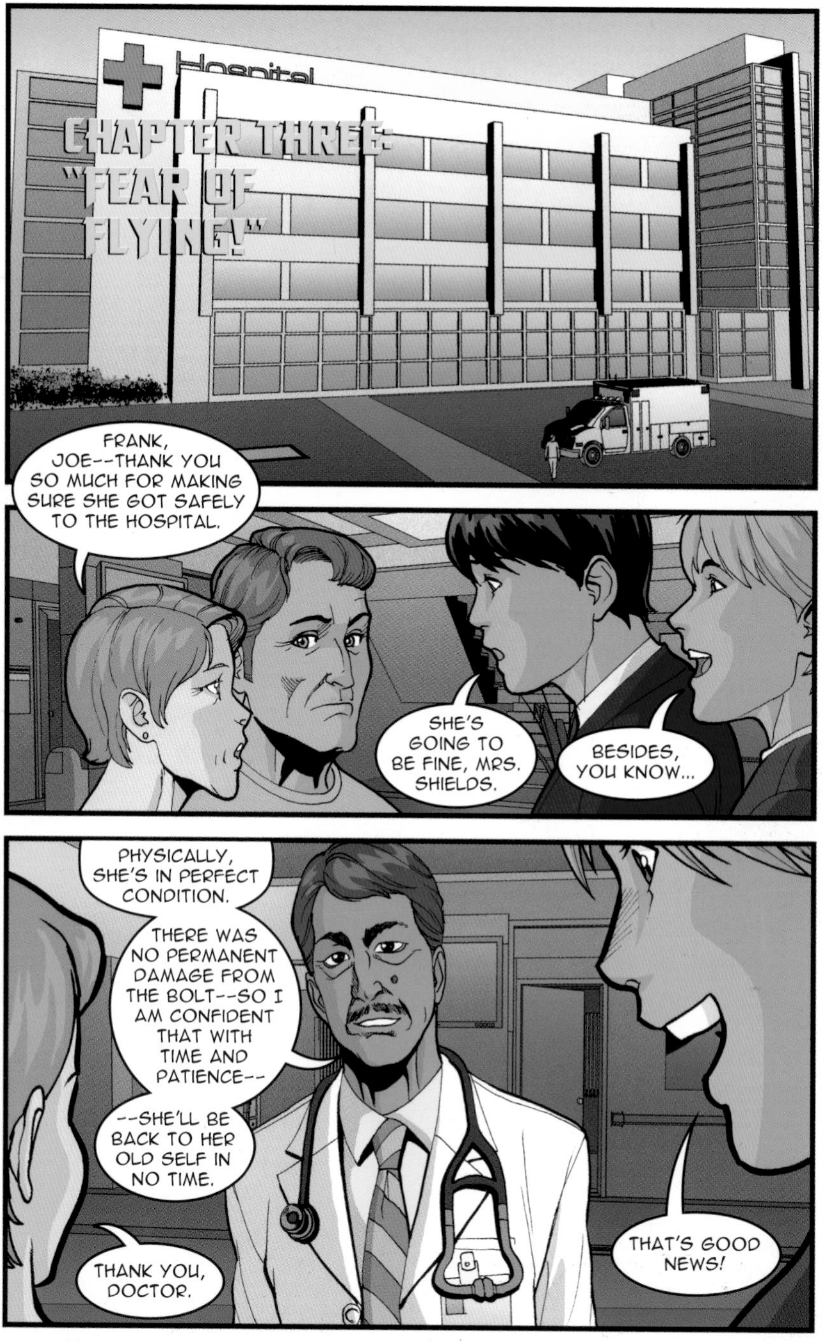
Hospital
CHAPTER THREE: "FEAR OF FLYING!"
FRANK, JOE--THANK YOU SO MUCH FOR MAKING SURE SHE GOT SAFELY TO THE HOSPITAL.
SHE'S GOING TO BE FINE, MRS. SHIELDS.
BESIDES, YOU KNOW...
PHYSICALLY, SHE'S IN PERFECT CONDITION.
THERE WAS NO PERMANENT DAMAGE FROM THE BOLT--SO I AM CONFIDENT THAT WITH TIME AND PATIENCE--
--SHE'LL BE BACK TO HER OLD SELF IN NO TIME.
THANK YOU, DOCTOR.
THAT'S GOOD NEWS!

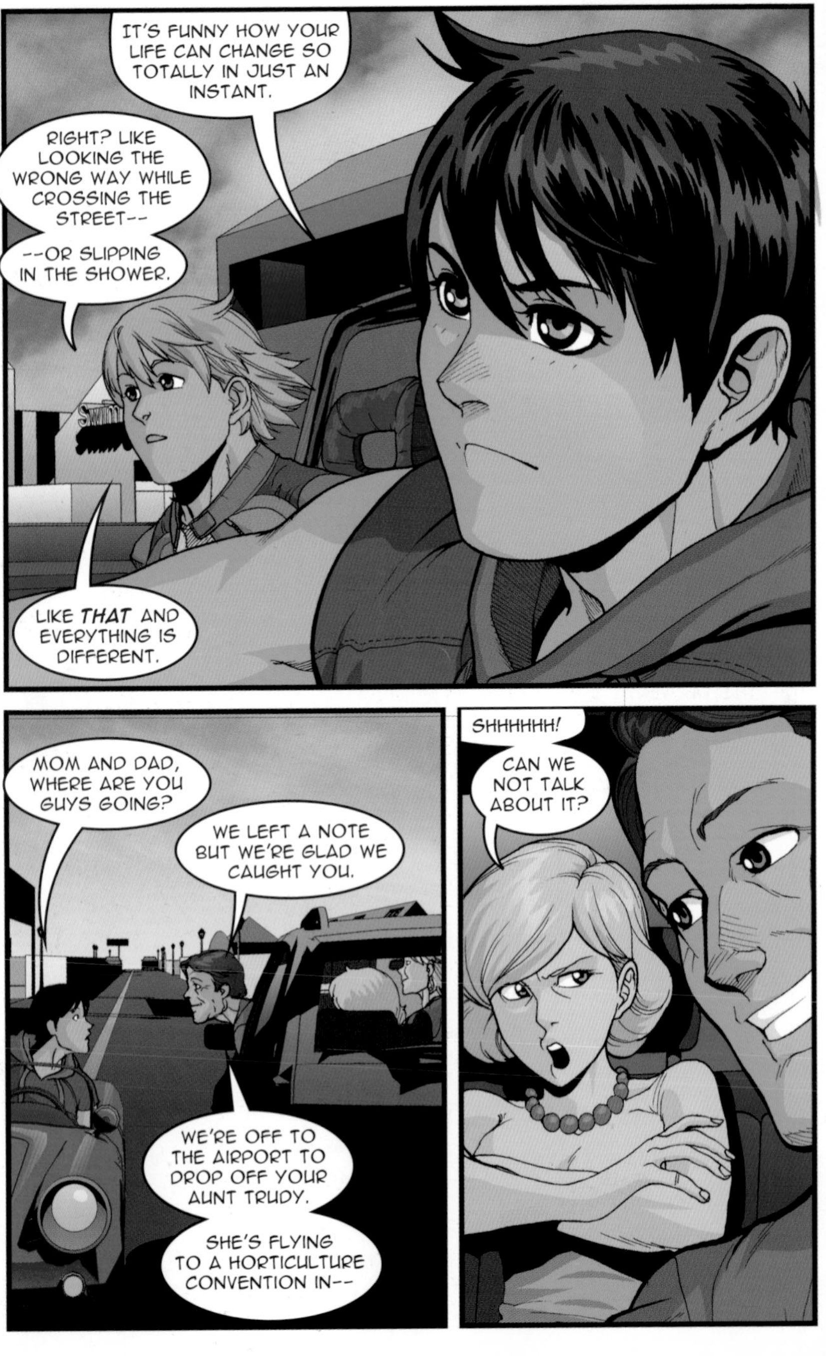
IT'S FUNNY HOW YOUR LIFE CAN CHANGE SO TOTALLY IN JUST AN INSTANT.
RIGHT? LIKE LOOKING THE WRONG WAY WHILE CROSSING THE STREET--
--OR SLIPPING IN THE SHOWER.
LIKE *THAT* AND EVERYTHING IS DIFFERENT.
MOM AND DAD, WHERE ARE YOU GUYS GOING?
WE LEFT A NOTE BUT WE'RE GLAD WE CAUGHT YOU.
WE'RE OFF TO THE AIRPORT TO DROP OFF YOUR AUNT TRUDY.
SHE'S FLYING TO A HORTICULTURE CONVENTION IN--
SHHHHHH!
CAN WE NOT TALK ABOUT IT?

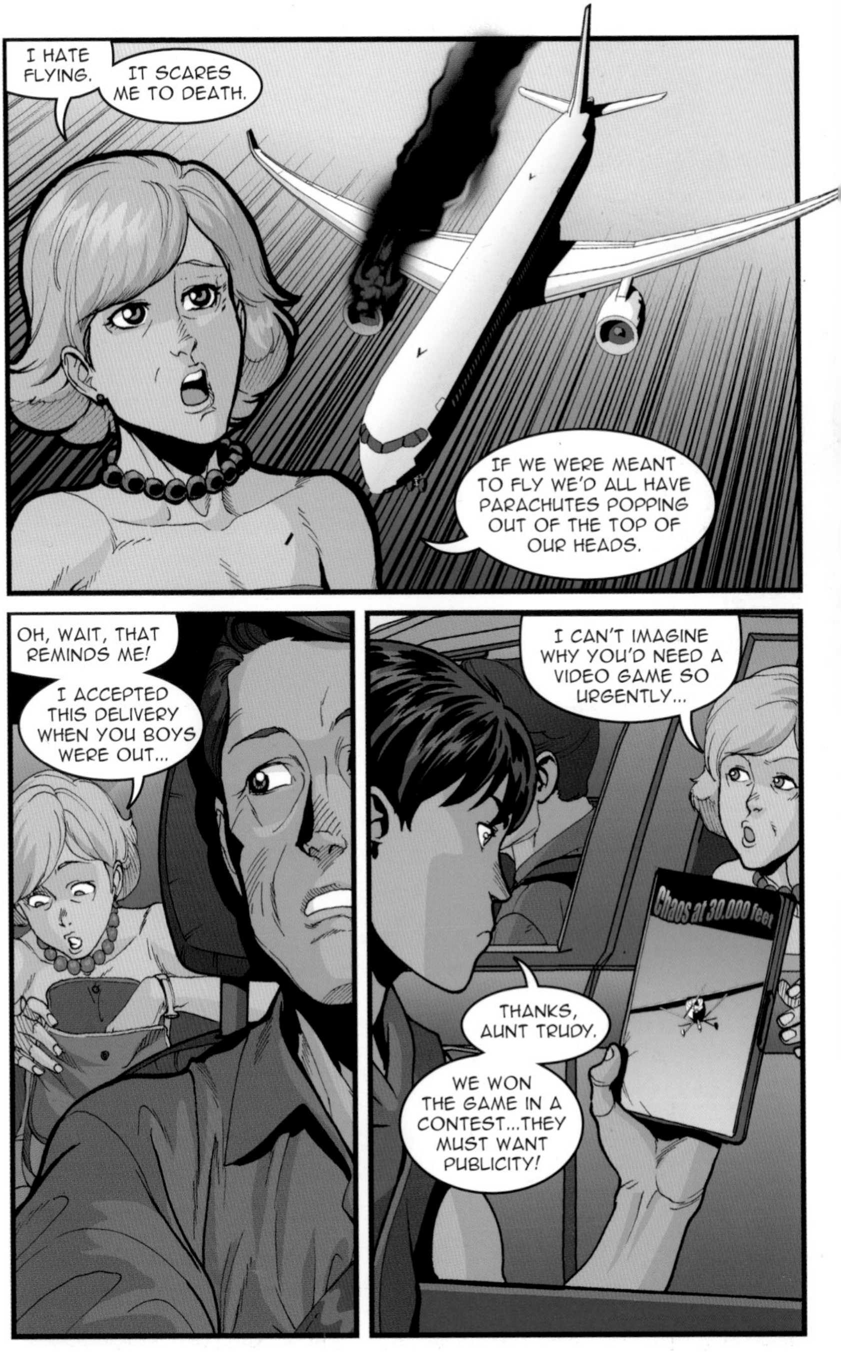
I HATE FLYING.
IT SCARES ME TO DEATH.
IF WE WERE MEANT TO FLY WE'D ALL HAVE PARACHUTES POPPING OUT OF THE TOP OF OUR HEADS.
OH, WAIT, THAT REMINDS ME!
I ACCEPTED THIS DELIVERY WHEN YOU BOYS WERE OUT...
I CAN'T IMAGINE WHY YOU'D NEED A VIDEO GAME SO URGENTLY...
Chaos at 30,000 feet
THANKS, AUNT TRUDY.
WE WON THE GAME IN A CONTEST...THEY MUST WANT PUBLICITY!

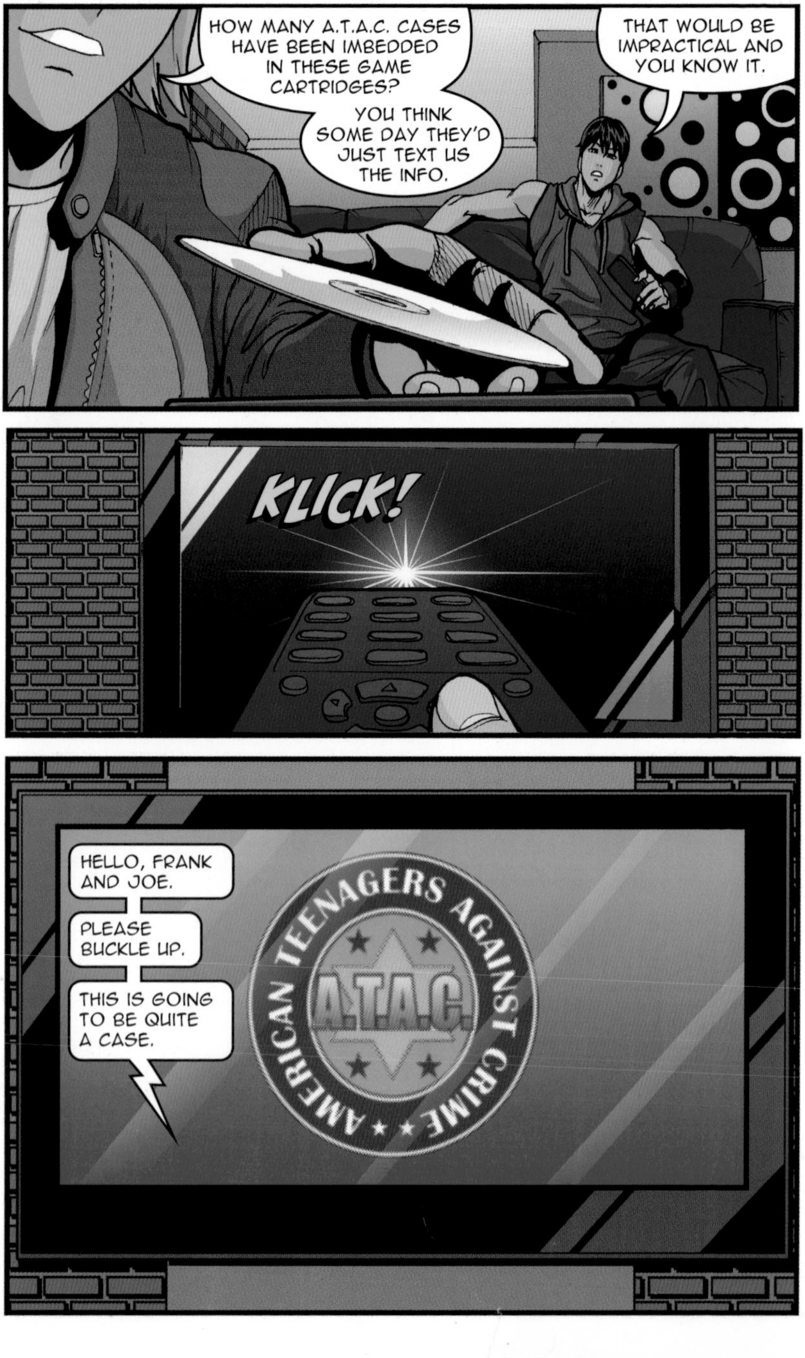
HOW MANY A.T.A.C. CASES HAVE BEEN IMBEDDED IN THESE GAME CARTRIDGES?
YOU THINK SOME DAY THEY'D JUST TEXT US THE INFO.
THAT WOULD BE IMPRACTICAL AND YOU KNOW IT.
KLICK!
HELLO, FRANK AND JOE.
PLEASE BUCKLE UP.
THIS IS GOING TO BE QUITE A CASE.
AMERICAN TEENAGERS AGAINST CRIME
A.T.A.C.

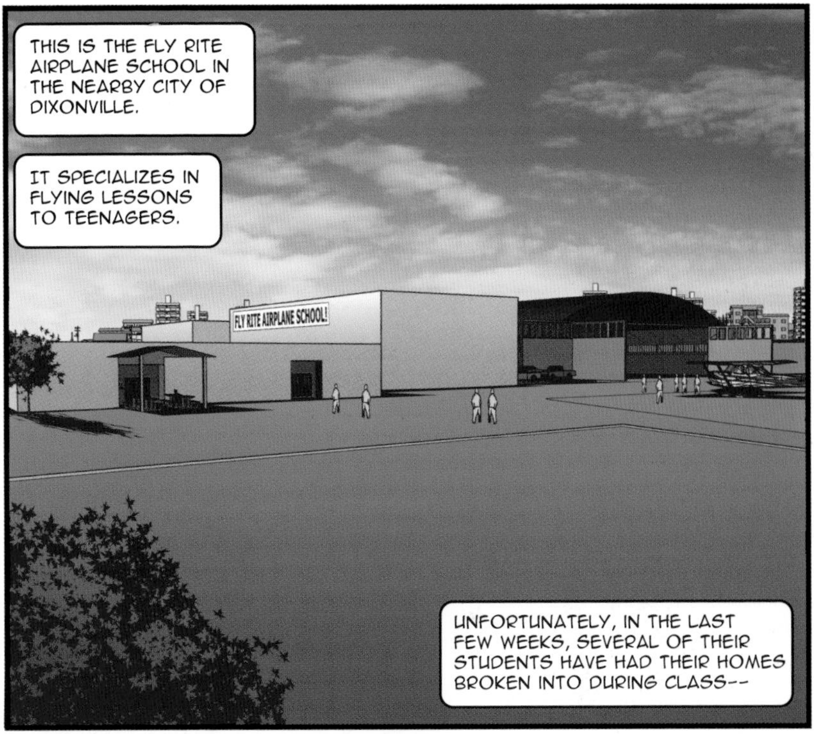
THIS IS THE FLY RITE AIRPLANE SCHOOL IN THE NEARBY CITY OF DIXONVILLE.
IT SPECIALIZES IN FLYING LESSONS TO TEENAGERS.
FLY RITE AIRPLANE SCHOOL!
UNFORTUNATELY, IN THE LAST FEW WEEKS, SEVERAL OF THEIR STUDENTS HAVE HAD THEIR HOMES BROKEN INTO DURING CLASS--

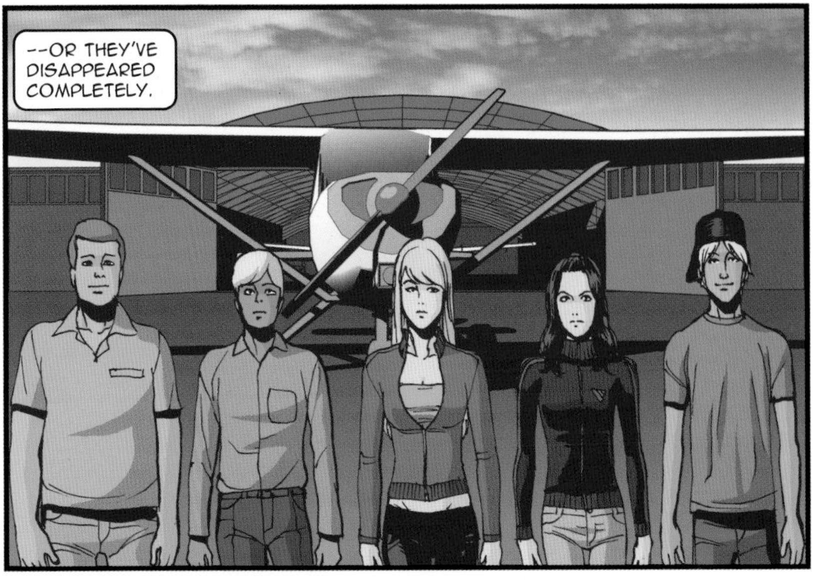
--OR THEY'VE DISAPPEARED COMPLETELY.

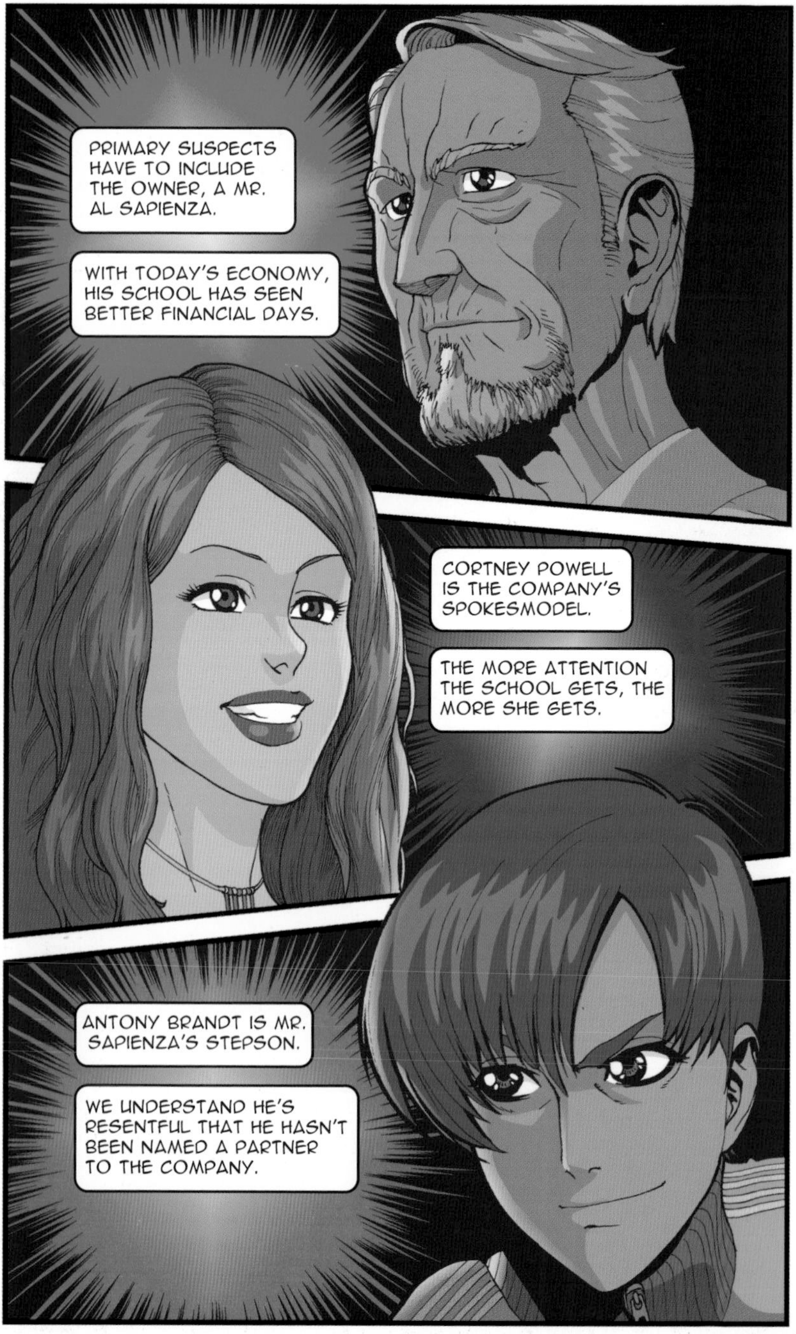
PRIMARY SUSPECTS HAVE TO INCLUDE THE OWNER, A MR. AL SAPIENZA.
WITH TODAY'S ECONOMY, HIS SCHOOL HAS SEEN BETTER FINANCIAL DAYS.
CORTNEY POWELL IS THE COMPANY'S SPOKESMODEL.
THE MORE ATTENTION THE SCHOOL GETS, THE MORE SHE GETS.
ANTONY BRANDT IS MR. SAPIENZA'S STEPSON.
WE UNDERSTAND HE'S RESENTFUL THAT HE HASN'T BEEN NAMED A PARTNER TO THE COMPANY.

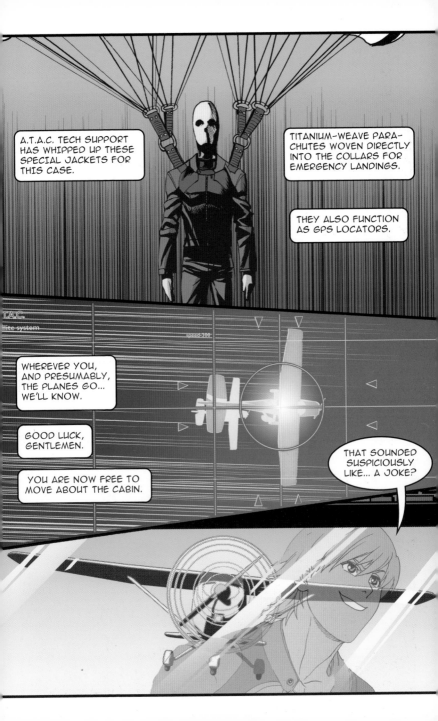

A.T.A.C. TECH SUPPORT HAS WHIPPED UP THESE SPECIAL JACKETS FOR THIS CASE.

TITANIUM-WEAVE PARACHUTES WOVEN DIRECTLY INTO THE COLLARS FOR EMERGENCY LANDINGS.

THEY ALSO FUNCTION AS GPS LOCATORS.

WHEREVER YOU, AND PRESUMABLY, THE PLANES GO... WE'LL KNOW.

GOOD LUCK, GENTLEMEN.

YOU ARE NOW FREE TO MOVE ABOUT THE CABIN.

THAT SOUNDED SUSPICIOUSLY LIKE... A JOKE?

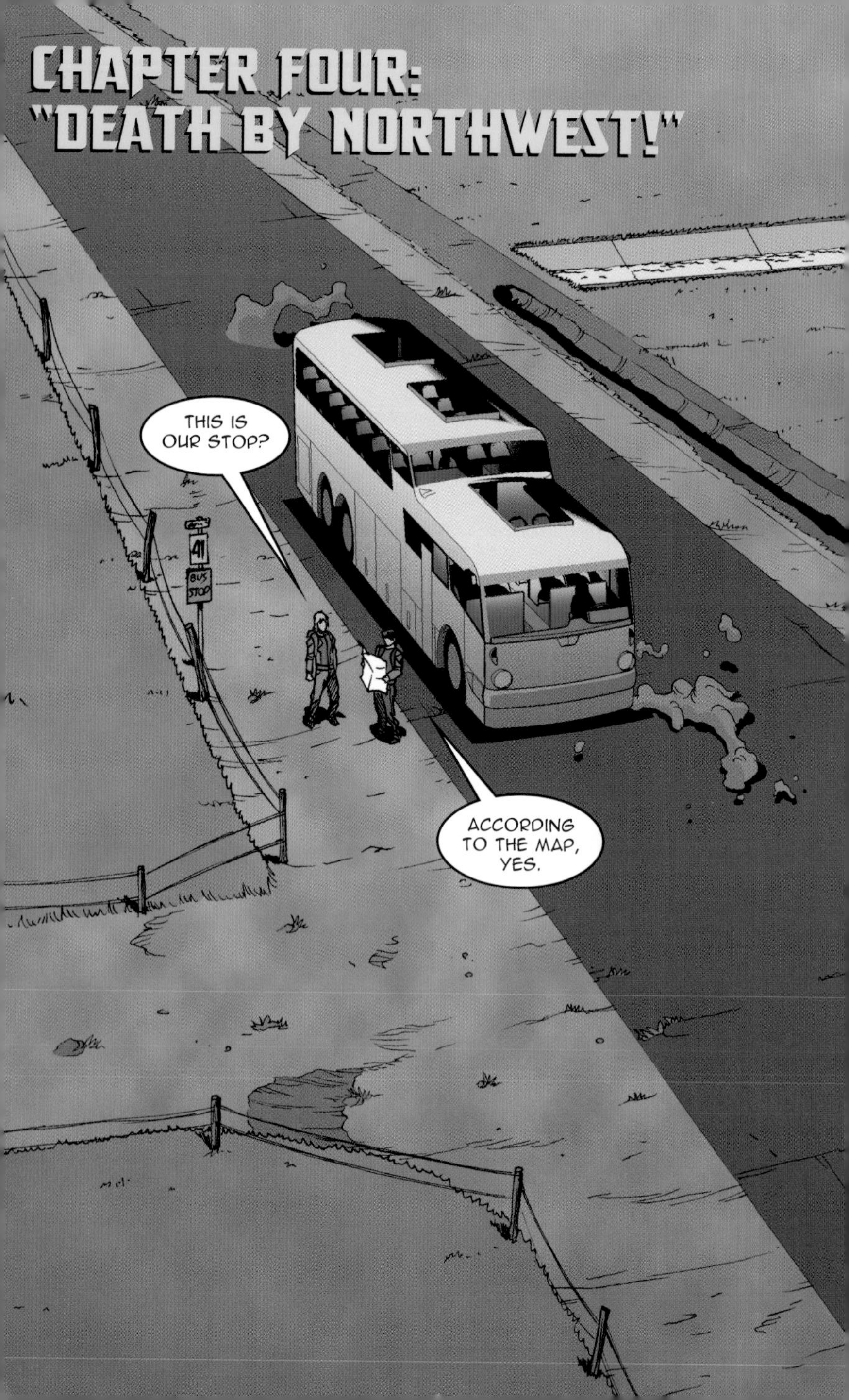
CHAPTER FOUR:
"DEATH BY NORTHWEST!"
41
BUS STOP
THIS IS OUR STOP?
ACCORDING TO THE MAP, YES.

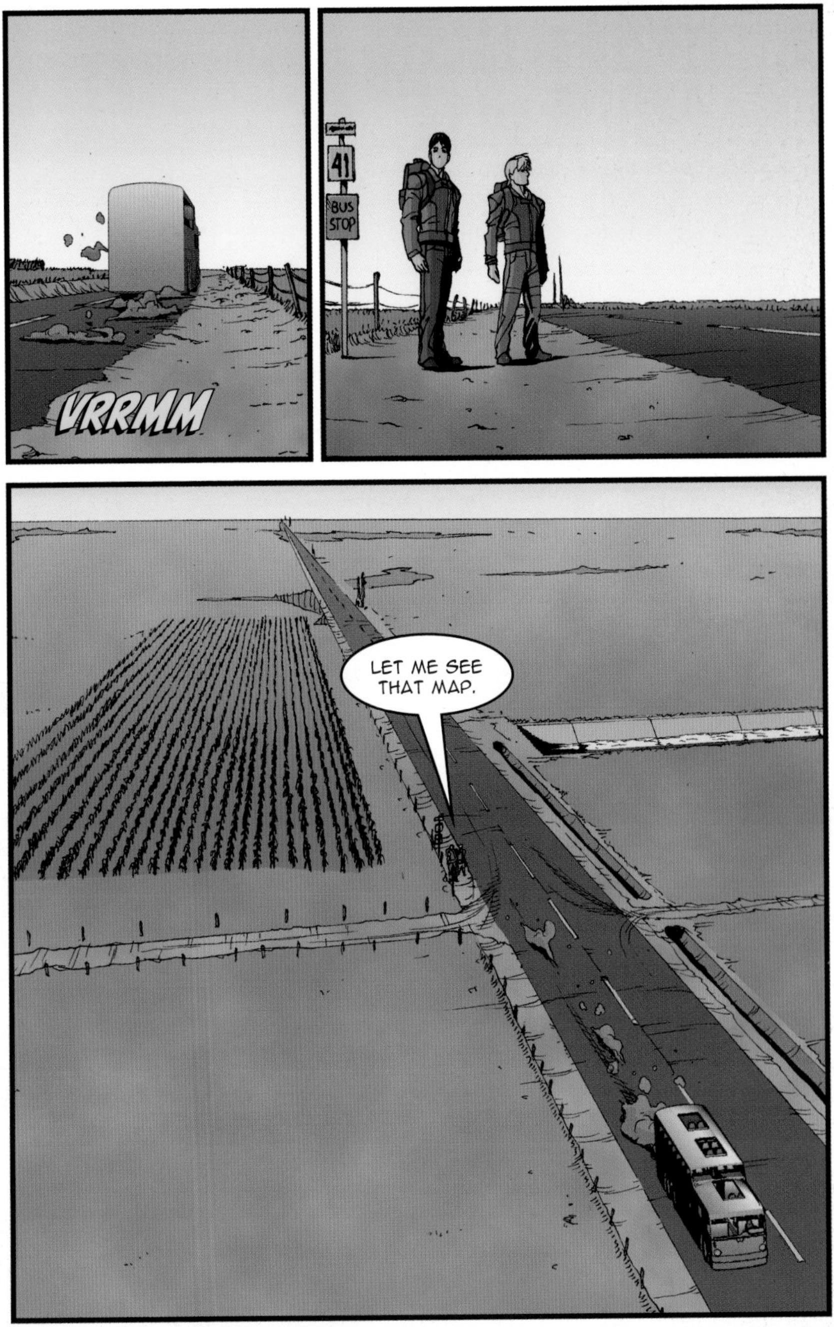
VRRMM
41
BUS STOP
LET ME SEE THAT MAP.

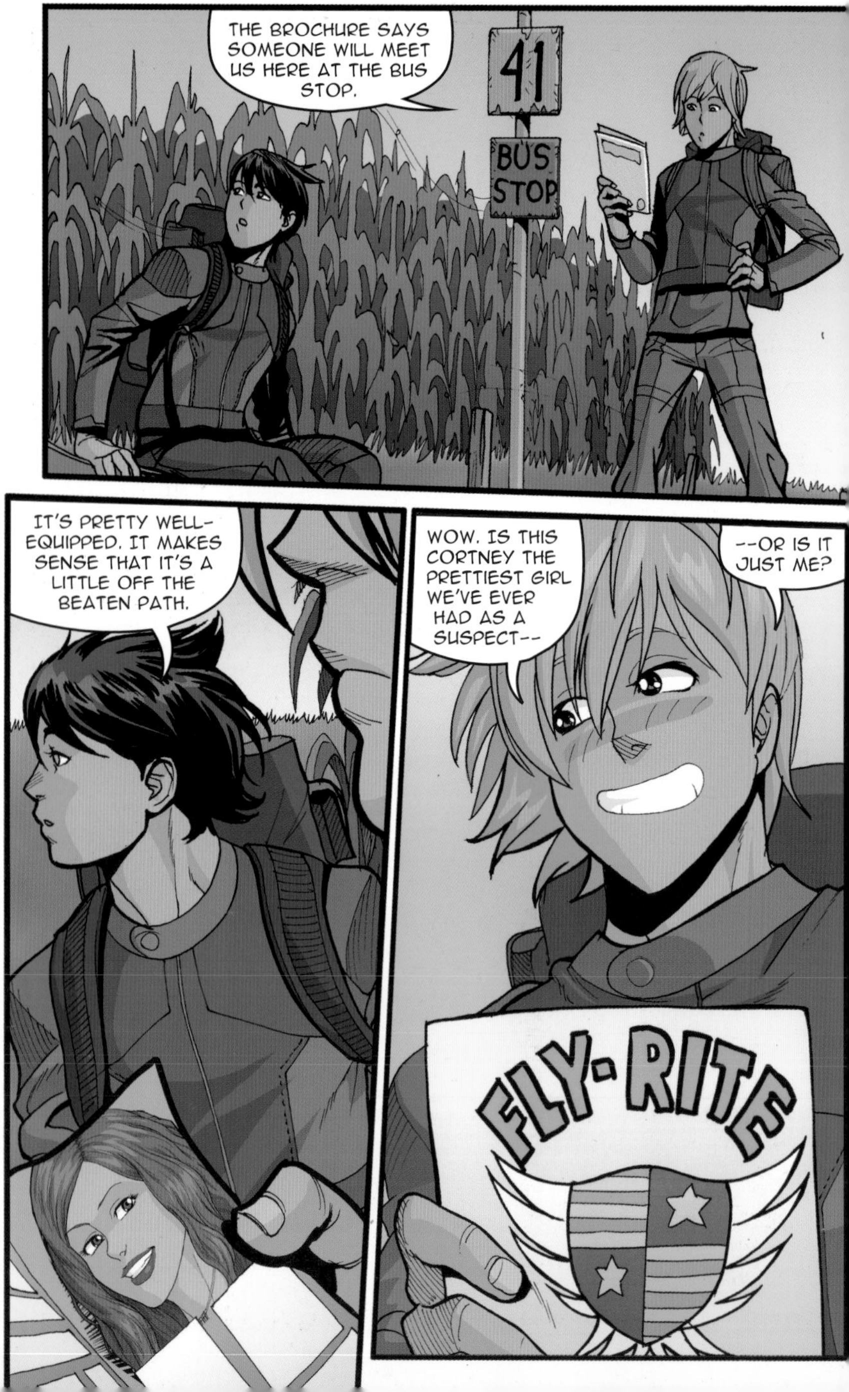
THE BROCHURE SAYS SOMEONE WILL MEET US HERE AT THE BUS STOP.
41
BUS STOP
IT'S PRETTY WELL-EQUIPPED. IT MAKES SENSE THAT IT'S A LITTLE OFF THE BEATEN PATH.
WOW. IS THIS CORTNEY THE PRETTIEST GIRL WE'VE EVER HAD AS A SUSPECT--
--OR IS IT JUST ME?
FLY-RITE

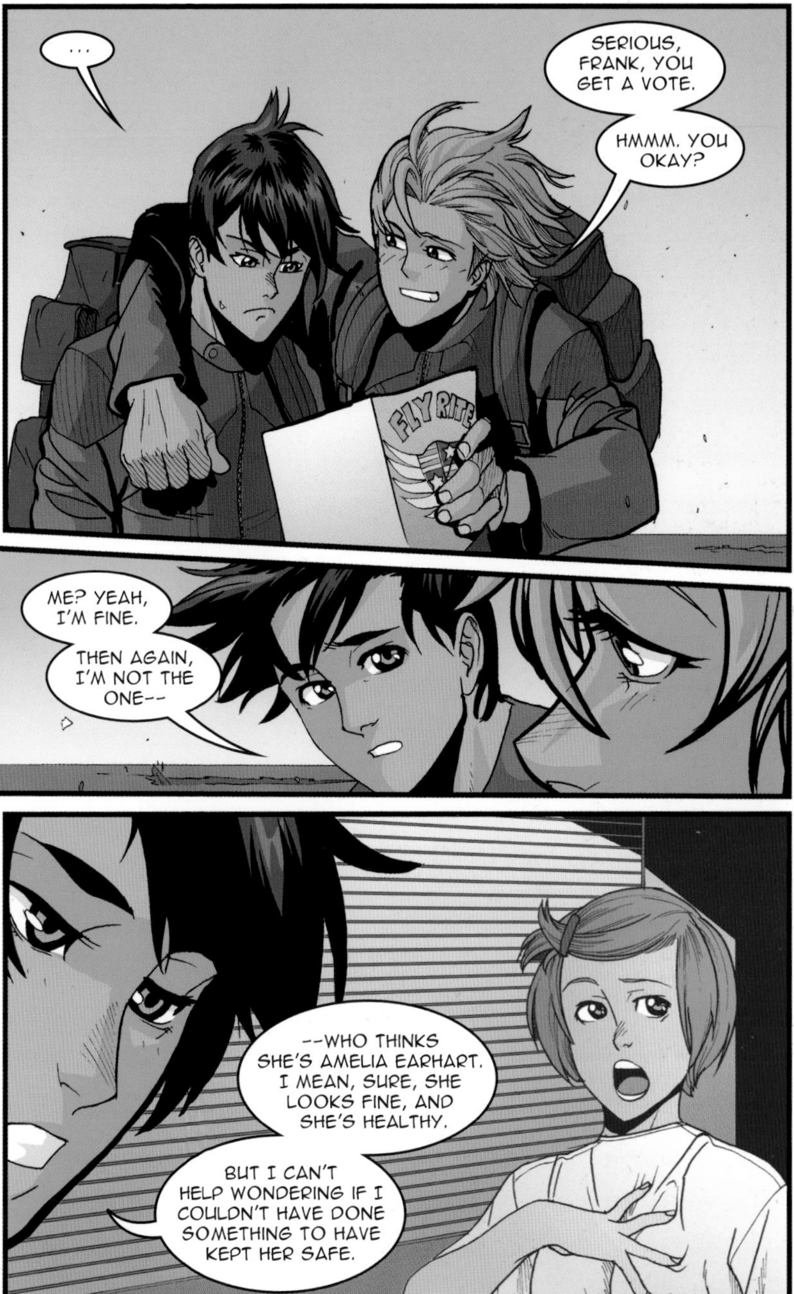
...
SERIOUS, FRANK, YOU GET A VOTE.
HMMM. YOU OKAY?
ME? YEAH, I'M FINE.
THEN AGAIN, I'M NOT THE ONE--
--WHO THINKS SHE'S AMELIA EARHART. I MEAN, SURE, SHE LOOKS FINE, AND SHE'S HEALTHY.
BUT I CAN'T HELP WONDERING IF I COULDN'T HAVE DONE SOMETHING TO HAVE KEPT HER SAFE.

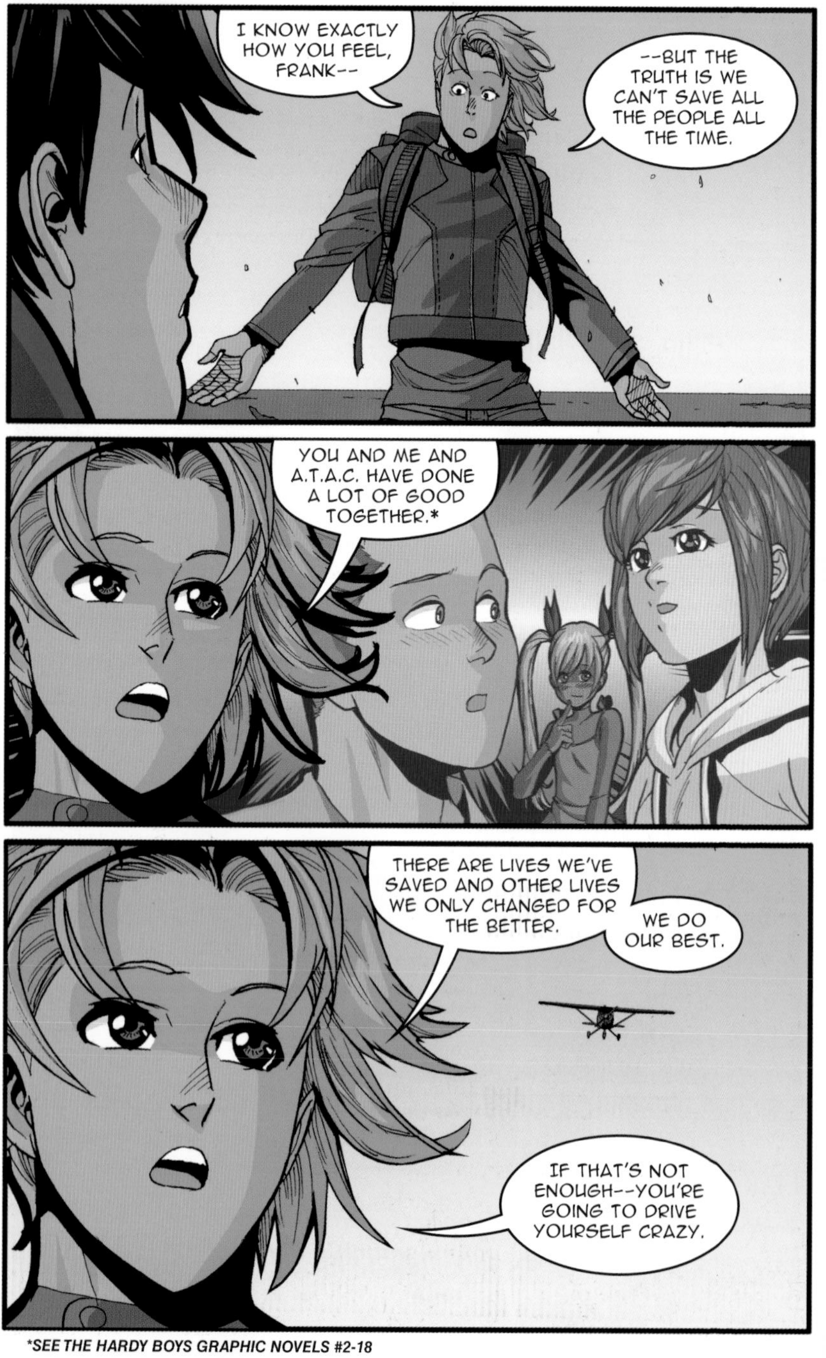
I KNOW EXACTLY HOW YOU FEEL, FRANK--
--BUT THE TRUTH IS WE CAN'T SAVE ALL THE PEOPLE ALL THE TIME.
YOU AND ME AND A.T.A.C. HAVE DONE A LOT OF GOOD TOGETHER.*
THERE ARE LIVES WE'VE SAVED AND OTHER LIVES WE ONLY CHANGED FOR THE BETTER.
WE DO OUR BEST.
IF THAT'S NOT ENOUGH--YOU'RE GOING TO DRIVE YOURSELF CRAZY.

***SEE THE HARDY BOYS GRAPHIC NOVELS #2-18**

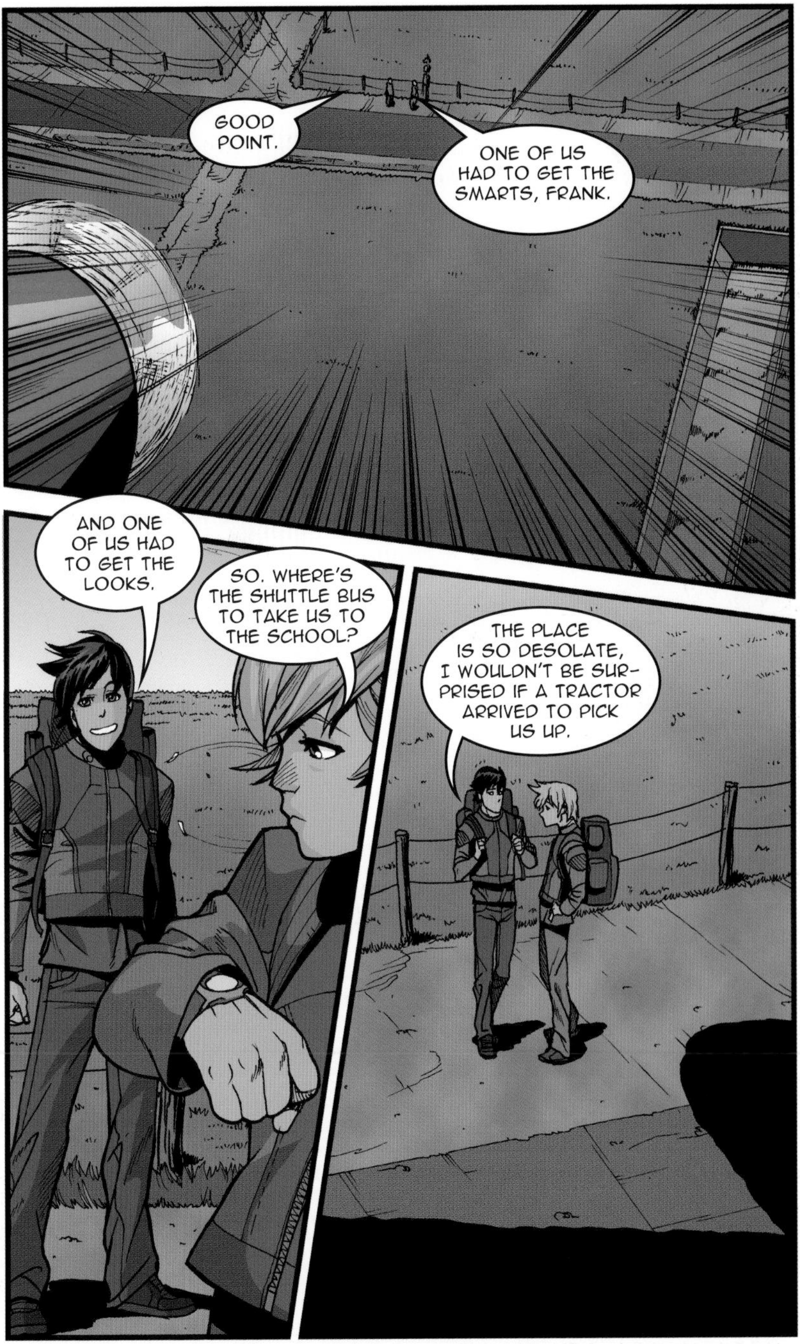
GOOD POINT.
ONE OF US HAD TO GET THE SMARTS, FRANK.
AND ONE OF US HAD TO GET THE LOOKS.
SO. WHERE'S THE SHUTTLE BUS TO TAKE US TO THE SCHOOL?
THE PLACE IS SO DESOLATE, I WOULDN'T BE SUR-PRISED IF A TRACTOR ARRIVED TO PICK US UP.

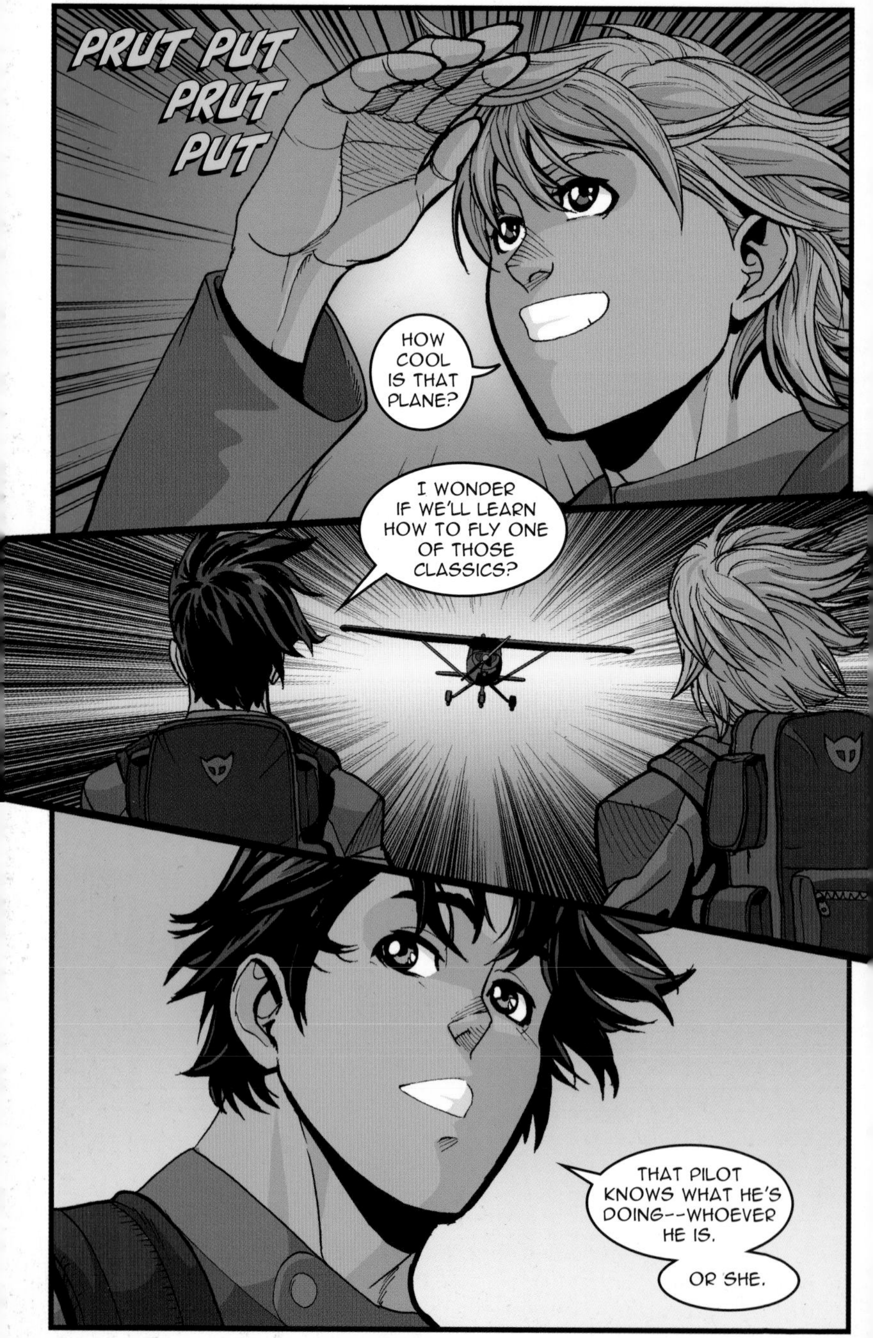
PRUT PUT PRUT PUT
HOW COOL IS THAT PLANE?
I WONDER IF WE'LL LEARN HOW TO FLY ONE OF THOSE CLASSICS?
THAT PILOT KNOWS WHAT HE'S DOING--WHOEVER HE IS.
OR SHE.

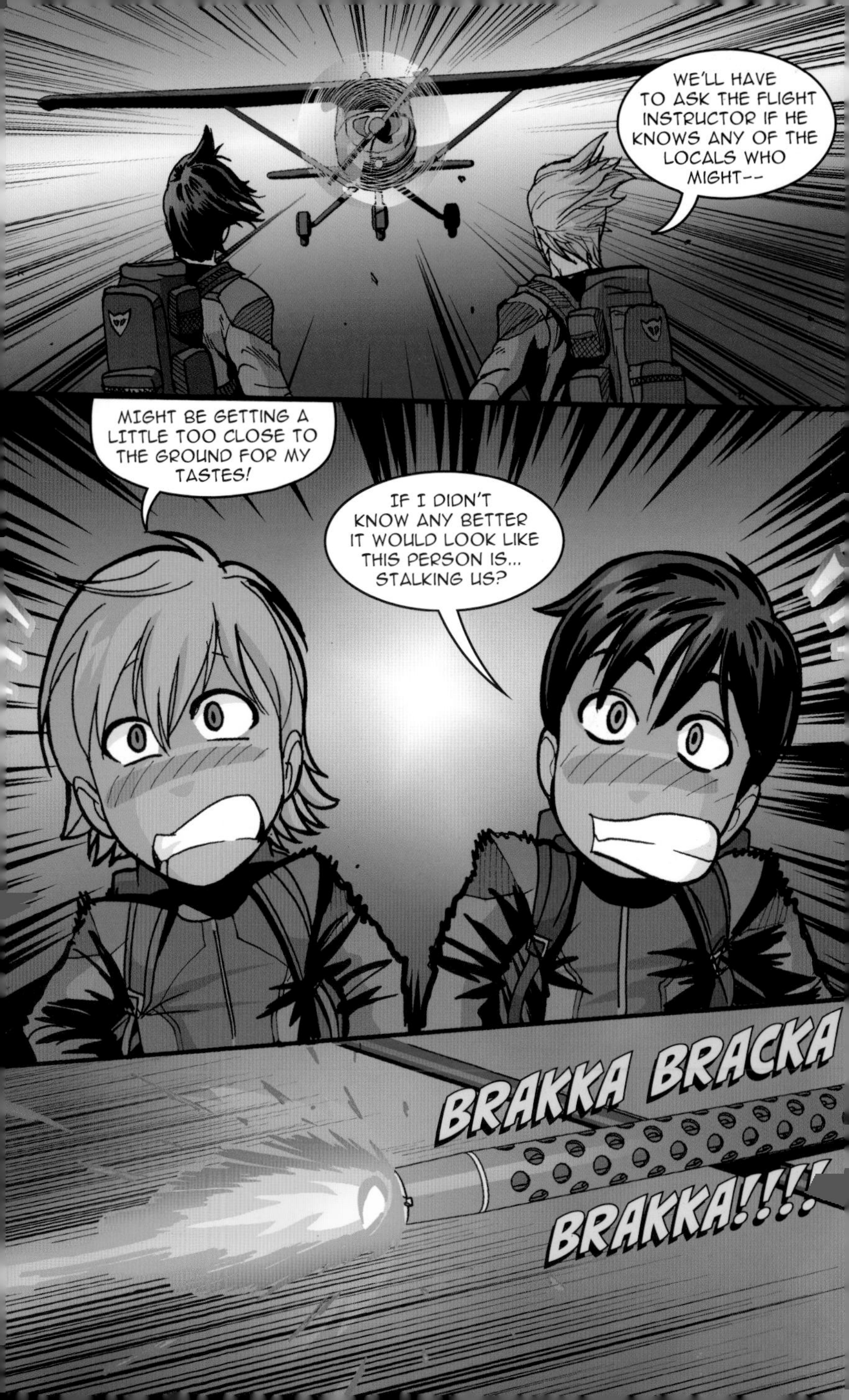
WE'LL HAVE TO ASK THE FLIGHT INSTRUCTOR IF HE KNOWS ANY OF THE LOCALS WHO MIGHT--
MIGHT BE GETTING A LITTLE TOO CLOSE TO THE GROUND FOR MY TASTES!
IF I DIDN'T KNOW ANY BETTER IT WOULD LOOK LIKE THIS PERSON IS... STALKING US?
BRAKKA BRACKA
BRAKKA!!!!

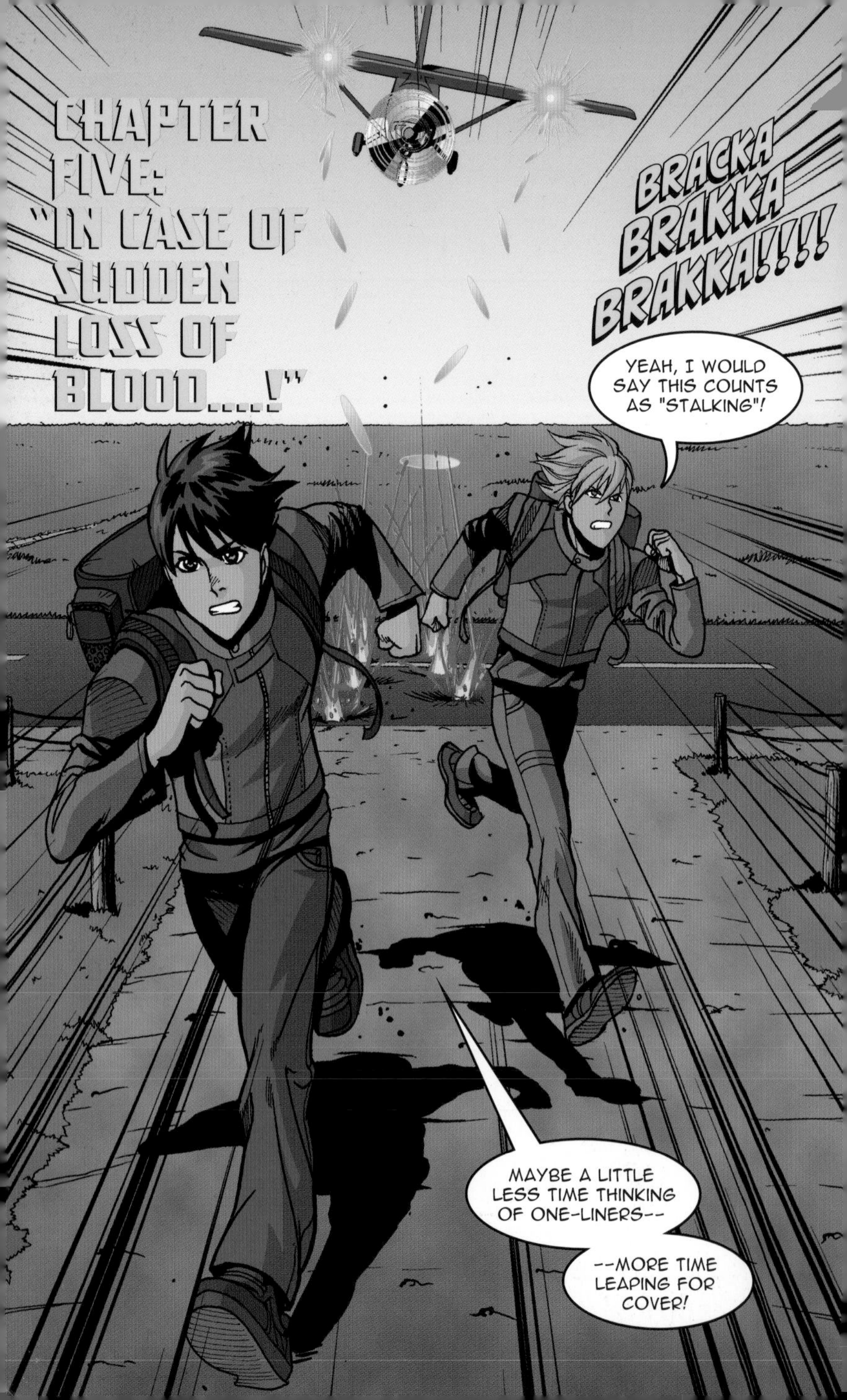
CHAPTER FIVE: "IN CASE OF SUDDEN LOSS OF BLOOD...!"
BRACKA BRAKKA BRAKKA!!!!
YEAH, I WOULD SAY THIS COUNTS AS "STALKING"!
MAYBE A LITTLE LESS TIME THINKING OF ONE-LINERS--
--MORE TIME LEAPING FOR COVER!

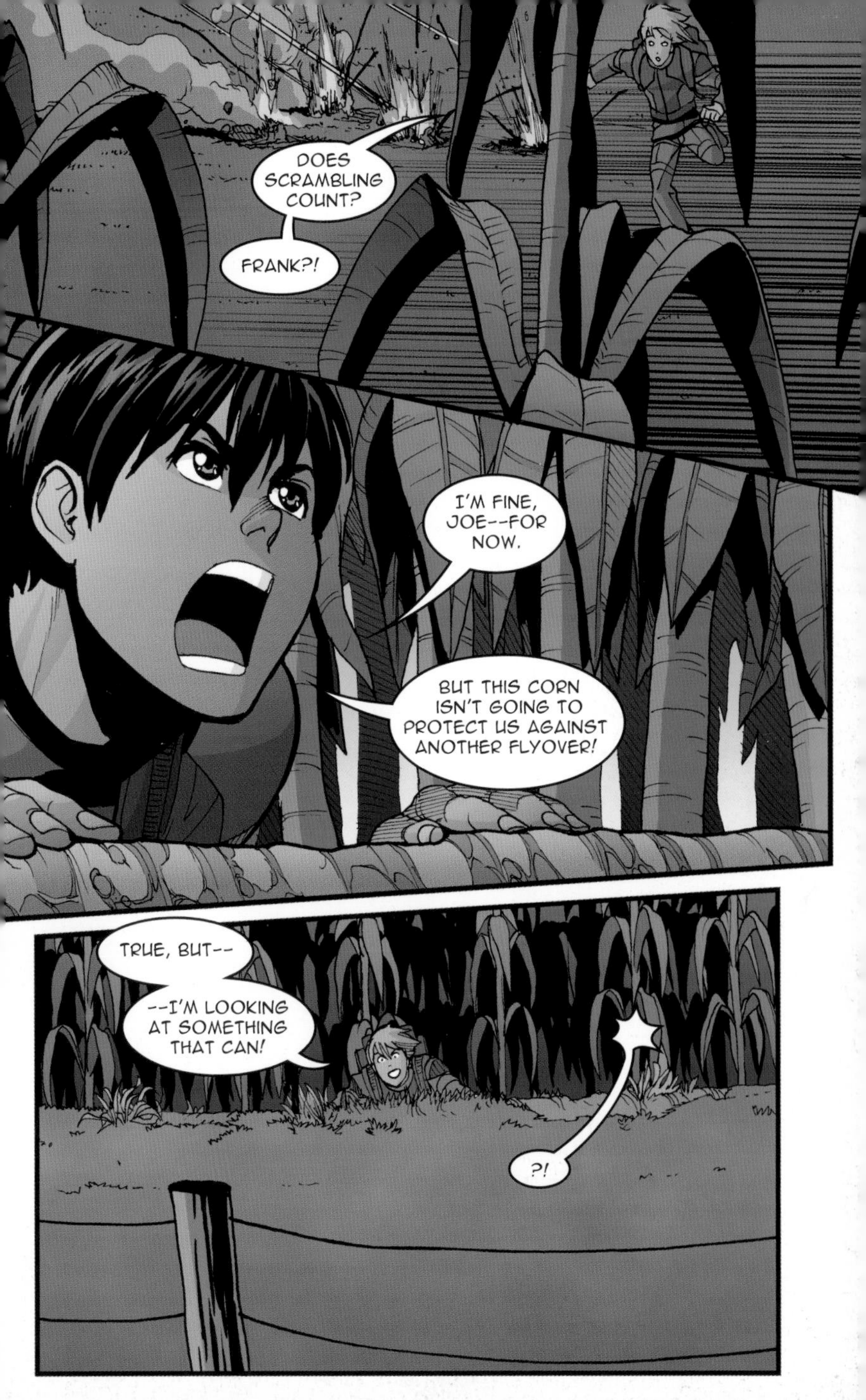
DOES SCRAMBLING COUNT?
FRANK?!
I'M FINE, JOE--FOR NOW.
BUT THIS CORN ISN'T GOING TO PROTECT US AGAINST ANOTHER FLYOVER!
TRUE, BUT--
--I'M LOOKING AT SOMETHING THAT CAN!
?!

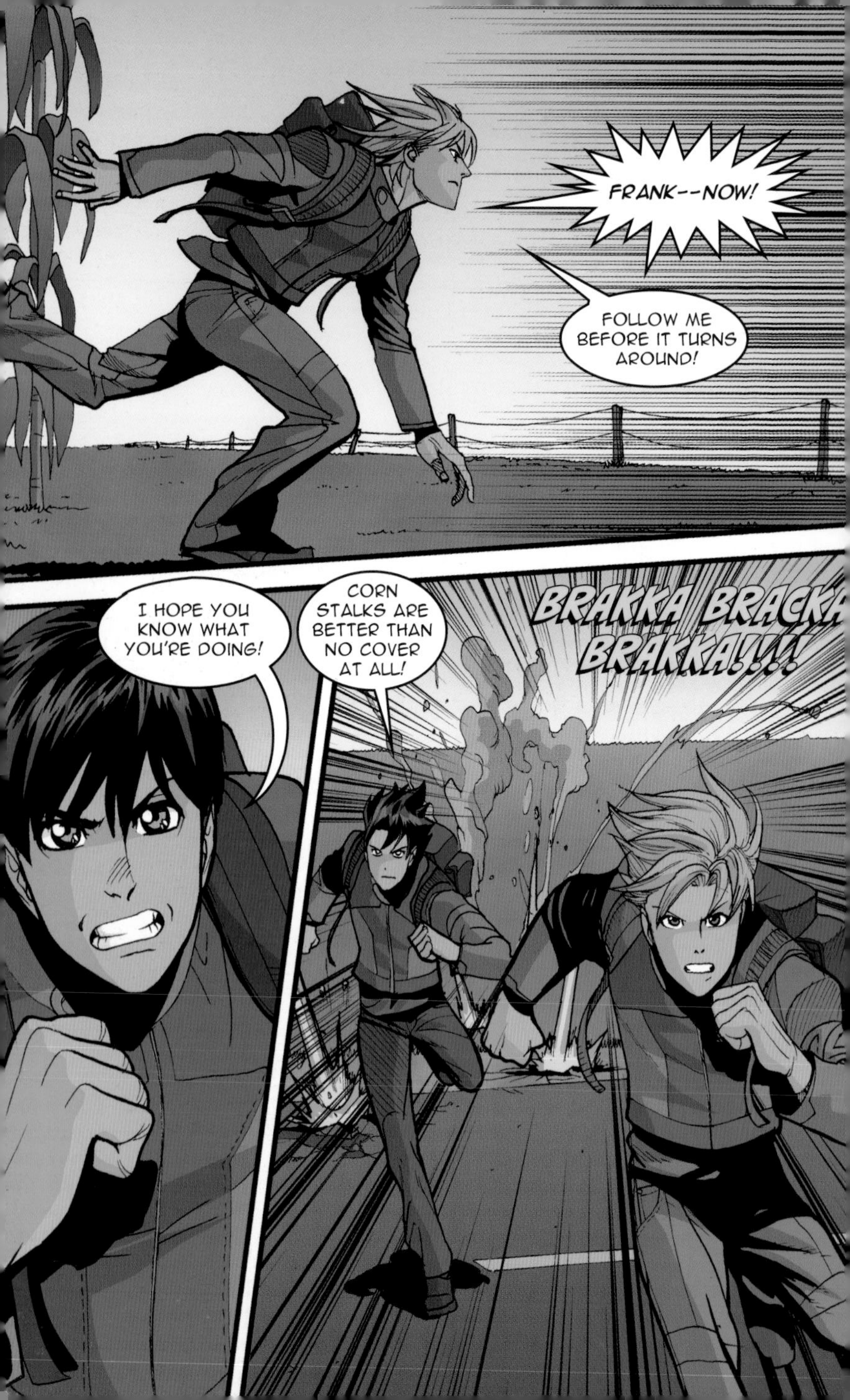
FRANK--NOW!
FOLLOW ME BEFORE IT TURNS AROUND!
I HOPE YOU KNOW WHAT YOU'RE DOING!
CORN STALKS ARE BETTER THAN NO COVER AT ALL!
BRAKKA BRACKA BRAKKA!!!!

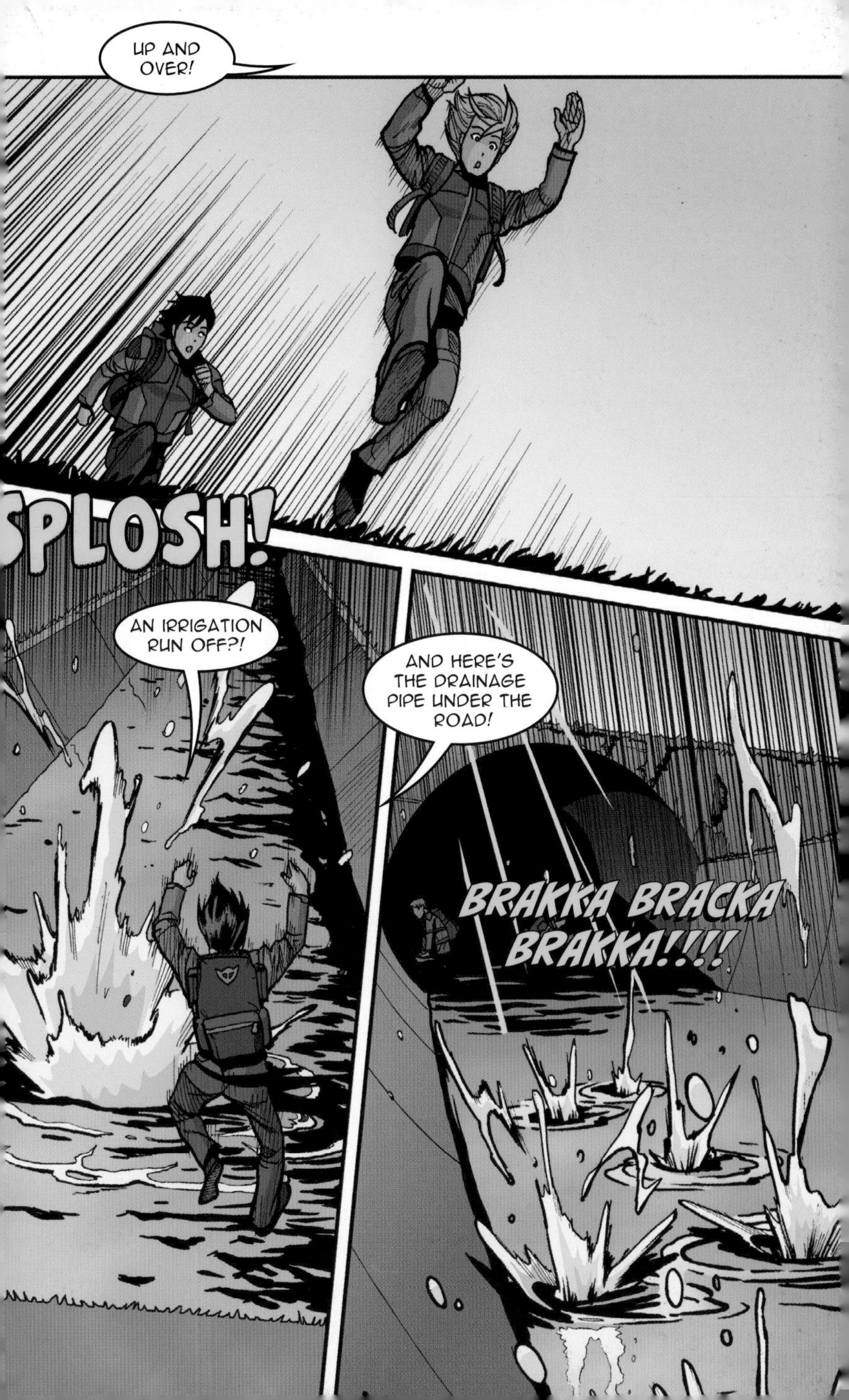
UP AND OVER!
SPLOSH!
AN IRRIGATION RUN OFF?!
AND HERE'S THE DRAINAGE PIPE UNDER THE ROAD!
BRAKKA BRACKA BRAKKA!!!!

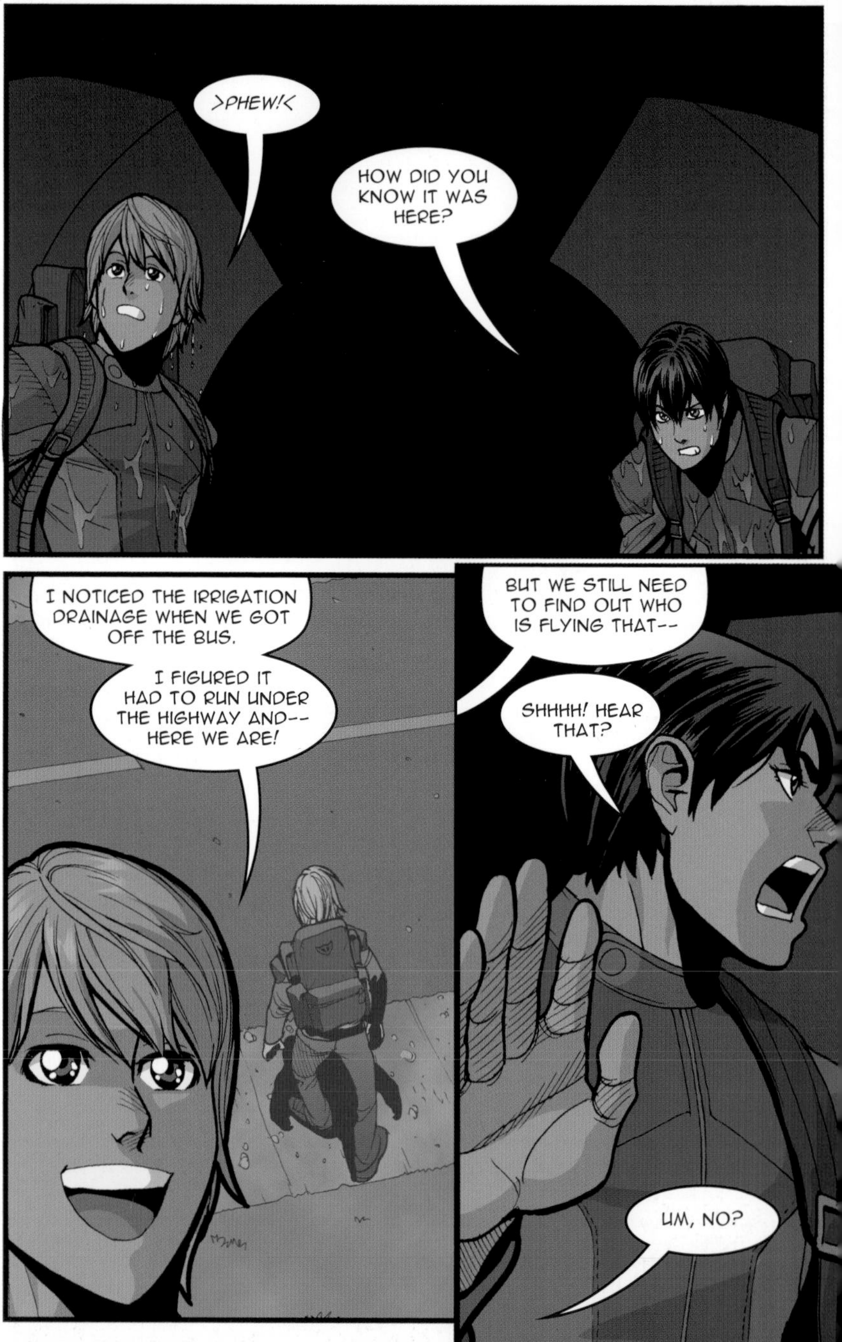
>PHEW!<
HOW DID YOU KNOW IT WAS HERE?
I NOTICED THE IRRIGATION DRAINAGE WHEN WE GOT OFF THE BUS.
I FIGURED IT HAD TO RUN UNDER THE HIGHWAY AND-- HERE WE ARE!
BUT WE STILL NEED TO FIND OUT WHO IS FLYING THAT--
SHHHH! HEAR THAT?
UM, NO?

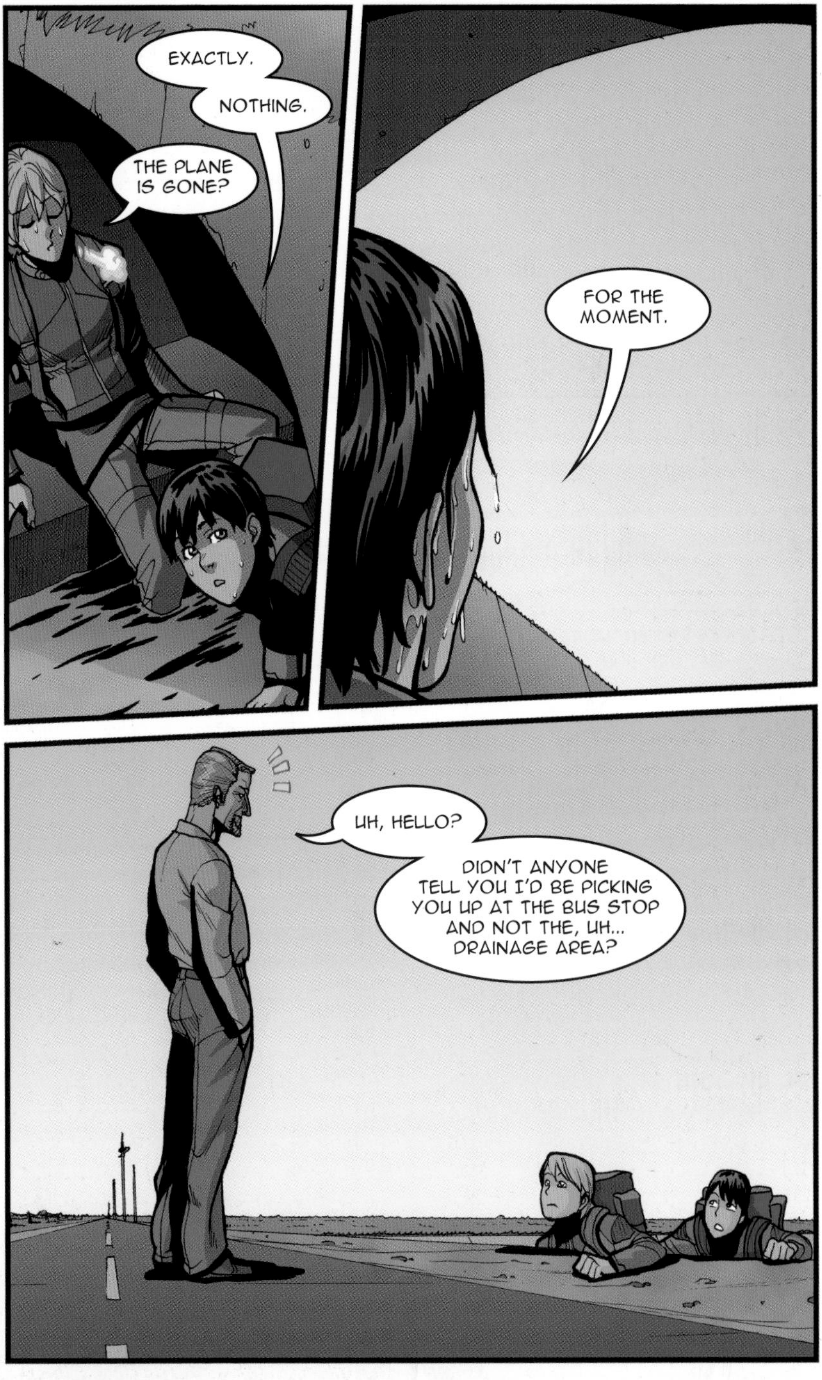
EXACTLY.
NOTHING.
THE PLANE IS GONE?
FOR THE MOMENT.
UH, HELLO?
DIDN'T ANYONE TELL YOU I'D BE PICKING YOU UP AT THE BUS STOP AND NOT THE, UH... DRAINAGE AREA?

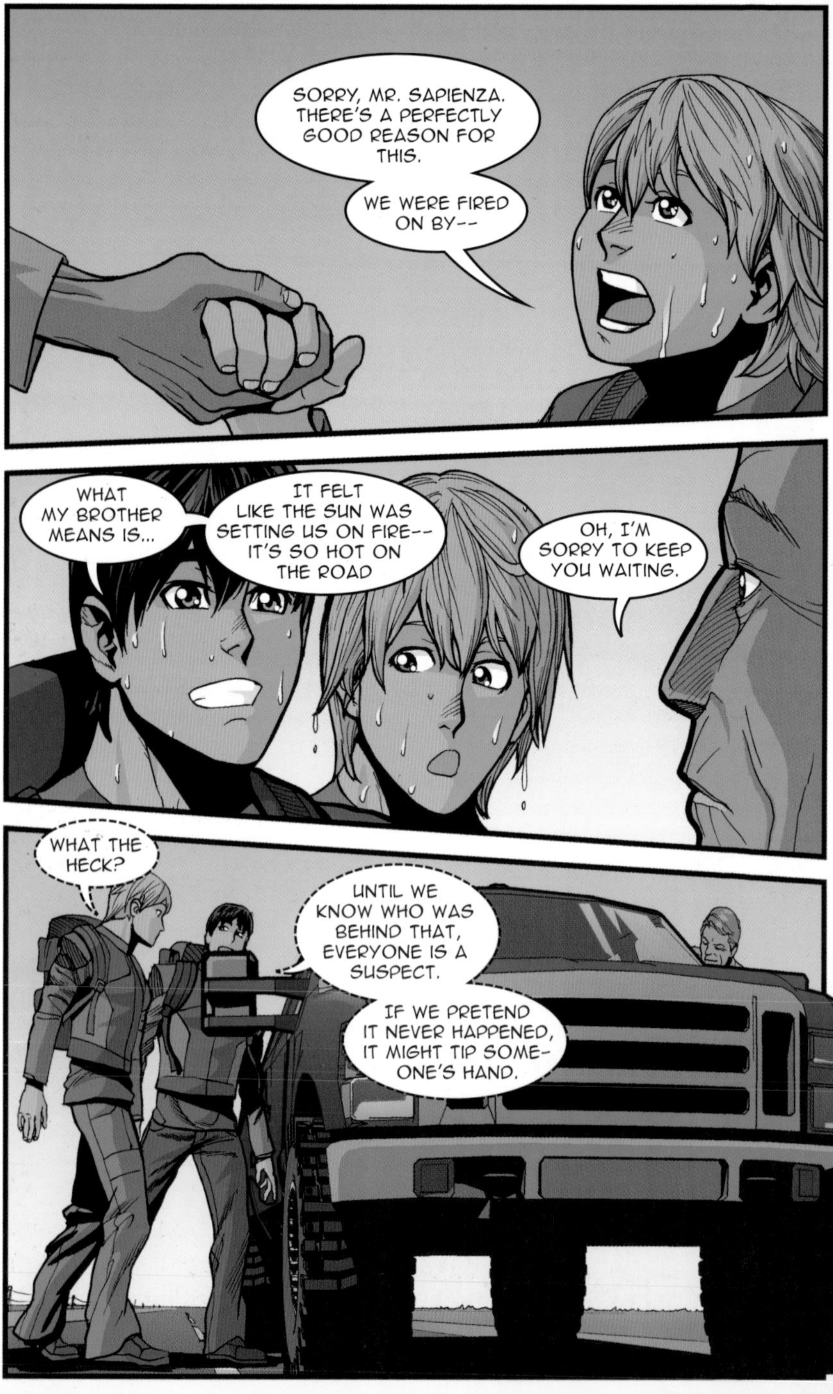
SORRY, MR. SAPIENZA. THERE'S A PERFECTLY GOOD REASON FOR THIS.
WE WERE FIRED ON BY--
WHAT MY BROTHER MEANS IS...
IT FELT LIKE THE SUN WAS SETTING US ON FIRE-- IT'S SO HOT ON THE ROAD
OH, I'M SORRY TO KEEP YOU WAITING.
WHAT THE HECK?
UNTIL WE KNOW WHO WAS BEHIND THAT, EVERYONE IS A SUSPECT.
IF WE PRETEND IT NEVER HAPPENED, IT MIGHT TIP SOME-ONE'S HAND.

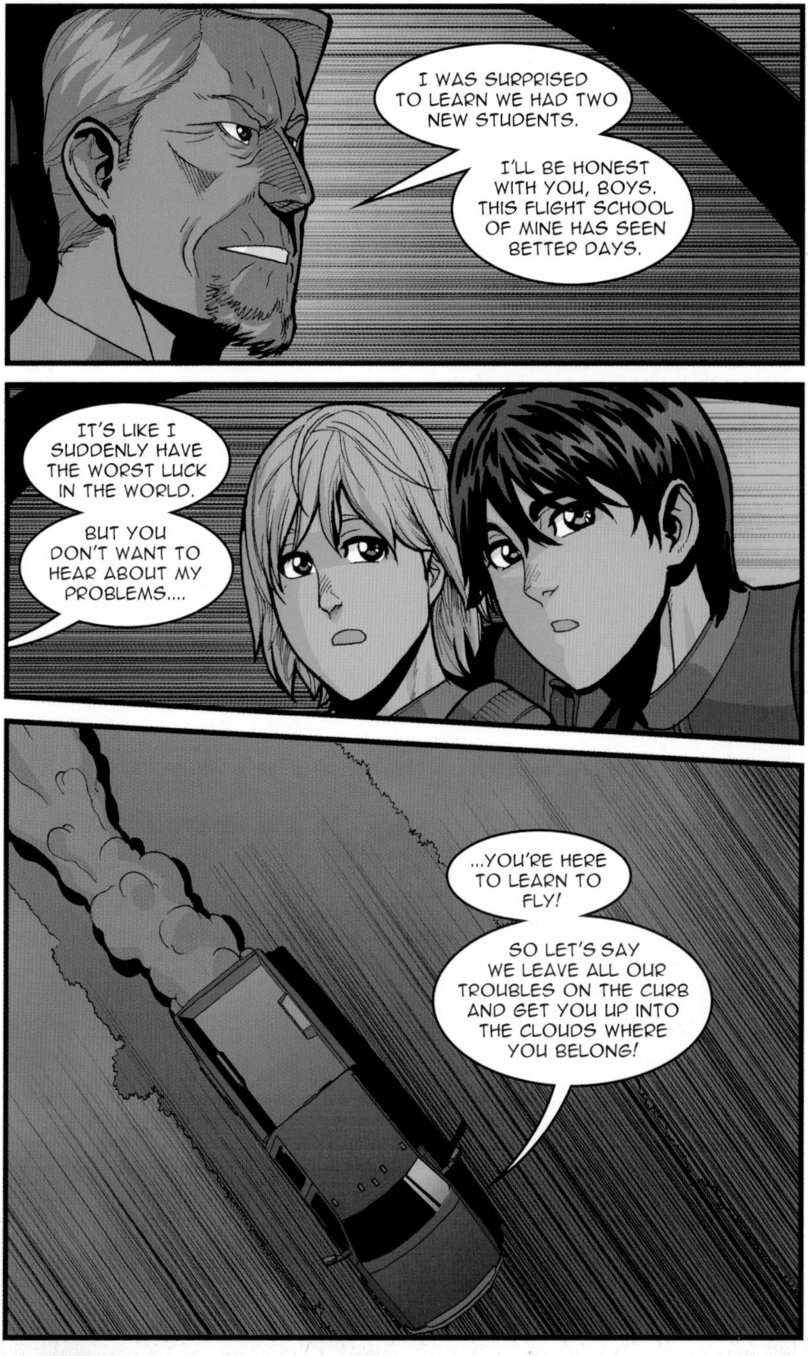
I WAS SURPRISED TO LEARN WE HAD TWO NEW STUDENTS.
I'LL BE HONEST WITH YOU, BOYS. THIS FLIGHT SCHOOL OF MINE HAS SEEN BETTER DAYS.
IT'S LIKE I SUDDENLY HAVE THE WORST LUCK IN THE WORLD.
BUT YOU DON'T WANT TO HEAR ABOUT MY PROBLEMS....
...YOU'RE HERE TO LEARN TO FLY!
SO LET'S SAY WE LEAVE ALL OUR TROUBLES ON THE CURB AND GET YOU UP INTO THE CLOUDS WHERE YOU BELONG!

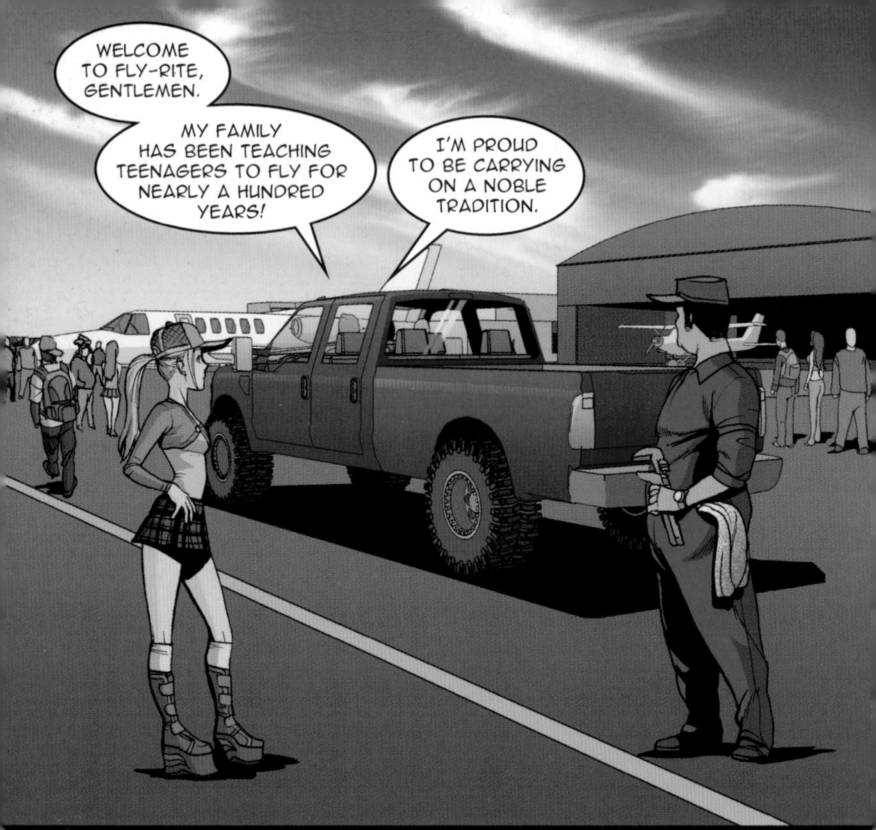
WELCOME TO FLY-RITE, GENTLEMEN.
MY FAMILY HAS BEEN TEACHING TEENAGERS TO FLY FOR NEARLY A HUNDRED YEARS!
I'M PROUD TO BE CARRYING ON A NOBLE TRADITION.

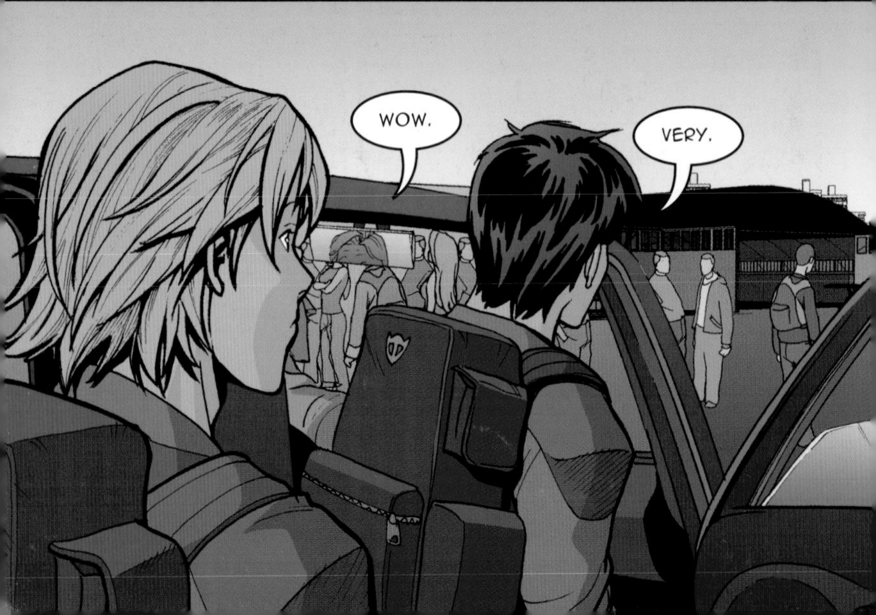
WOW.
VERY.

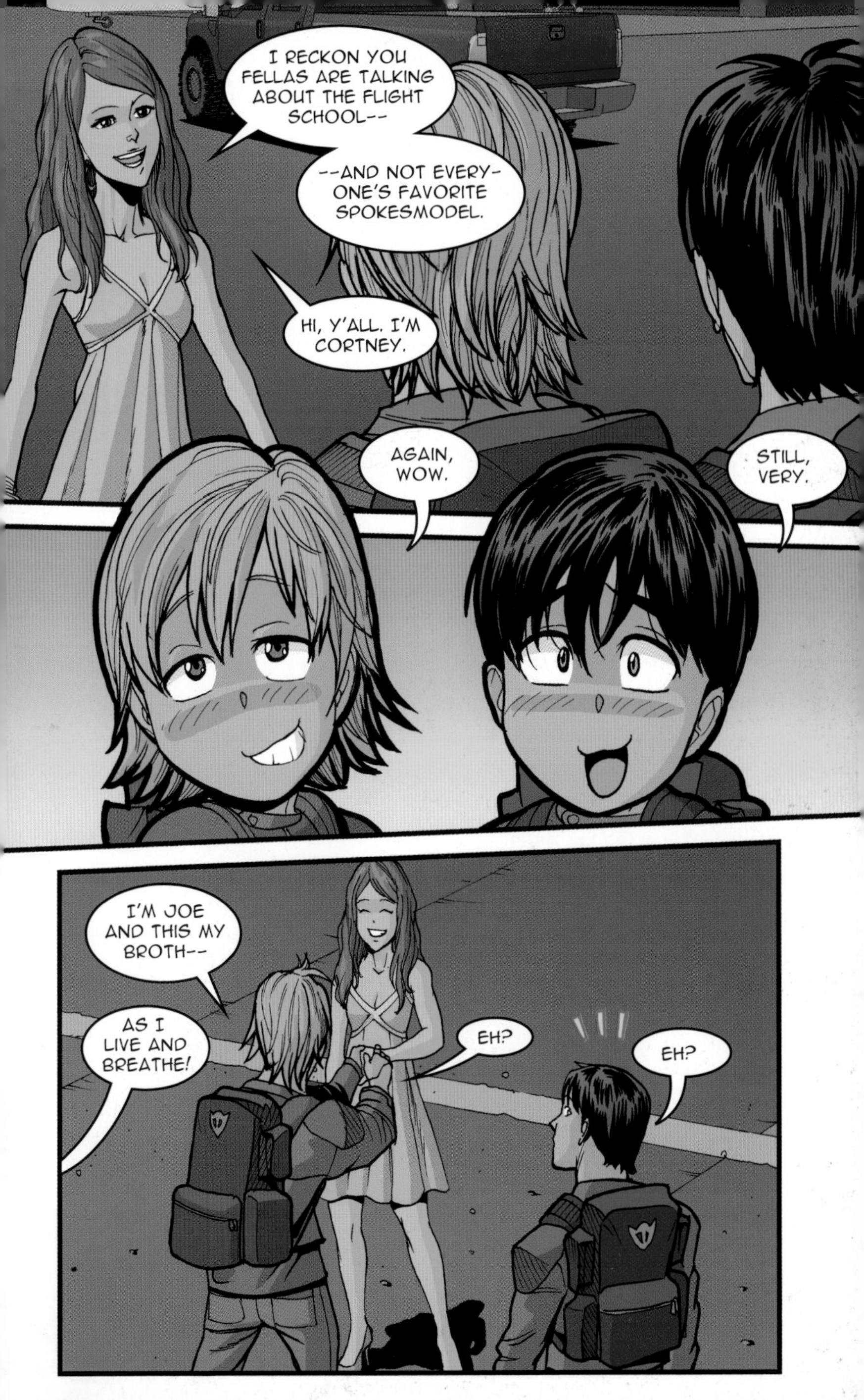
I RECKON YOU FELLAS ARE TALKING ABOUT THE FLIGHT SCHOOL--
--AND NOT EVERY-ONE'S FAVORITE SPOKESMODEL.
HI, Y'ALL. I'M CORTNEY.
AGAIN, WOW.
STILL, VERY.
I'M JOE AND THIS MY BROTH--
AS I LIVE AND BREATHE!
EH?
EH?

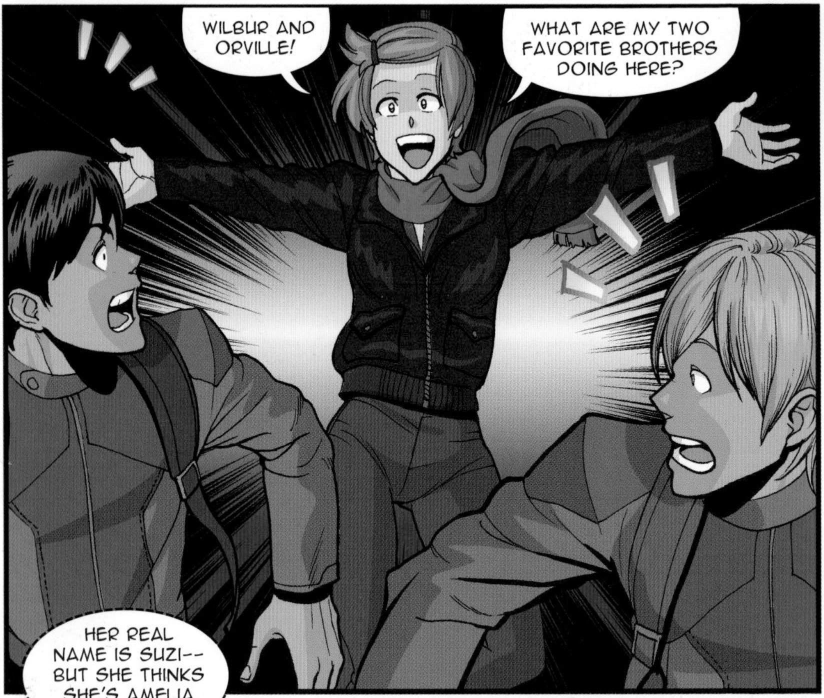
WILBUR AND ORVILLE!
WHAT ARE MY TWO FAVORITE BROTHERS DOING HERE?
HER REAL NAME IS SUZI-- BUT SHE THINKS SHE'S AMELIA EARHART.

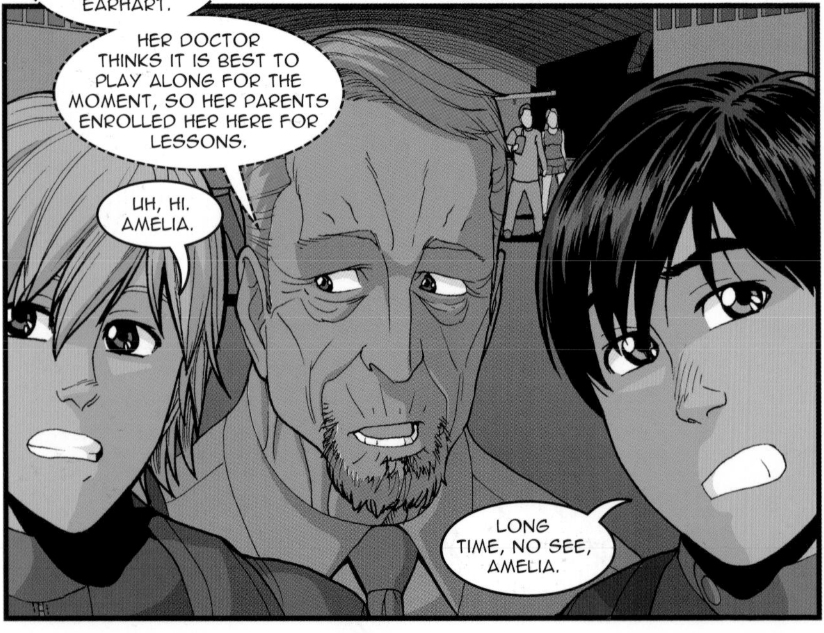
HER DOCTOR THINKS IT IS BEST TO PLAY ALONG FOR THE MOMENT, SO HER PARENTS ENROLLED HER HERE FOR LESSONS.
UH, HI. AMELIA.
LONG TIME, NO SEE, AMELIA.

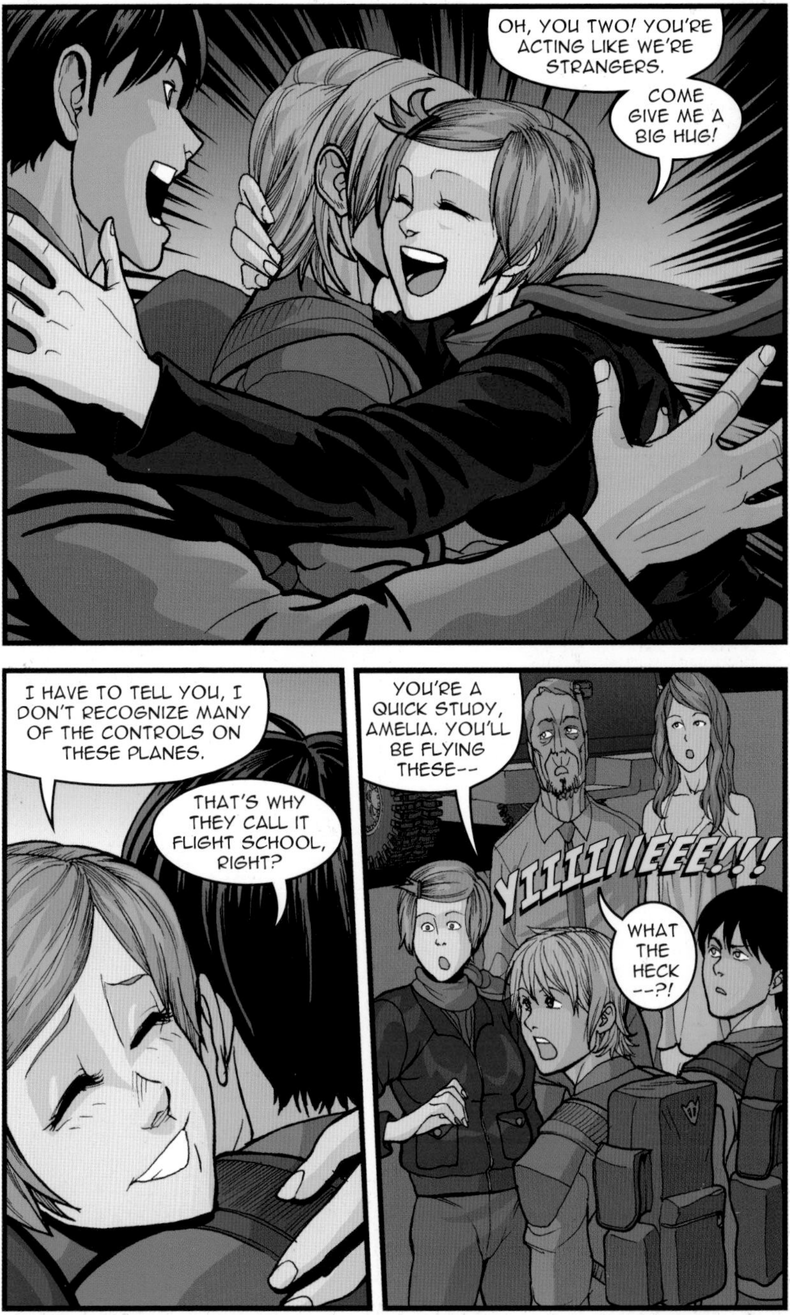

OH, YOU TWO! YOU'RE ACTING LIKE WE'RE STRANGERS.
COME GIVE ME A BIG HUG!
I HAVE TO TELL YOU, I DON'T RECOGNIZE MANY OF THE CONTROLS ON THESE PLANES.
THAT'S WHY THEY CALL IT FLIGHT SCHOOL, RIGHT?
YOU'RE A QUICK STUDY, AMELIA. YOU'LL BE FLYING THESE--
YIIIIIIEEE!!!
WHAT THE HECK --?!

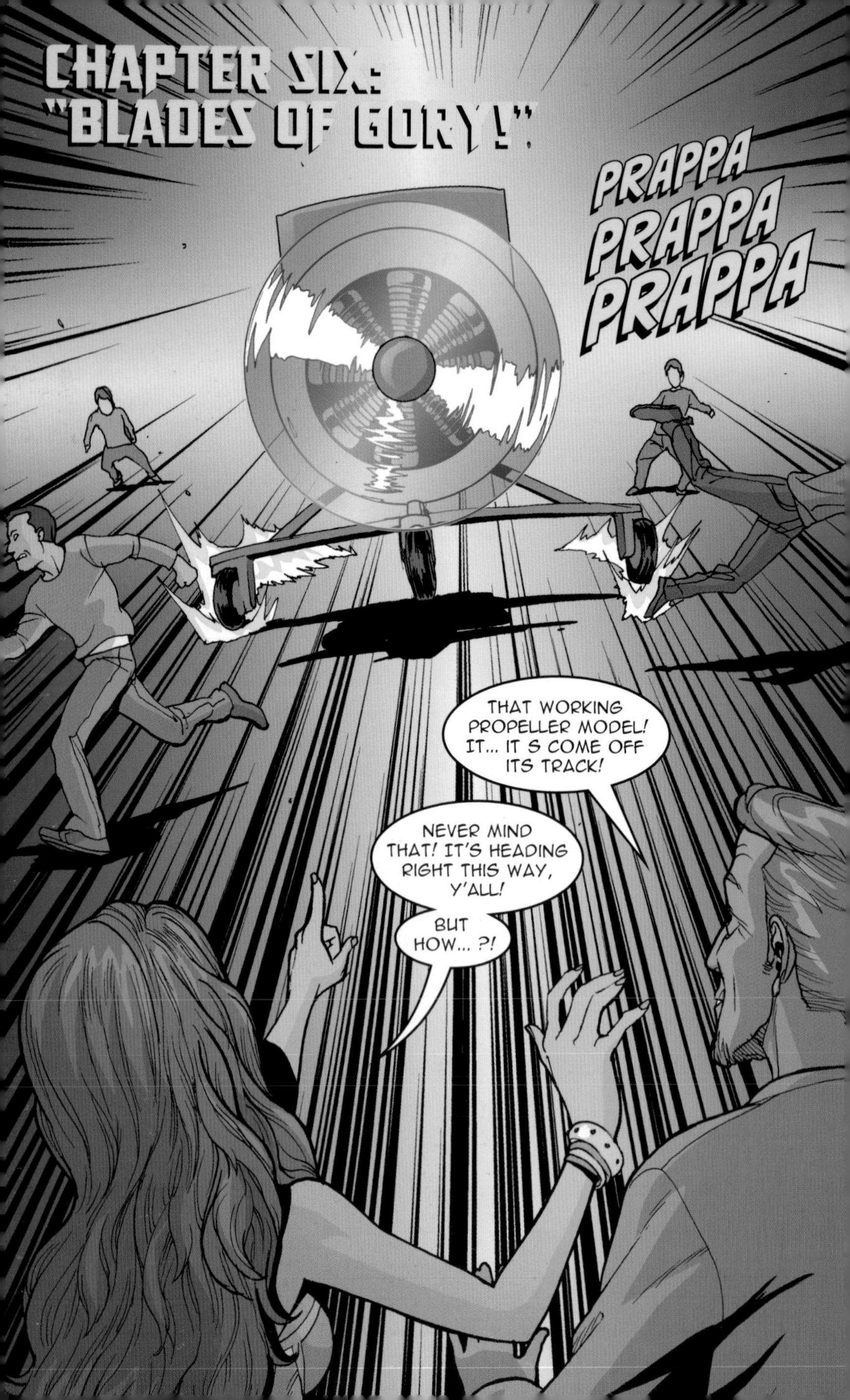
CHAPTER SIX:
"BLADES OF GORY!"
PRAPPA
PRAPPA
PRAPPA
THAT WORKING PROPELLER MODEL! IT... IT S COME OFF ITS TRACK!
NEVER MIND THAT! IT'S HEADING RIGHT THIS WAY, Y'ALL!
BUT HOW... ?!

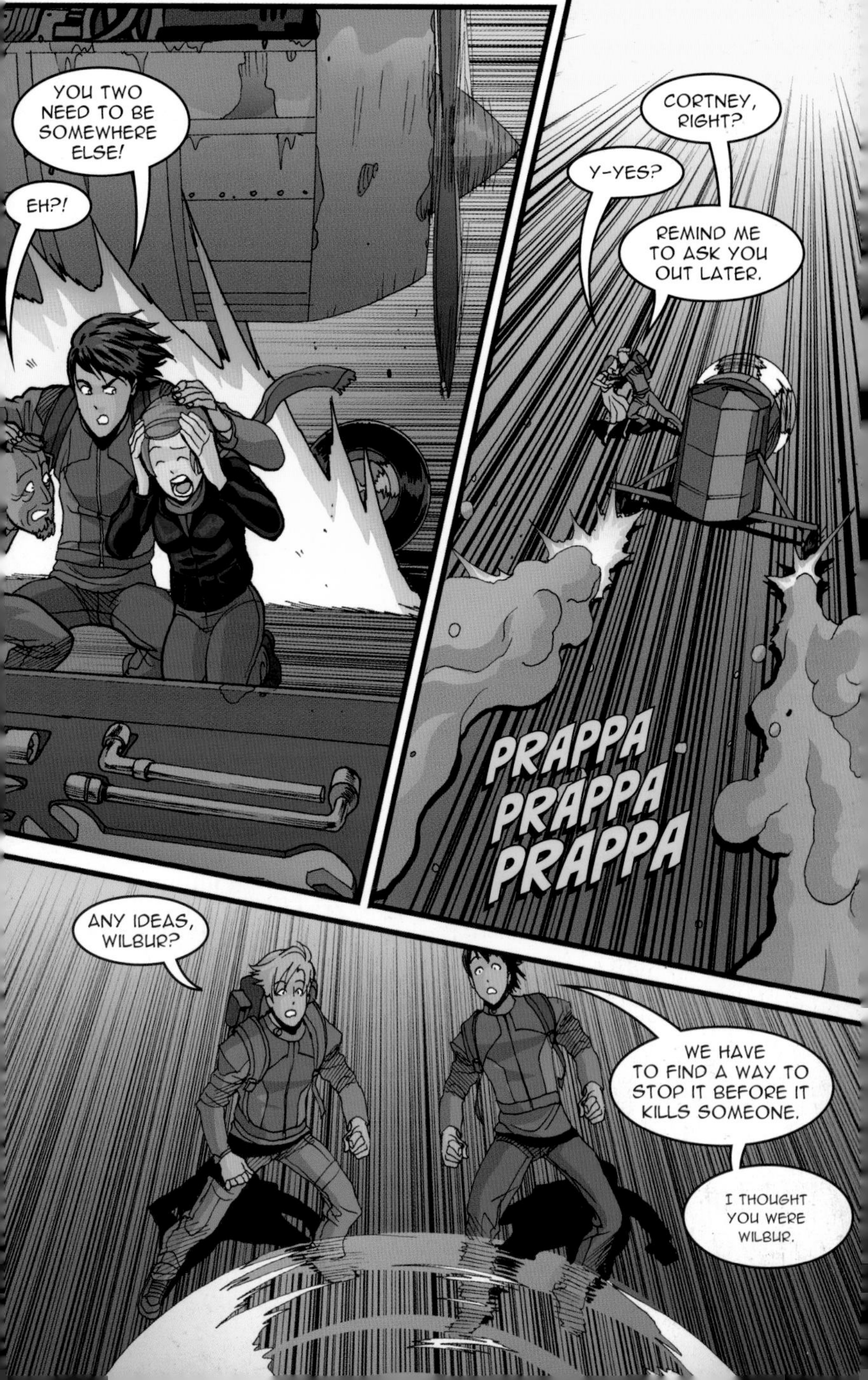
YOU TWO NEED TO BE SOMEWHERE ELSE!
EH?!
CORTNEY, RIGHT?
Y-YES?
REMIND ME TO ASK YOU OUT LATER.
PRAPPA PRAPPA PRAPPA
ANY IDEAS, WILBUR?
WE HAVE TO FIND A WAY TO STOP IT BEFORE IT KILLS SOMEONE.
I THOUGHT YOU WERE WILBUR.

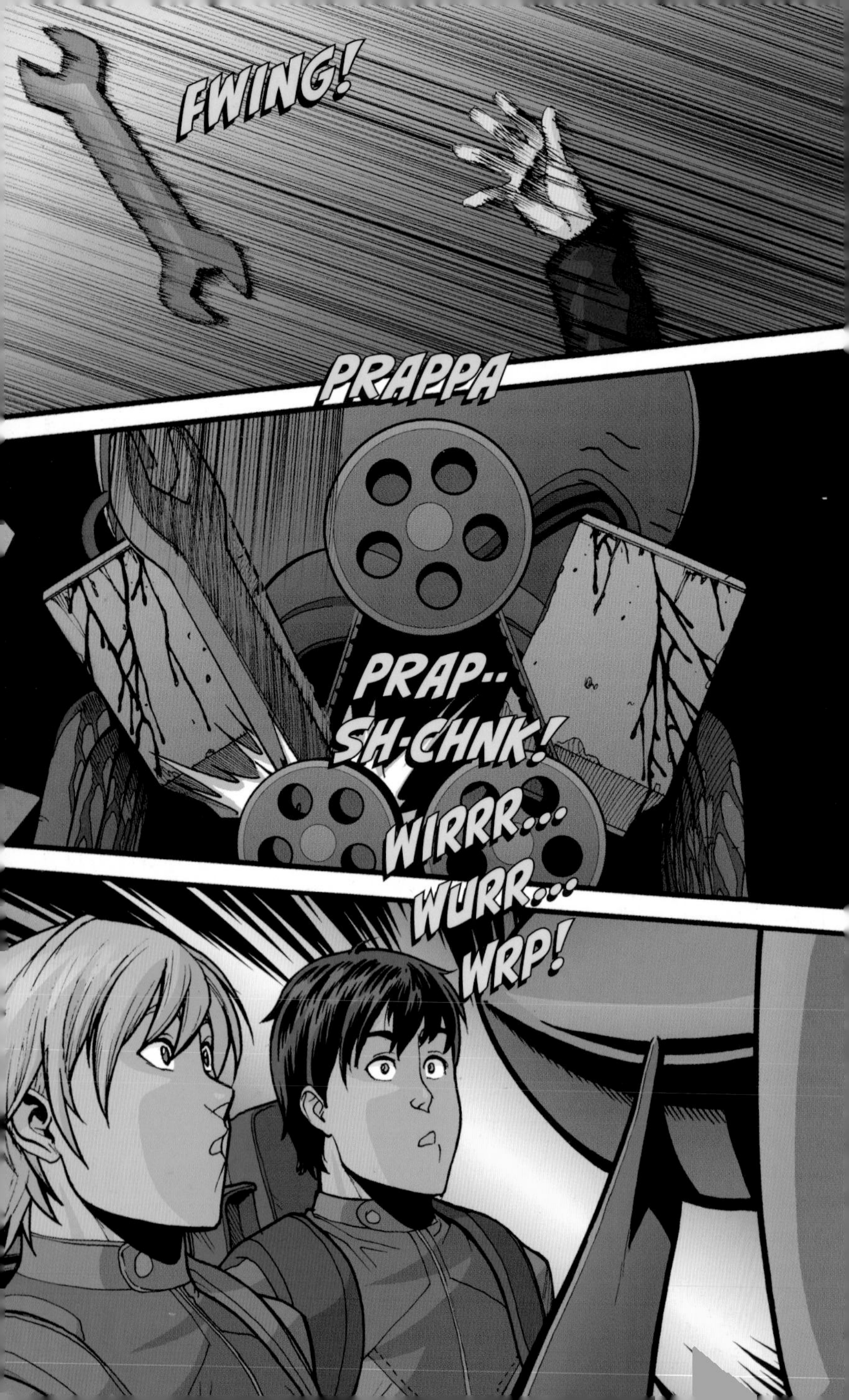
FWING!
PRAPPA
PRAP..
SH-CHNK!
WIRRR...
WURR...
WRP!

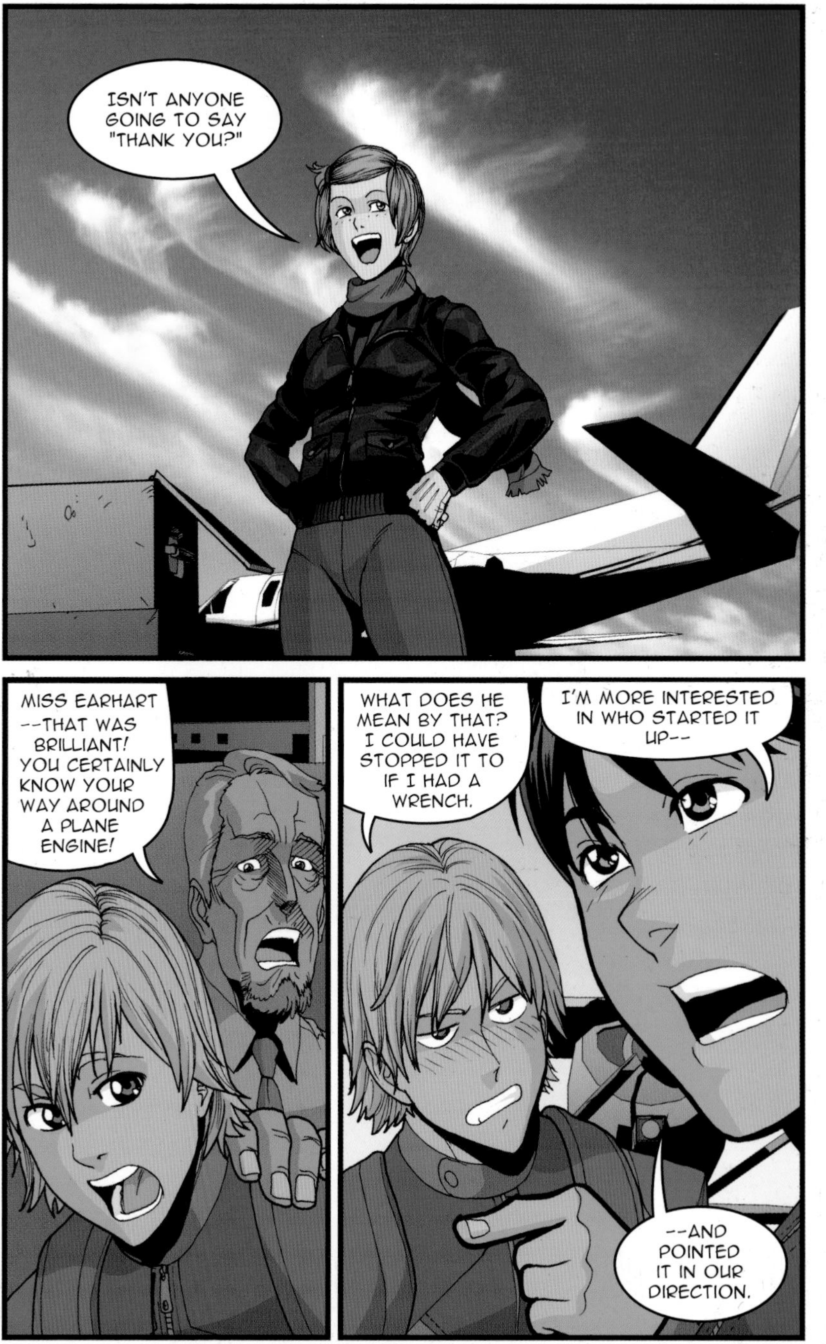
ISN'T ANYONE GOING TO SAY "THANK YOU?"
MISS EARHART --THAT WAS BRILLIANT! YOU CERTAINLY KNOW YOUR WAY AROUND A PLANE ENGINE!
WHAT DOES HE MEAN BY THAT? I COULD HAVE STOPPED IT TO IF I HAD A WRENCH.
I'M MORE INTERESTED IN WHO STARTED IT UP--
--AND POINTED IT IN OUR DIRECTION.

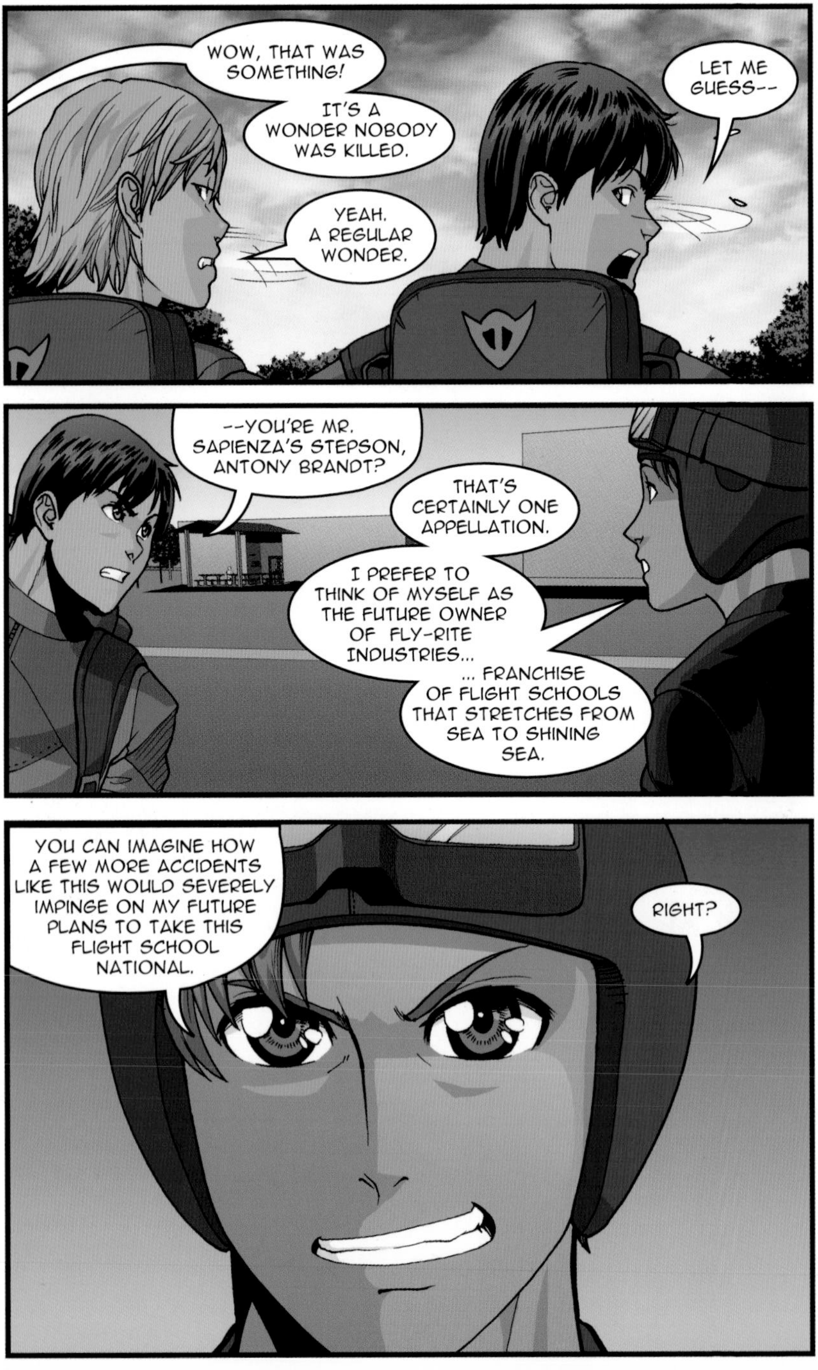
WOW, THAT WAS SOMETHING!
IT'S A WONDER NOBODY WAS KILLED.
YEAH. A REGULAR WONDER.
LET ME GUESS--
--YOU'RE MR. SAPIENZA'S STEPSON, ANTONY BRANDT?
THAT'S CERTAINLY ONE APPELLATION.
I PREFER TO THINK OF MYSELF AS THE FUTURE OWNER OF FLY-RITE INDUSTRIES...
... FRANCHISE OF FLIGHT SCHOOLS THAT STRETCHES FROM SEA TO SHINING SEA.
YOU CAN IMAGINE HOW A FEW MORE ACCIDENTS LIKE THIS WOULD SEVERELY IMPINGE ON MY FUTURE PLANS TO TAKE THIS FLIGHT SCHOOL NATIONAL.
RIGHT?

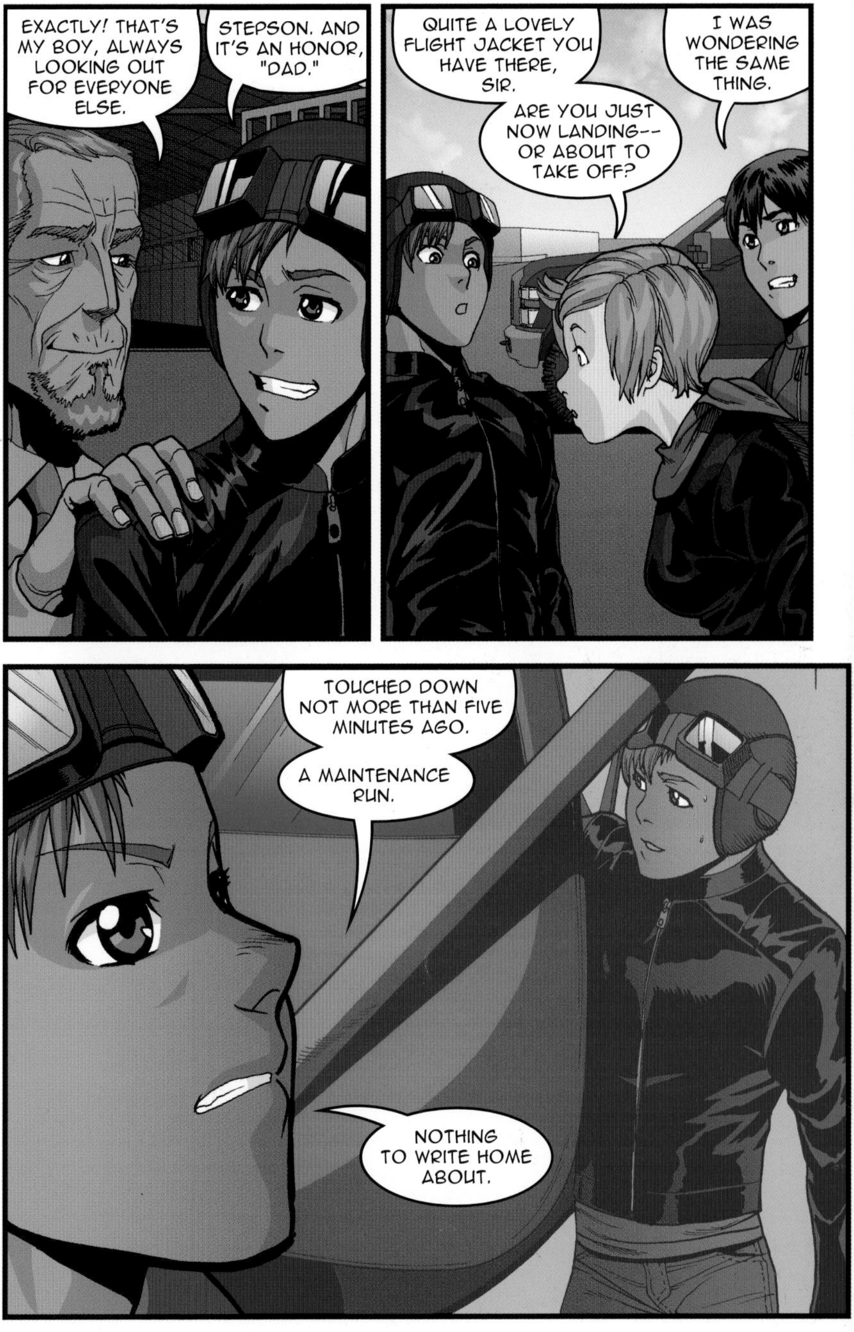

EXACTLY! THAT'S MY BOY, ALWAYS LOOKING OUT FOR EVERYONE ELSE.
STEPSON. AND IT'S AN HONOR, "DAD."
QUITE A LOVELY FLIGHT JACKET YOU HAVE THERE, SIR.
ARE YOU JUST NOW LANDING-- OR ABOUT TO TAKE OFF?
I WAS WONDERING THE SAME THING.
TOUCHED DOWN NOT MORE THAN FIVE MINUTES AGO.
A MAINTENANCE RUN.
NOTHING TO WRITE HOME ABOUT.

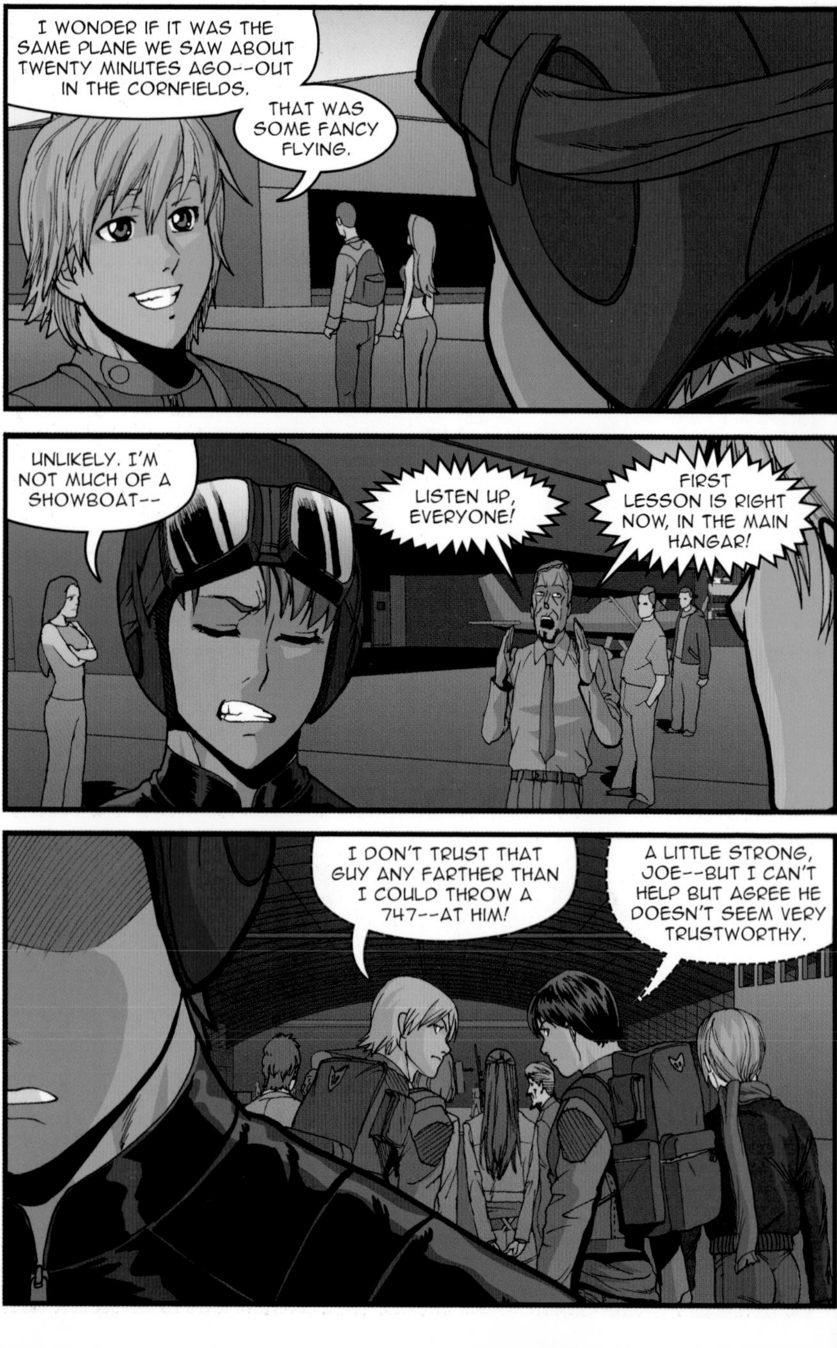
I WONDER IF IT WAS THE SAME PLANE WE SAW ABOUT TWENTY MINUTES AGO--OUT IN THE CORNFIELDS.
THAT WAS SOME FANCY FLYING.
UNLIKELY. I'M NOT MUCH OF A SHOWBOAT--
LISTEN UP, EVERYONE!
FIRST LESSON IS RIGHT NOW, IN THE MAIN HANGAR!
I DON'T TRUST THAT GUY ANY FARTHER THAN I COULD THROW A 747--AT HIM!
A LITTLE STRONG, JOE--BUT I CAN'T HELP BUT AGREE HE DOESN'T SEEM VERY TRUSTWORTHY.

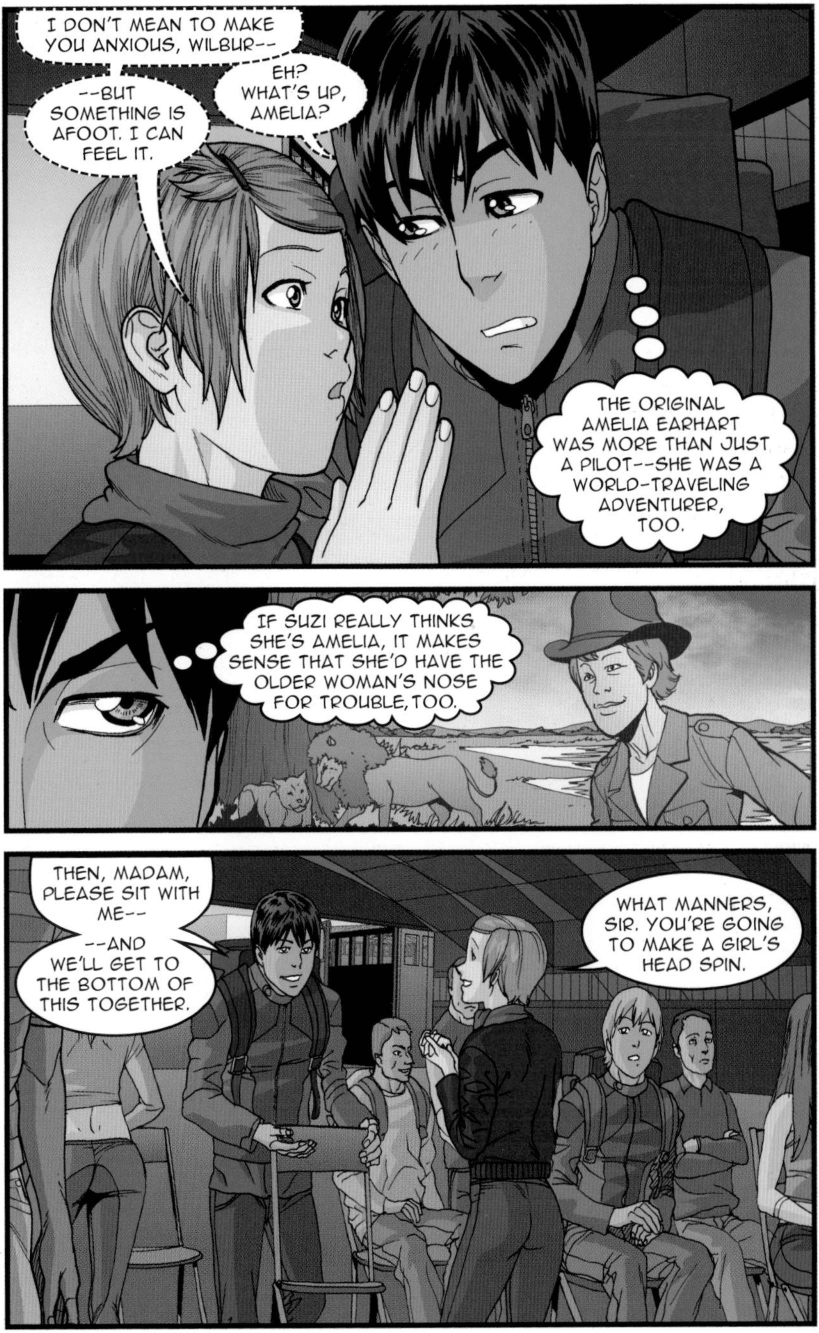
I DON'T MEAN TO MAKE YOU ANXIOUS, WILBUR--
--BUT SOMETHING IS AFOOT. I CAN FEEL IT.
EH? WHAT'S UP, AMELIA?
THE ORIGINAL AMELIA EARHART WAS MORE THAN JUST A PILOT--SHE WAS A WORLD-TRAVELING ADVENTURER, TOO.
IF SUZI REALLY THINKS SHE'S AMELIA, IT MAKES SENSE THAT SHE'D HAVE THE OLDER WOMAN'S NOSE FOR TROUBLE, TOO.
THEN, MADAM, PLEASE SIT WITH ME--
--AND WE'LL GET TO THE BOTTOM OF THIS TOGETHER.
WHAT MANNERS, SIR. YOU'RE GOING TO MAKE A GIRL'S HEAD SPIN.

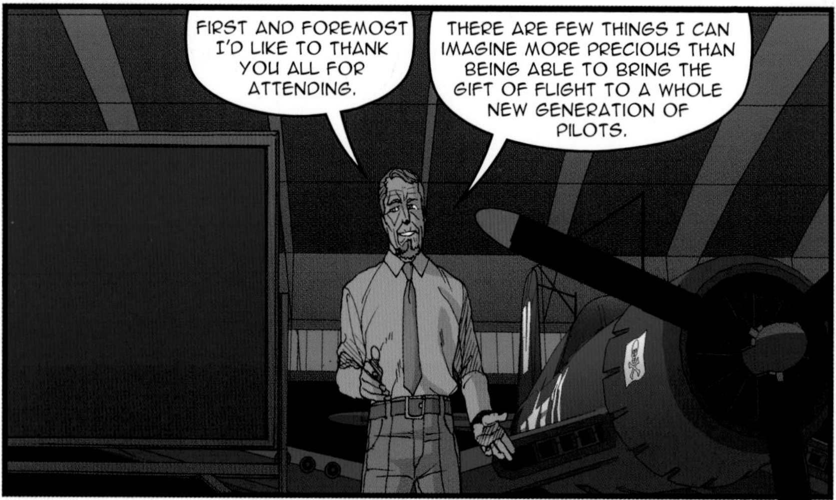
FIRST AND FOREMOST I'D LIKE TO THANK YOU ALL FOR ATTENDING.
THERE ARE FEW THINGS I CAN IMAGINE MORE PRECIOUS THAN BEING ABLE TO BRING THE GIFT OF FLIGHT TO A WHOLE NEW GENERATION OF PILOTS.

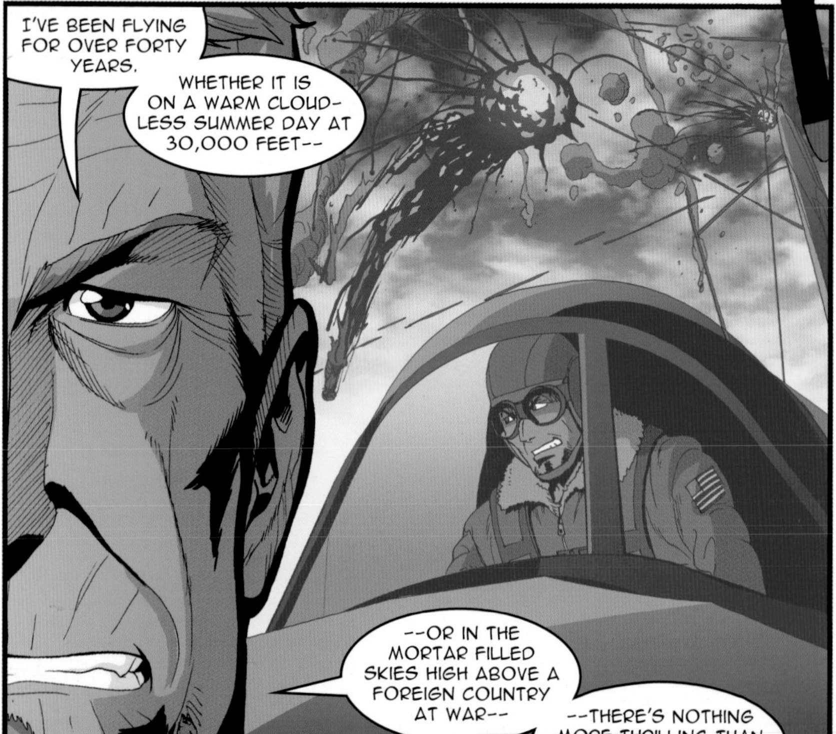
I'VE BEEN FLYING FOR OVER FORTY YEARS.
WHETHER IT IS ON A WARM CLOUD-LESS SUMMER DAY AT 30,000 FEET--
--OR IN THE MORTAR FILLED SKIES HIGH ABOVE A FOREIGN COUNTRY AT WAR--
--THERE'S NOTHING MORE THRILLING THAN BEING THE PILOT OF YOUR OWN DESTINY.

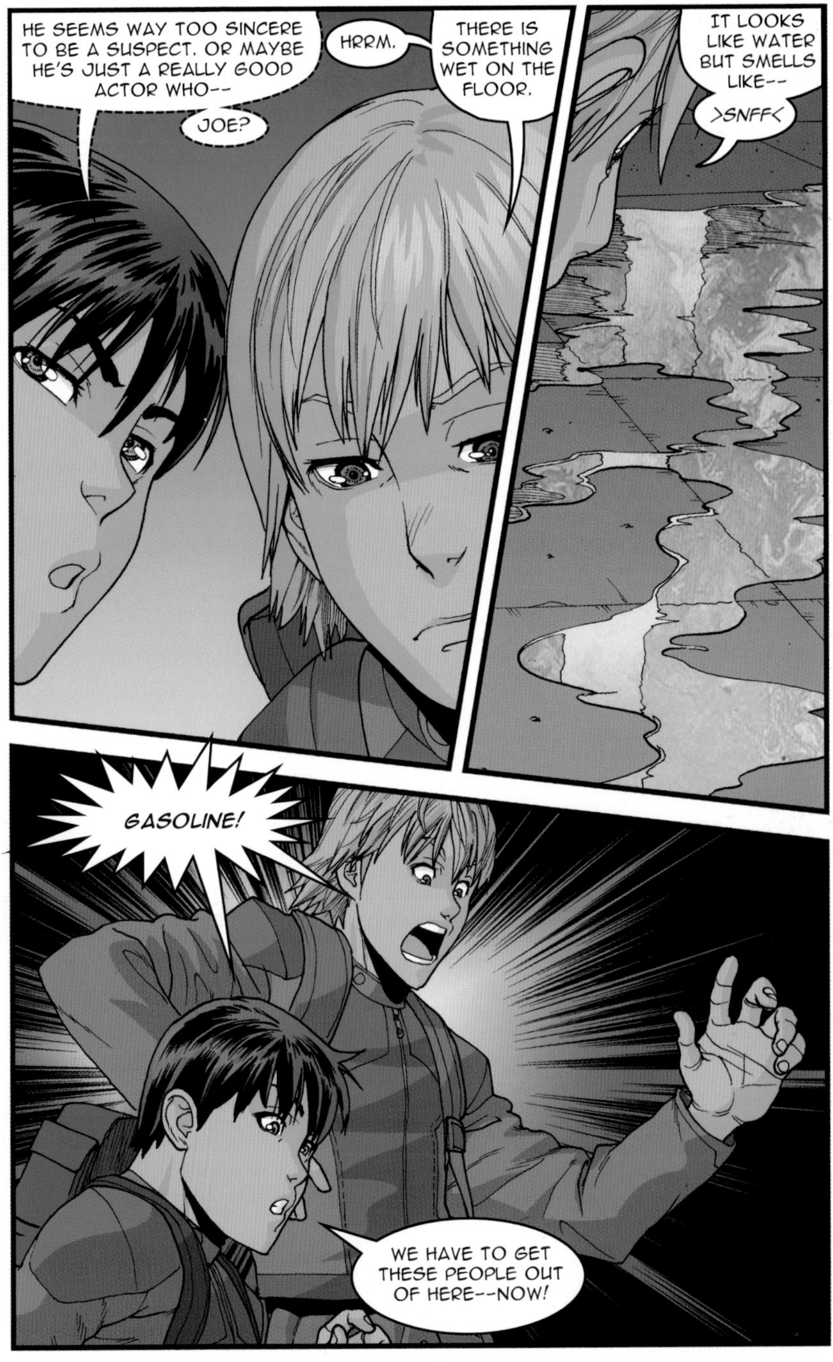
HE SEEMS WAY TOO SINCERE TO BE A SUSPECT. OR MAYBE HE'S JUST A REALLY GOOD ACTOR WHO--
JOE?
HRRM.
THERE IS SOMETHING WET ON THE FLOOR.
IT LOOKS LIKE WATER BUT SMELLS LIKE--
>SNFF<
GASOLINE!
WE HAVE TO GET THESE PEOPLE OUT OF HERE--NOW!

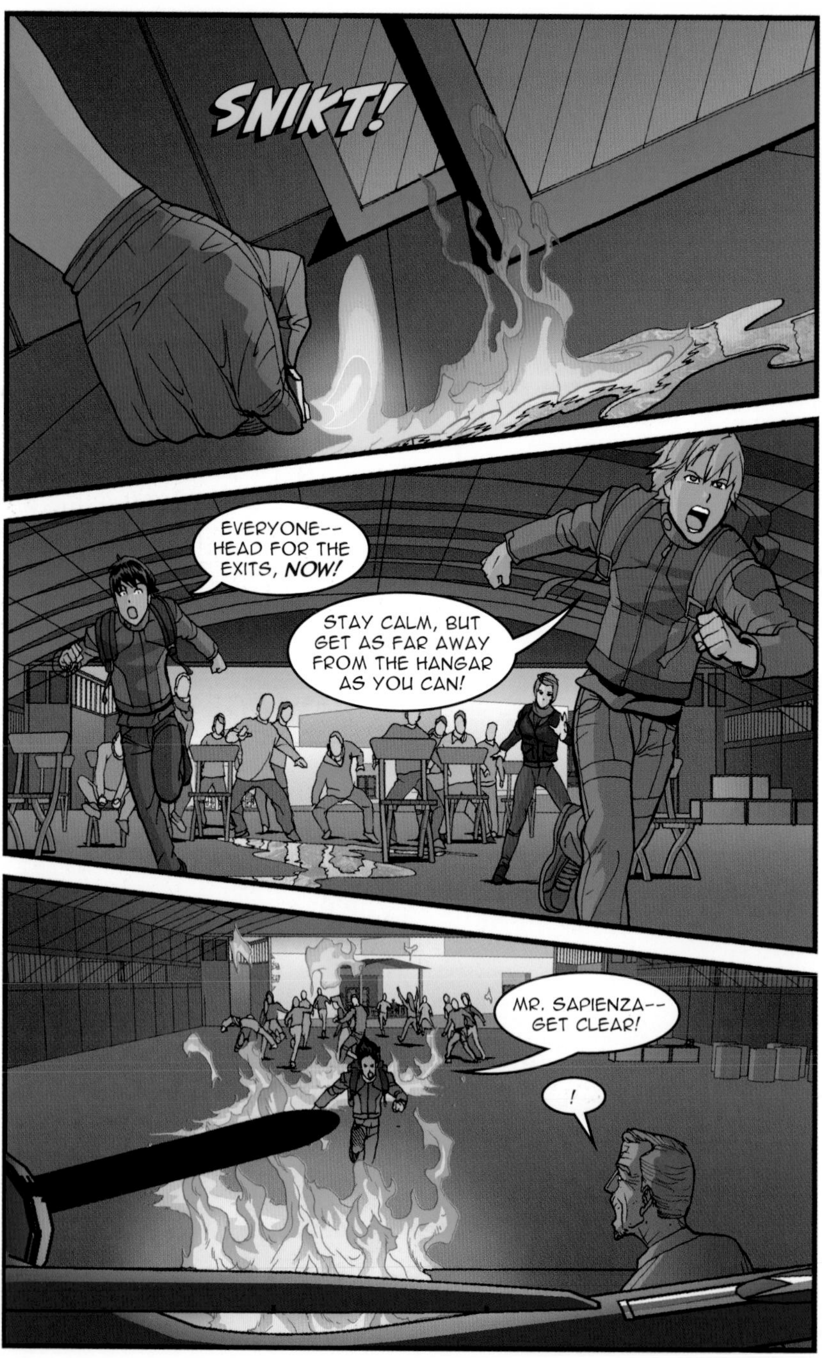
SNIKT!
EVERYONE--
HEAD FOR THE
EXITS, NOW!
STAY CALM, BUT
GET AS FAR AWAY
FROM THE HANGAR
AS YOU CAN!
MR. SAPIENZA--
GET CLEAR!
!

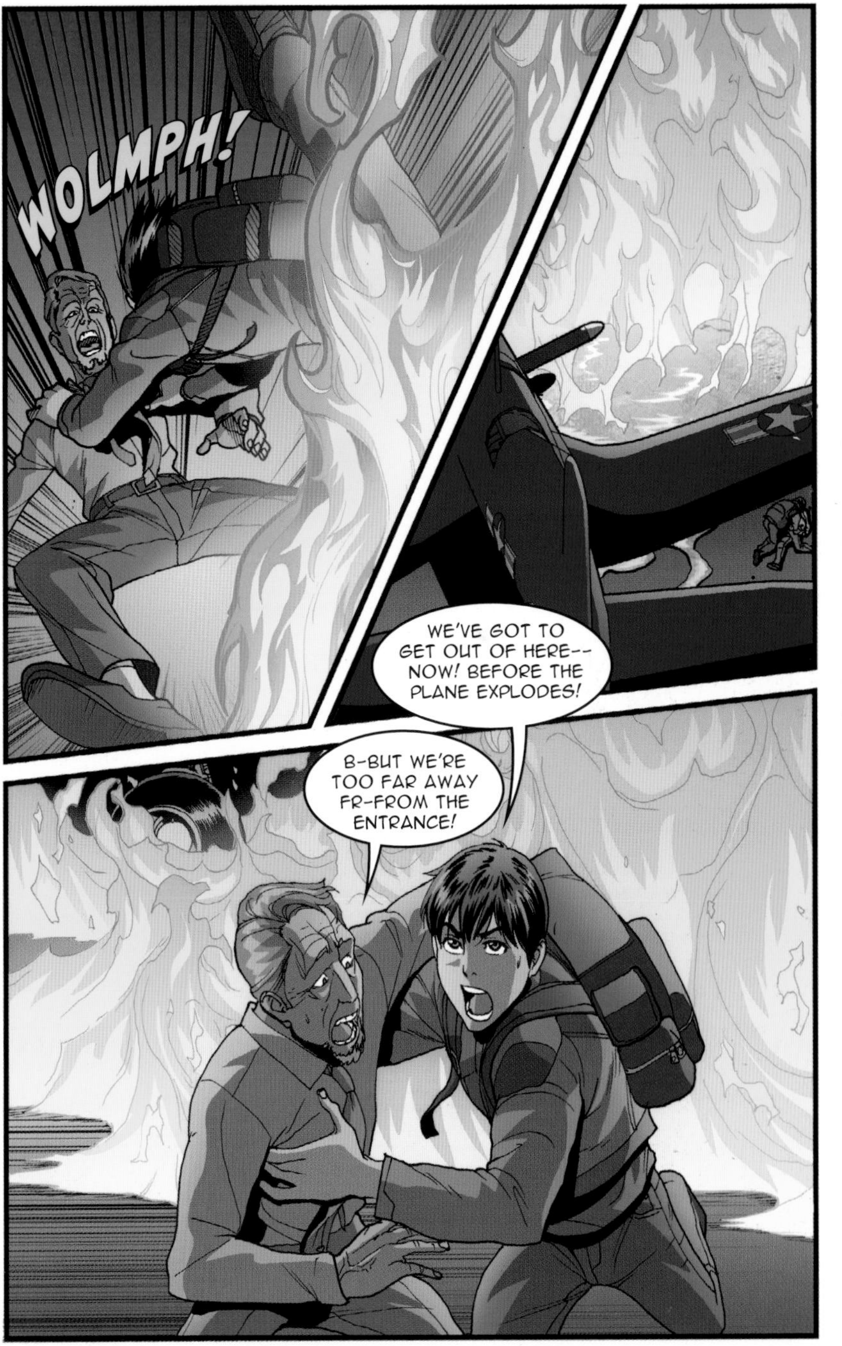
WOLMPH!
WE'VE GOT TO GET OUT OF HERE--NOW! BEFORE THE PLANE EXPLODES!
B-BUT WE'RE TOO FAR AWAY FR-FROM THE ENTRANCE!

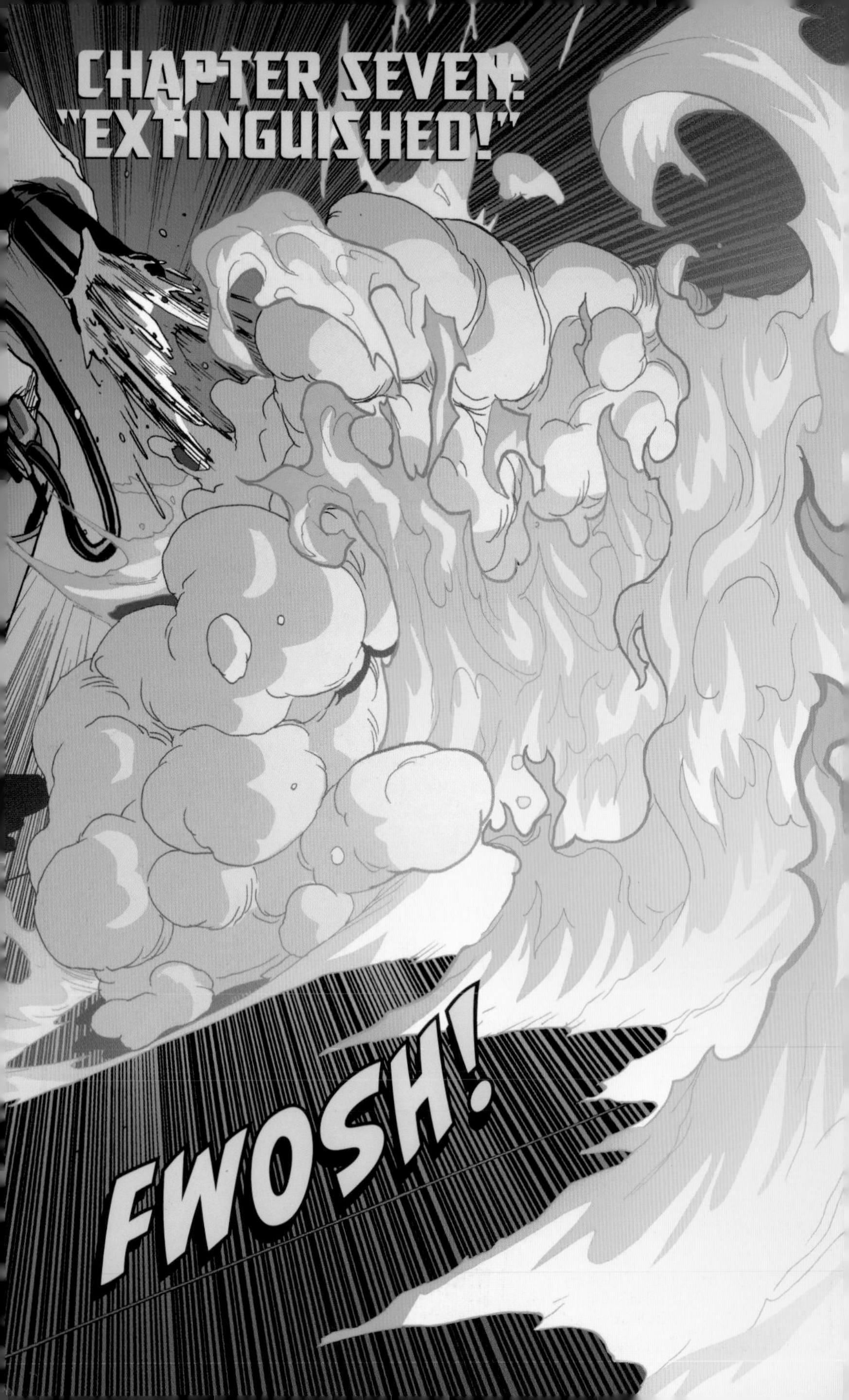
CHAPTER SEVEN:
"EXTINGUISHED!"
FWOSH!

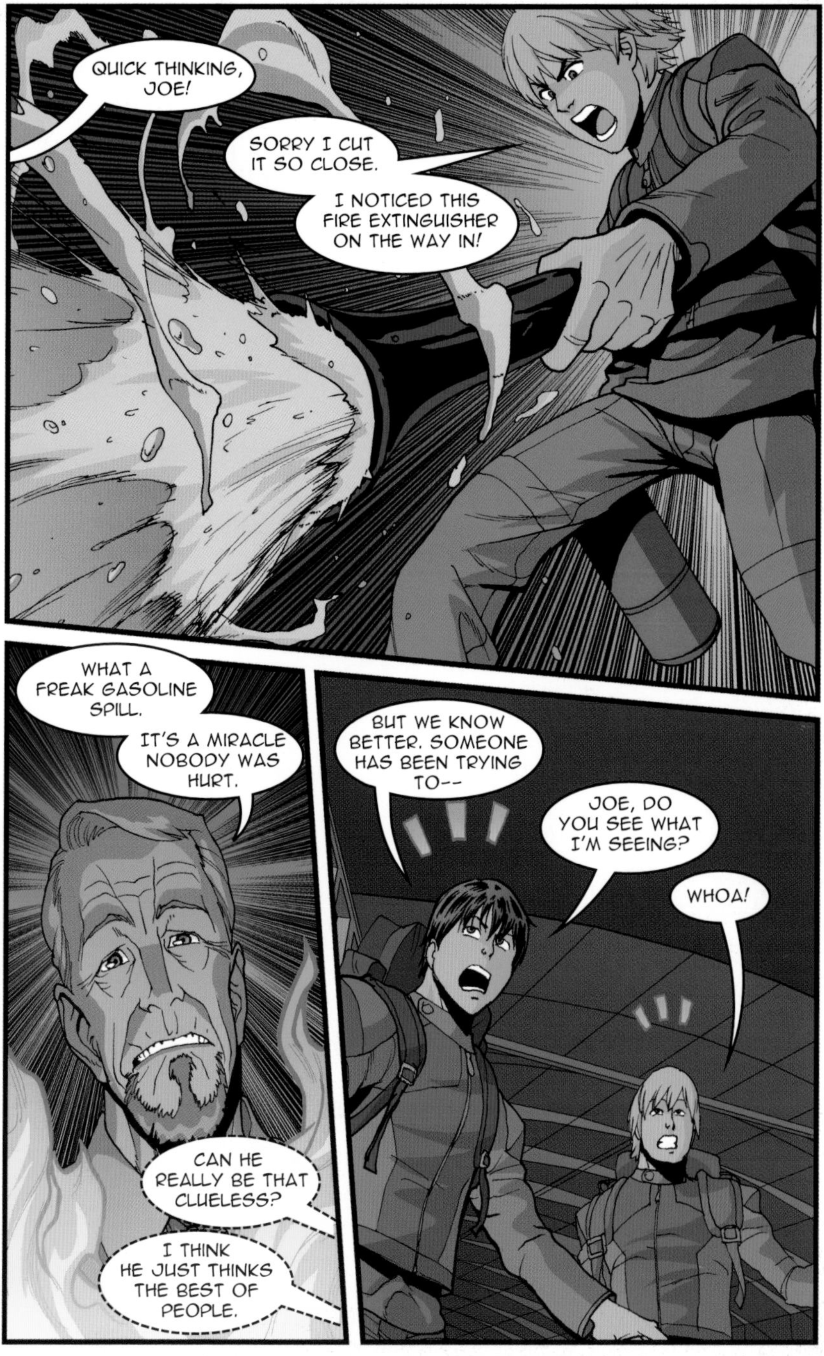
QUICK THINKING, JOE!
SORRY I CUT IT SO CLOSE.
I NOTICED THIS FIRE EXTINGUISHER ON THE WAY IN!
WHAT A FREAK GASOLINE SPILL.
IT'S A MIRACLE NOBODY WAS HURT.
CAN HE REALLY BE THAT CLUELESS?
I THINK HE JUST THINKS THE BEST OF PEOPLE.
BUT WE KNOW BETTER. SOMEONE HAS BEEN TRYING TO--
JOE, DO YOU SEE WHAT I'M SEEING?
WHOA!

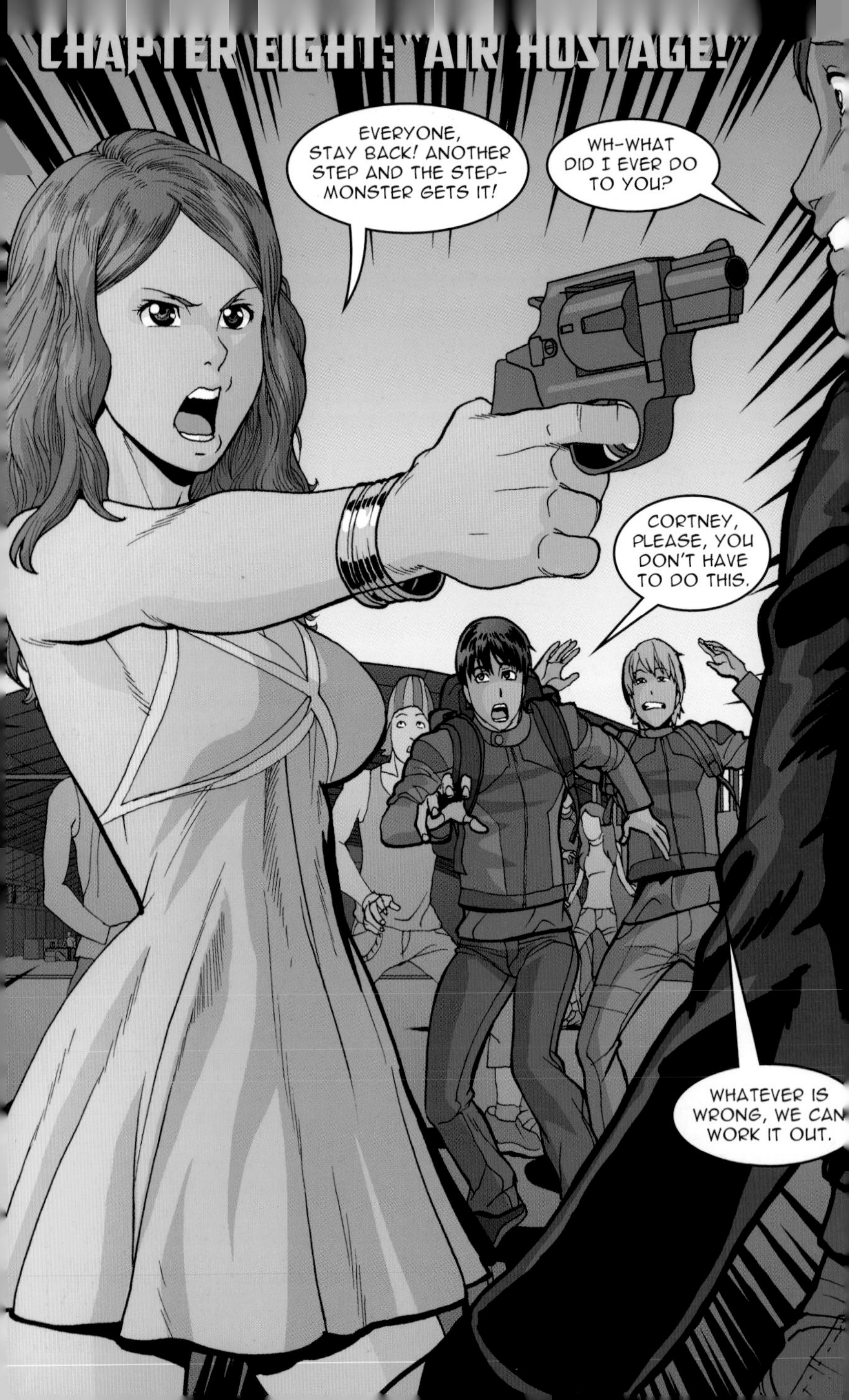
CHAPTER EIGHT: AIR HOSTAGE!
EVERYONE, STAY BACK! ANOTHER STEP AND THE STEP-MONSTER GETS IT!
WH-WHAT DID I EVER DO TO YOU?
CORTNEY, PLEASE, YOU DON'T HAVE TO DO THIS.
WHATEVER IS WRONG, WE CAN WORK IT OUT.

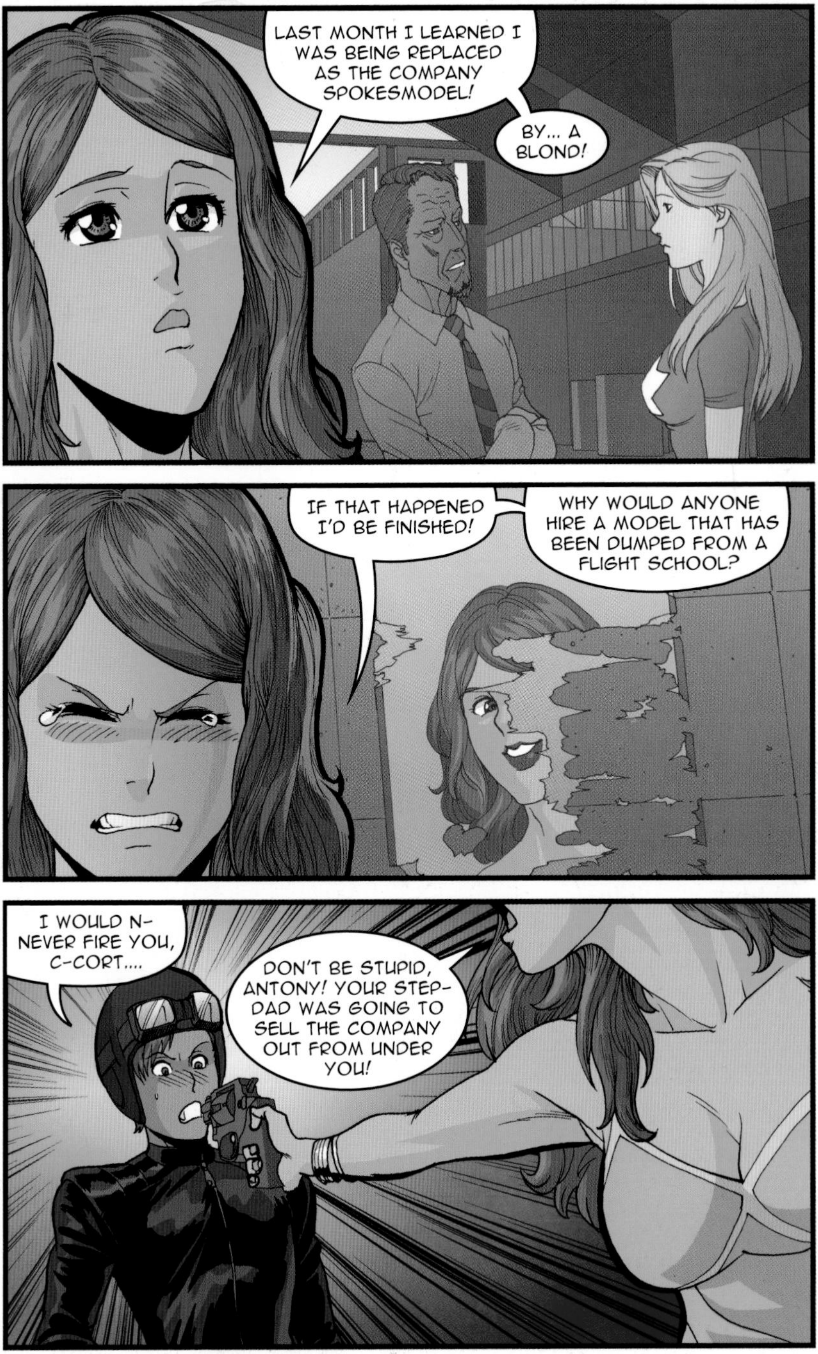
LAST MONTH I LEARNED I WAS BEING REPLACED AS THE COMPANY SPOKESMODEL!
BY... A BLOND!
IF THAT HAPPENED I'D BE FINISHED!
WHY WOULD ANYONE HIRE A MODEL THAT HAS BEEN DUMPED FROM A FLIGHT SCHOOL?
I WOULD N- NEVER FIRE YOU, C-CORT....
DON'T BE STUPID, ANTONY! YOUR STEP-DAD WAS GOING TO SELL THE COMPANY OUT FROM UNDER YOU!

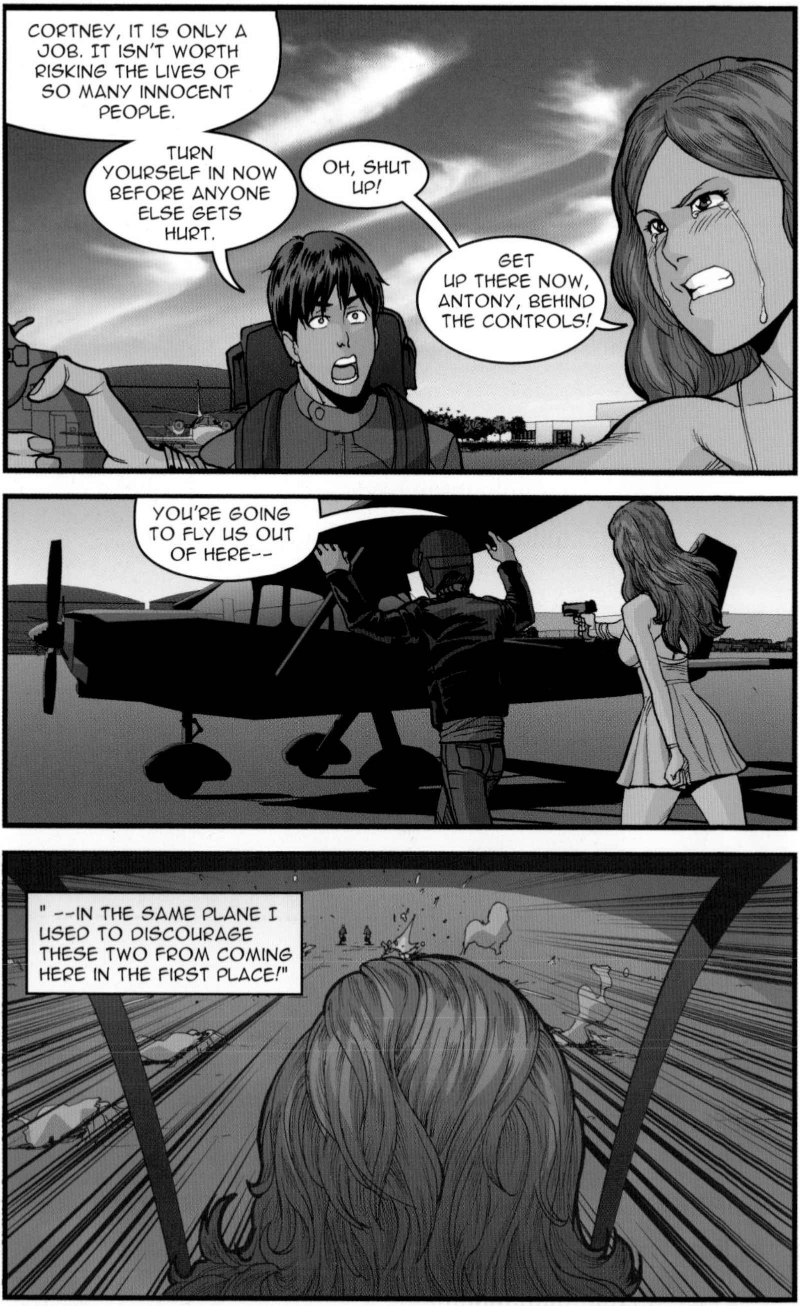
CORTNEY, IT IS ONLY A JOB. IT ISN'T WORTH RISKING THE LIVES OF SO MANY INNOCENT PEOPLE.
TURN YOURSELF IN NOW BEFORE ANYONE ELSE GETS HURT.
OH, SHUT UP!
GET UP THERE NOW, ANTONY, BEHIND THE CONTROLS!
YOU'RE GOING TO FLY US OUT OF HERE--
" --IN THE SAME PLANE I USED TO DISCOURAGE THESE TWO FROM COMING HERE IN THE FIRST PLACE!"

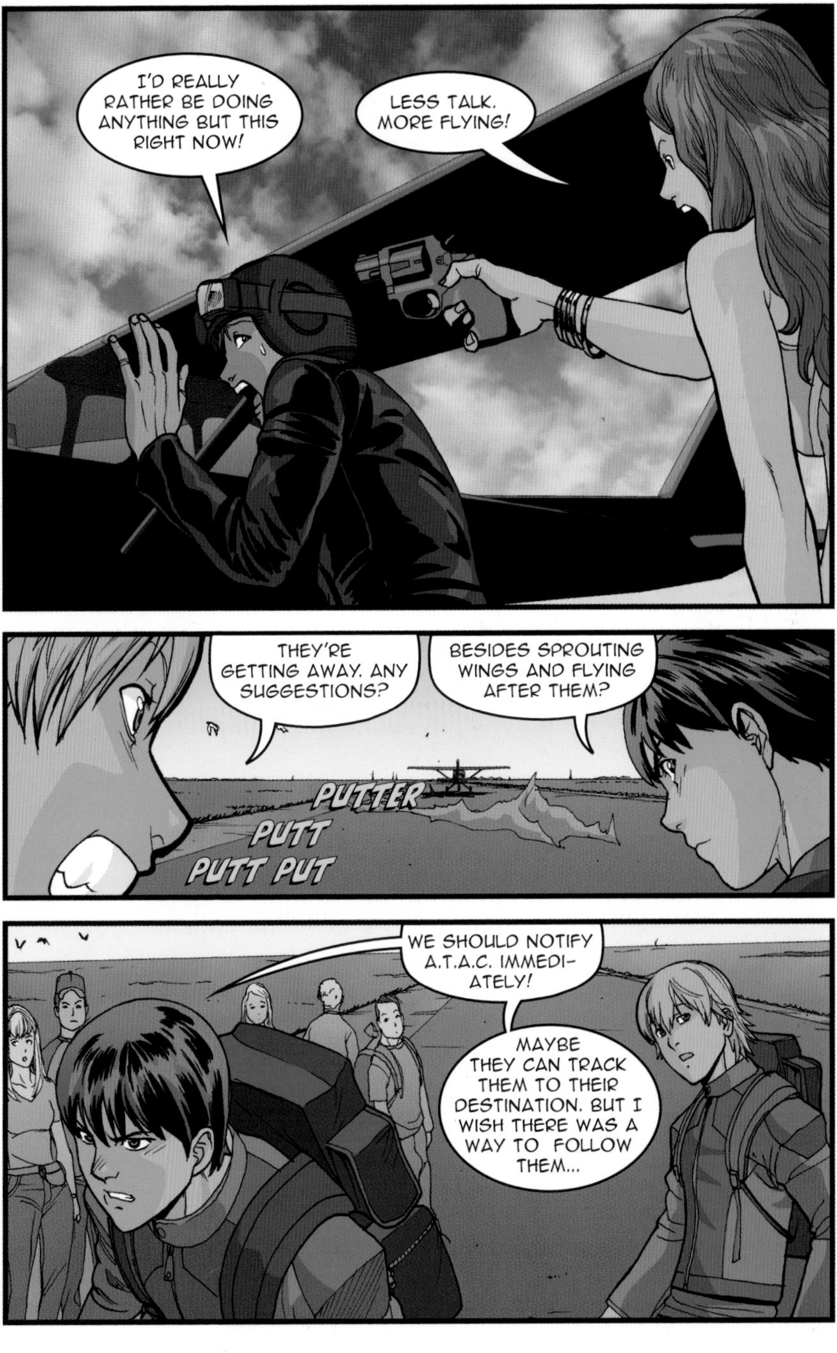
I'D REALLY RATHER BE DOING ANYTHING BUT THIS RIGHT NOW!
LESS TALK. MORE FLYING!
THEY'RE GETTING AWAY. ANY SUGGESTIONS?
BESIDES SPROUTING WINGS AND FLYING AFTER THEM?
PUTTER
PUTT
PUTT PUT
WE SHOULD NOTIFY A.T.A.C. IMMEDI-ATELY!
MAYBE THEY CAN TRACK THEM TO THEIR DESTINATION. BUT I WISH THERE WAS A WAY TO FOLLOW THEM...

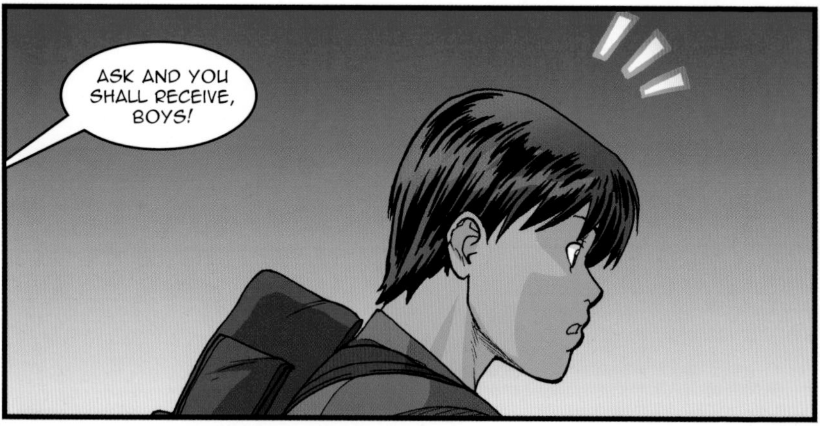
ASK AND YOU SHALL RECEIVE, BOYS!

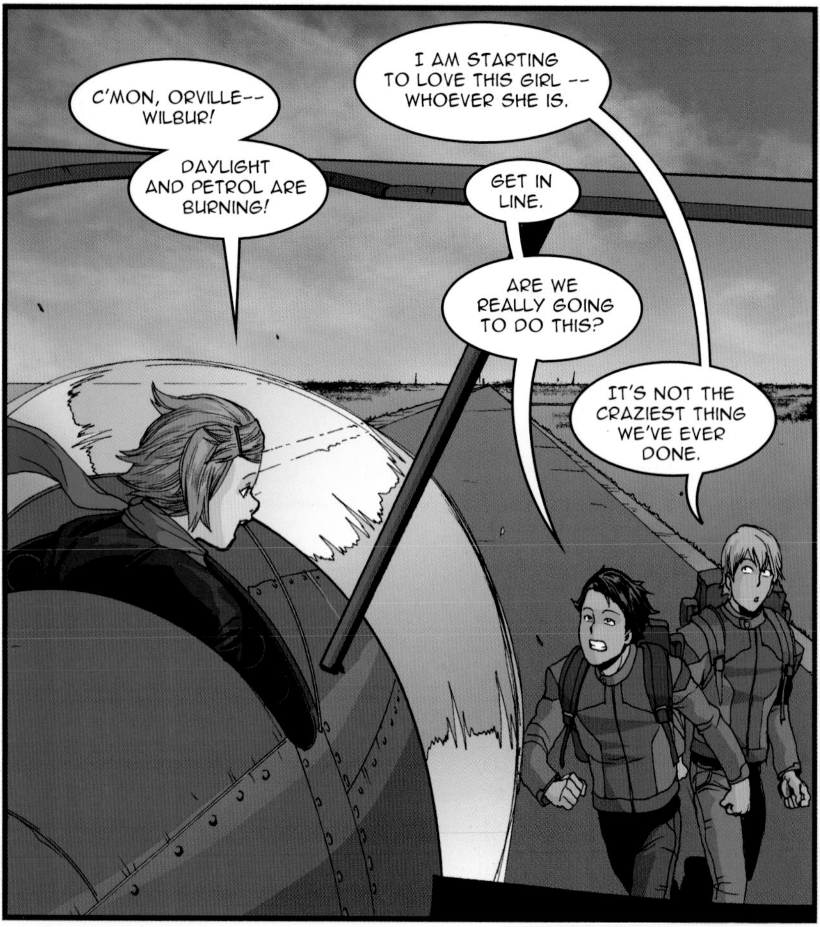
C'MON, ORVILLE-- WILBUR!
DAYLIGHT AND PETROL ARE BURNING!
I AM STARTING TO LOVE THIS GIRL -- WHOEVER SHE IS.
GET IN LINE.
ARE WE REALLY GOING TO DO THIS?
IT'S NOT THE CRAZIEST THING WE'VE EVER DONE.

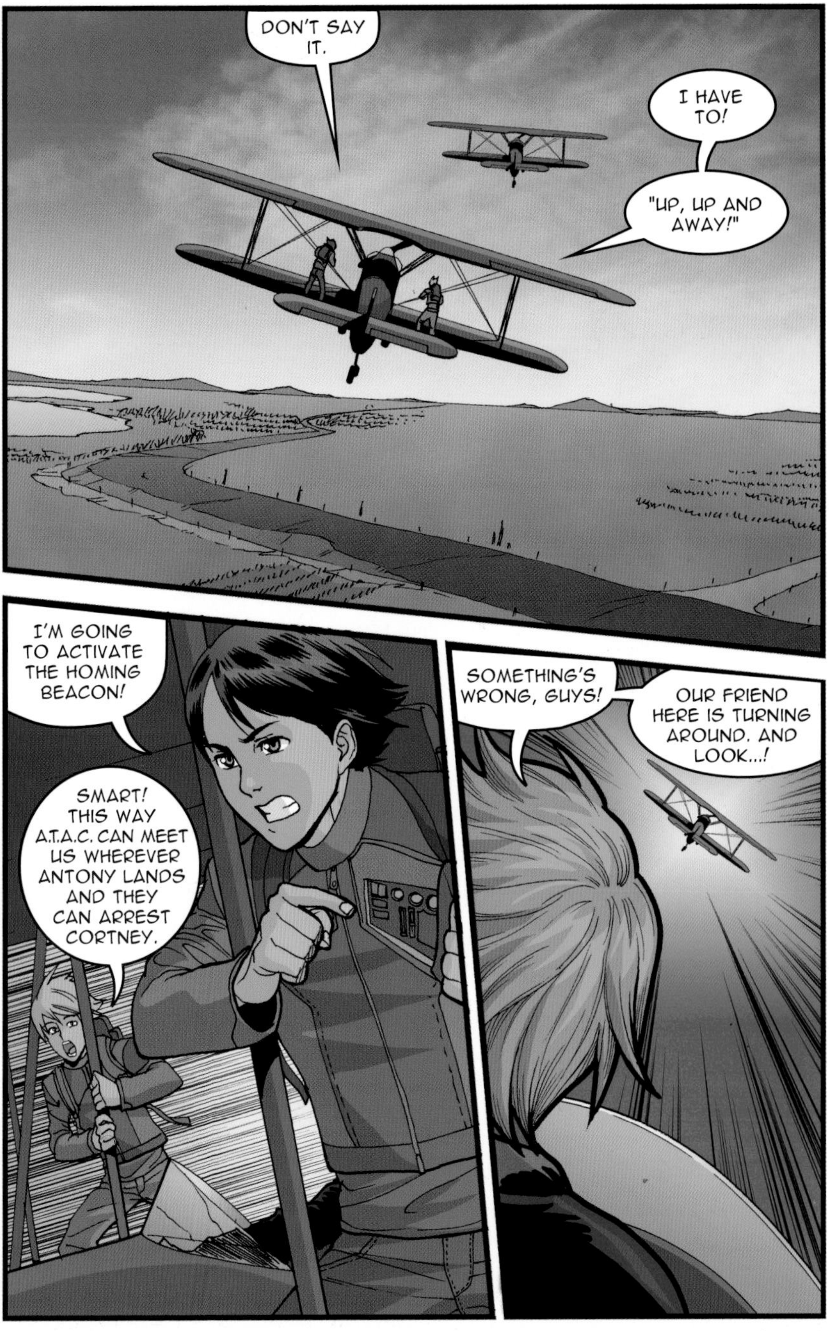
DON'T SAY IT.
I HAVE TO!
"UP, UP AND AWAY!"
I'M GOING TO ACTIVATE THE HOMING BEACON!
SMART! THIS WAY A.T.A.C. CAN MEET US WHEREVER ANTONY LANDS AND THEY CAN ARREST CORTNEY.
SOMETHING'S WRONG, GUYS!
OUR FRIEND HERE IS TURNING AROUND. AND LOOK...!

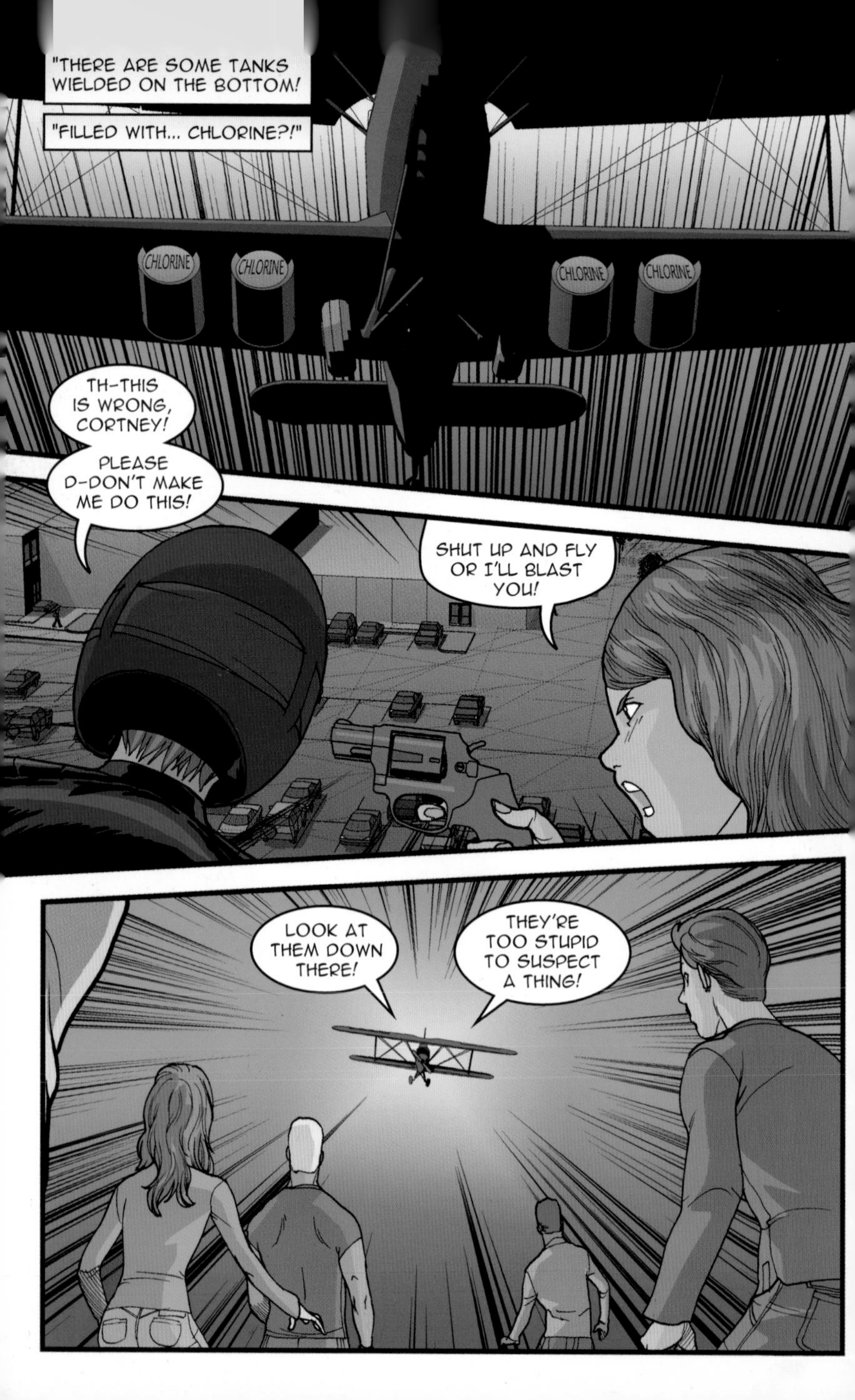
"THERE ARE SOME TANKS WIELDED ON THE BOTTOM!
"FILLED WITH... CHLORINE?!"
CHLORINE
CHLORINE
CHLORINE
CHLORINE
TH-THIS IS WRONG, CORTNEY!
PLEASE D-DON'T MAKE ME DO THIS!
SHUT UP AND FLY OR I'LL BLAST YOU!
LOOK AT THEM DOWN THERE!
THEY'RE TOO STUPID TO SUSPECT A THING!

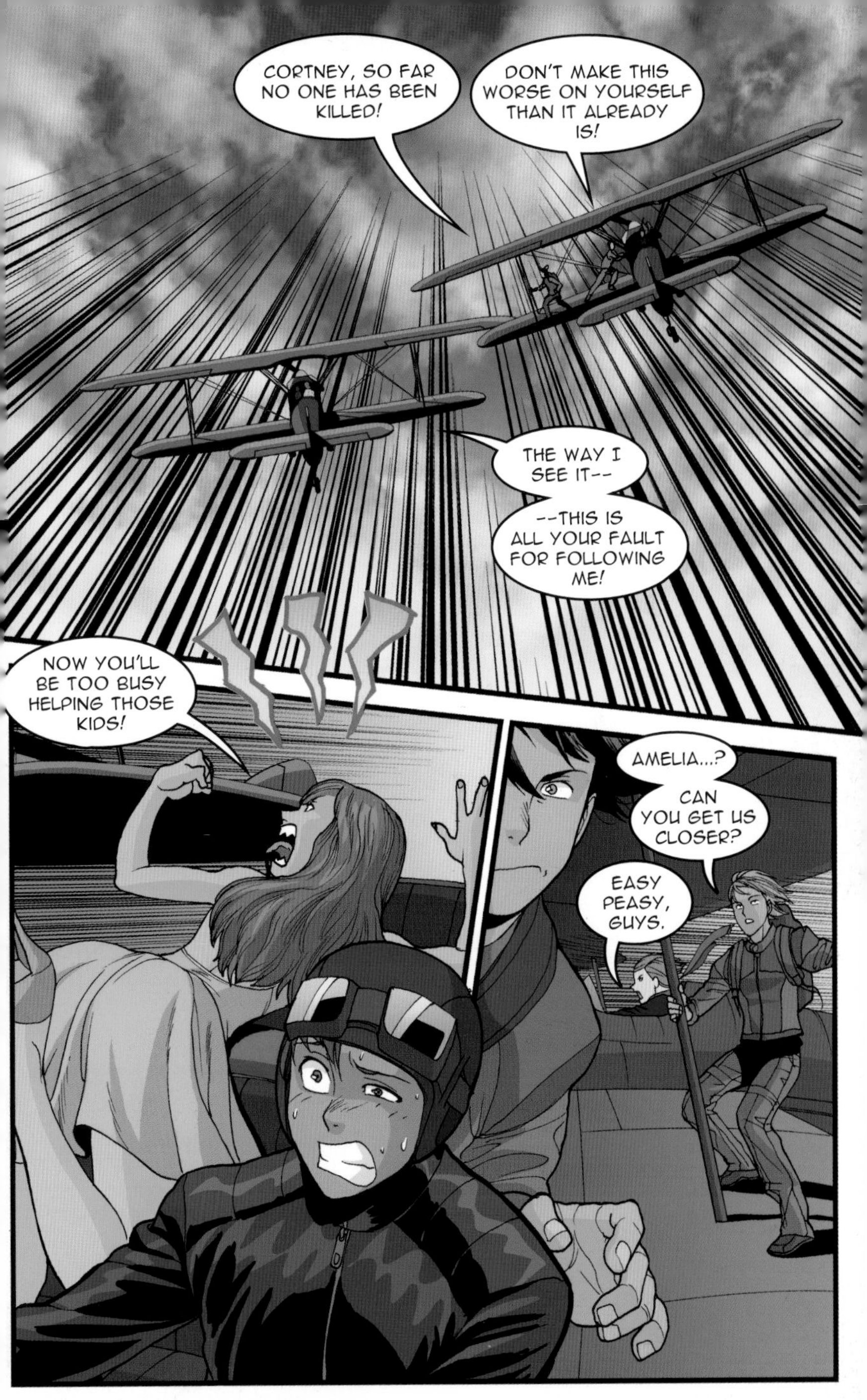
CORTNEY, SO FAR NO ONE HAS BEEN KILLED!
DON'T MAKE THIS WORSE ON YOURSELF THAN IT ALREADY IS!
THE WAY I SEE IT--
--THIS IS ALL YOUR FAULT FOR FOLLOWING ME!
NOW YOU'LL BE TOO BUSY HELPING THOSE KIDS!
AMELIA...?
CAN YOU GET US CLOSER?
EASY PEASY, GUYS.

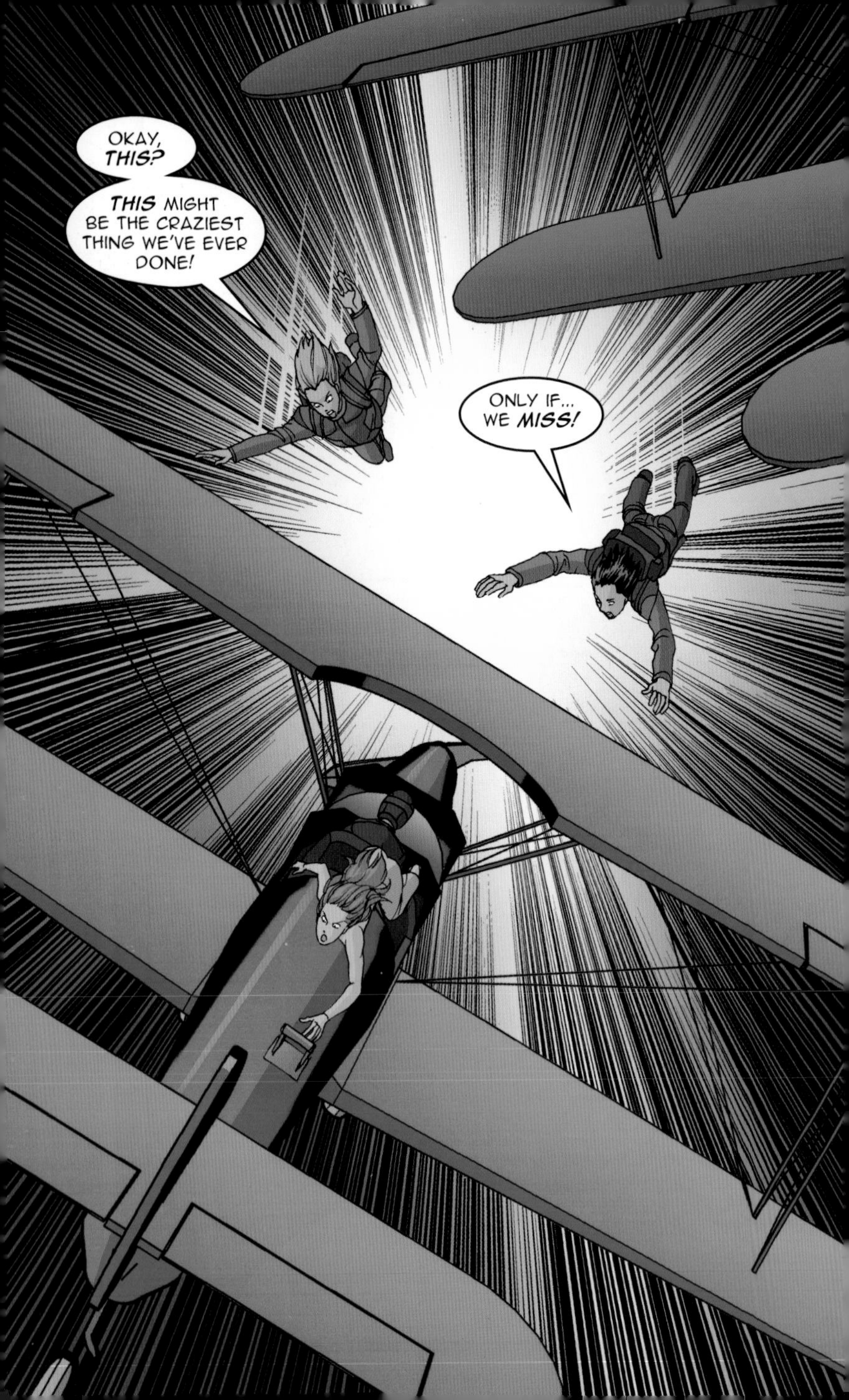
OKAY, THIS?
THIS MIGHT BE THE CRAZIEST THING WE'VE EVER DONE!
ONLY IF... WE MISS!

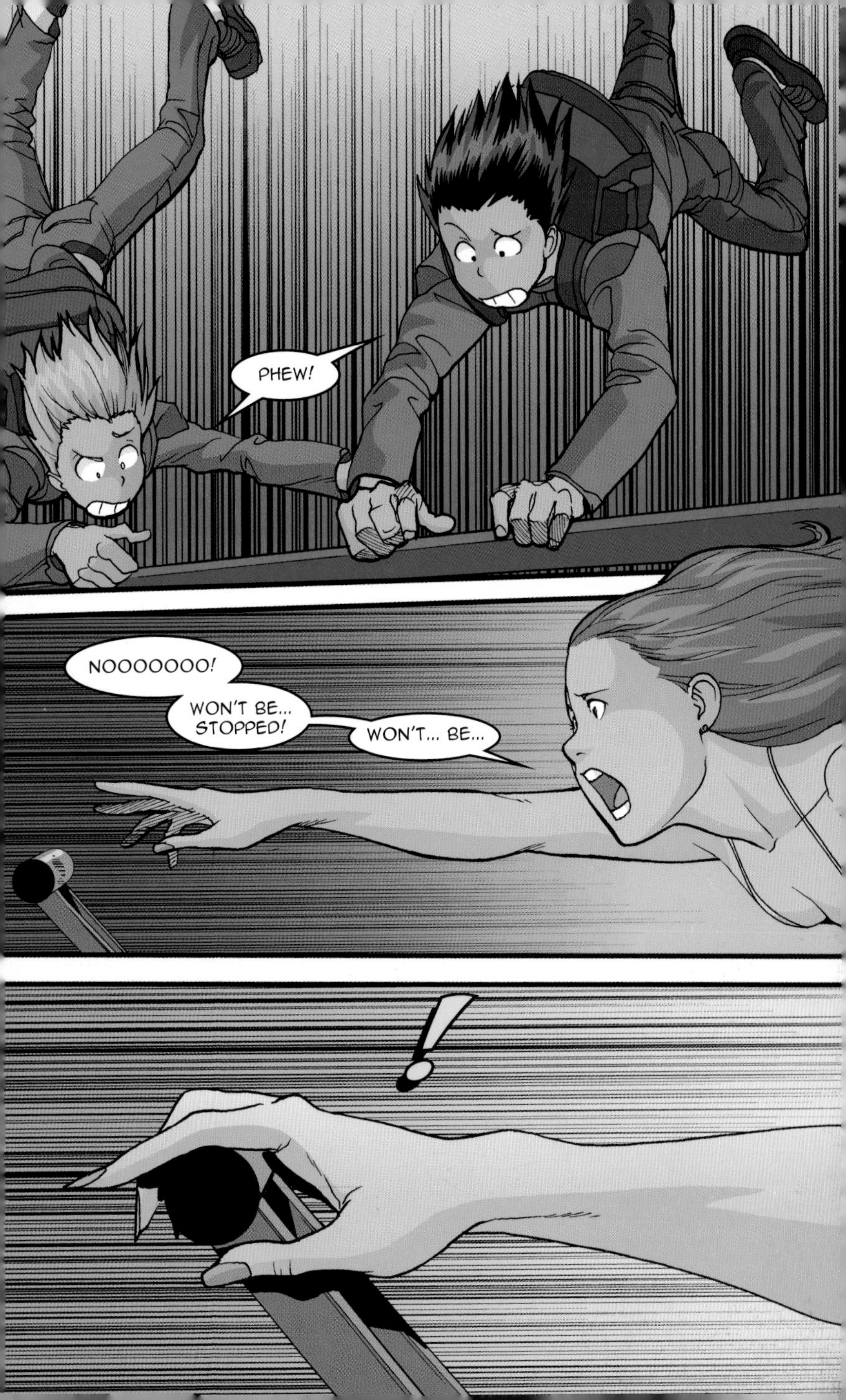
PHEW!
NOOOOOOO!
WON'T BE...
STOPPED!
WON'T... BE...
!

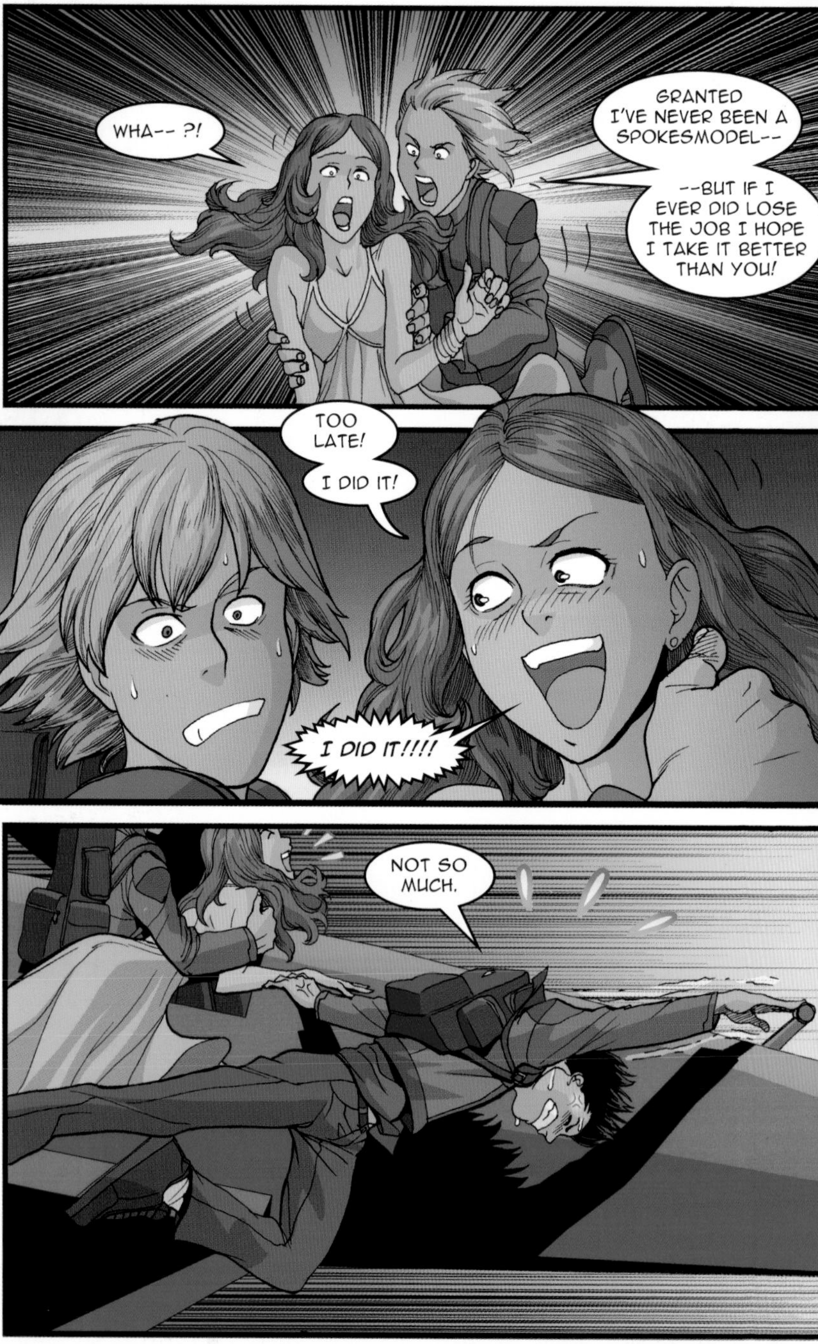
WHA-- ?!
GRANTED I'VE NEVER BEEN A SPOKESMODEL--
--BUT IF I EVER DID LOSE THE JOB I HOPE I TAKE IT BETTER THAN YOU!
TOO LATE!
I DID IT!
I DID IT!!!!
NOT SO MUCH.

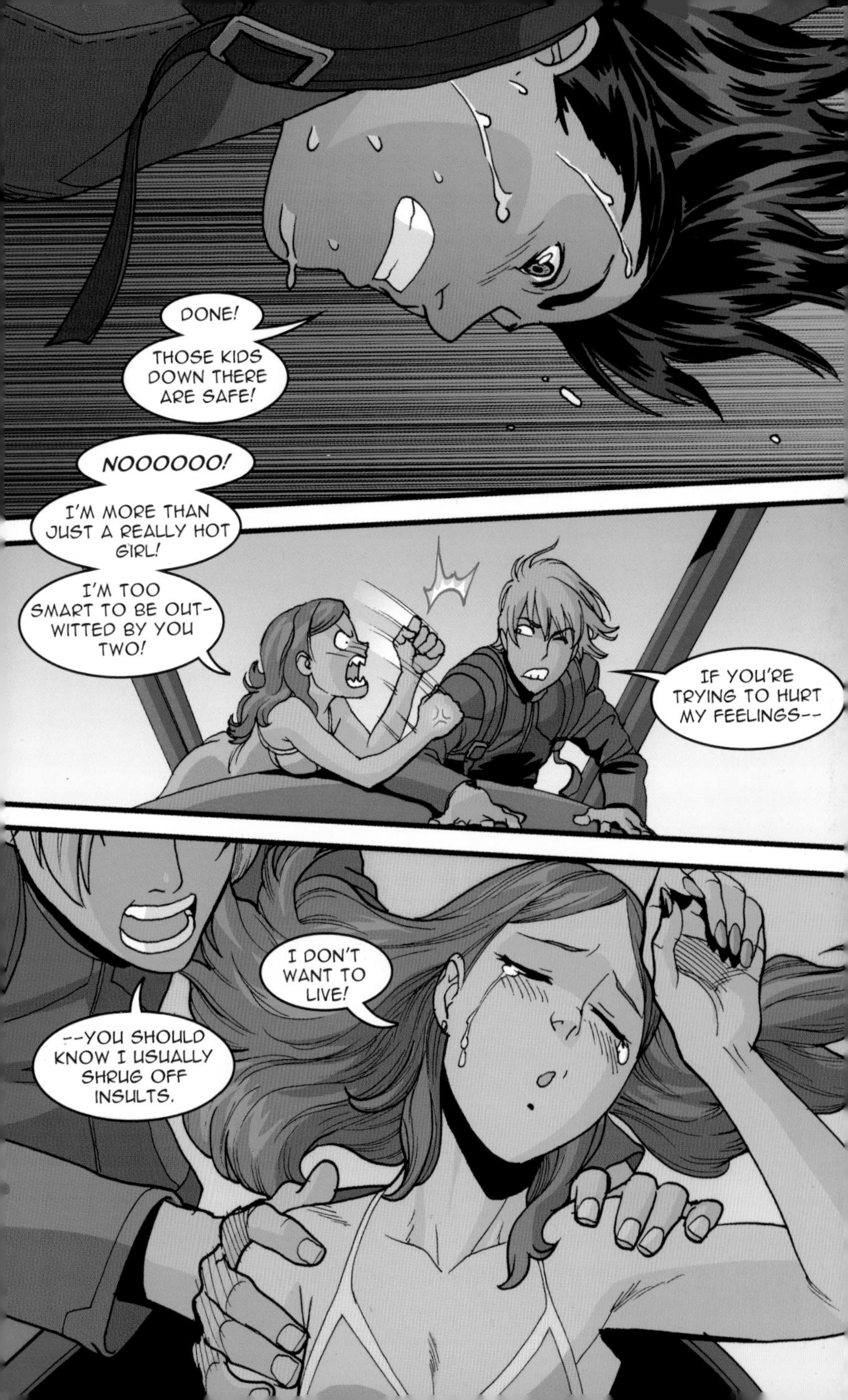
DONE!
THOSE KIDS DOWN THERE ARE SAFE!
NOOOOOO!
I'M MORE THAN JUST A REALLY HOT GIRL!
I'M TOO SMART TO BE OUT-WITTED BY YOU TWO!
IF YOU'RE TRYING TO HURT MY FEELINGS--
I DON'T WANT TO LIVE!
--YOU SHOULD KNOW I USUALLY SHRUG OFF INSULTS.

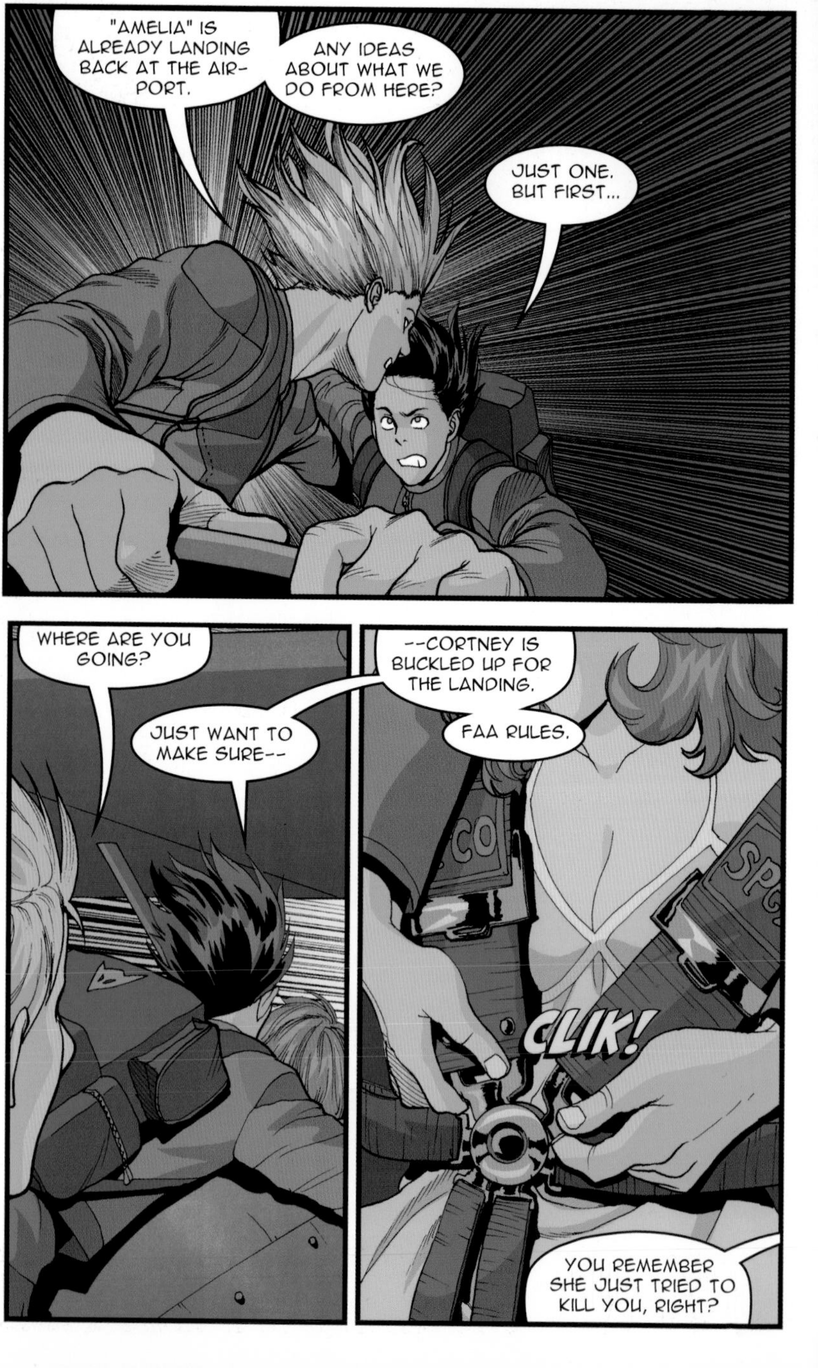
"AMELIA" IS ALREADY LANDING BACK AT THE AIR-PORT.
ANY IDEAS ABOUT WHAT WE DO FROM HERE?
JUST ONE. BUT FIRST...
WHERE ARE YOU GOING?
JUST WANT TO MAKE SURE--
--CORTNEY IS BUCKLED UP FOR THE LANDING.
FAA RULES.
CLIK!
YOU REMEMBER SHE JUST TRIED TO KILL YOU, RIGHT?

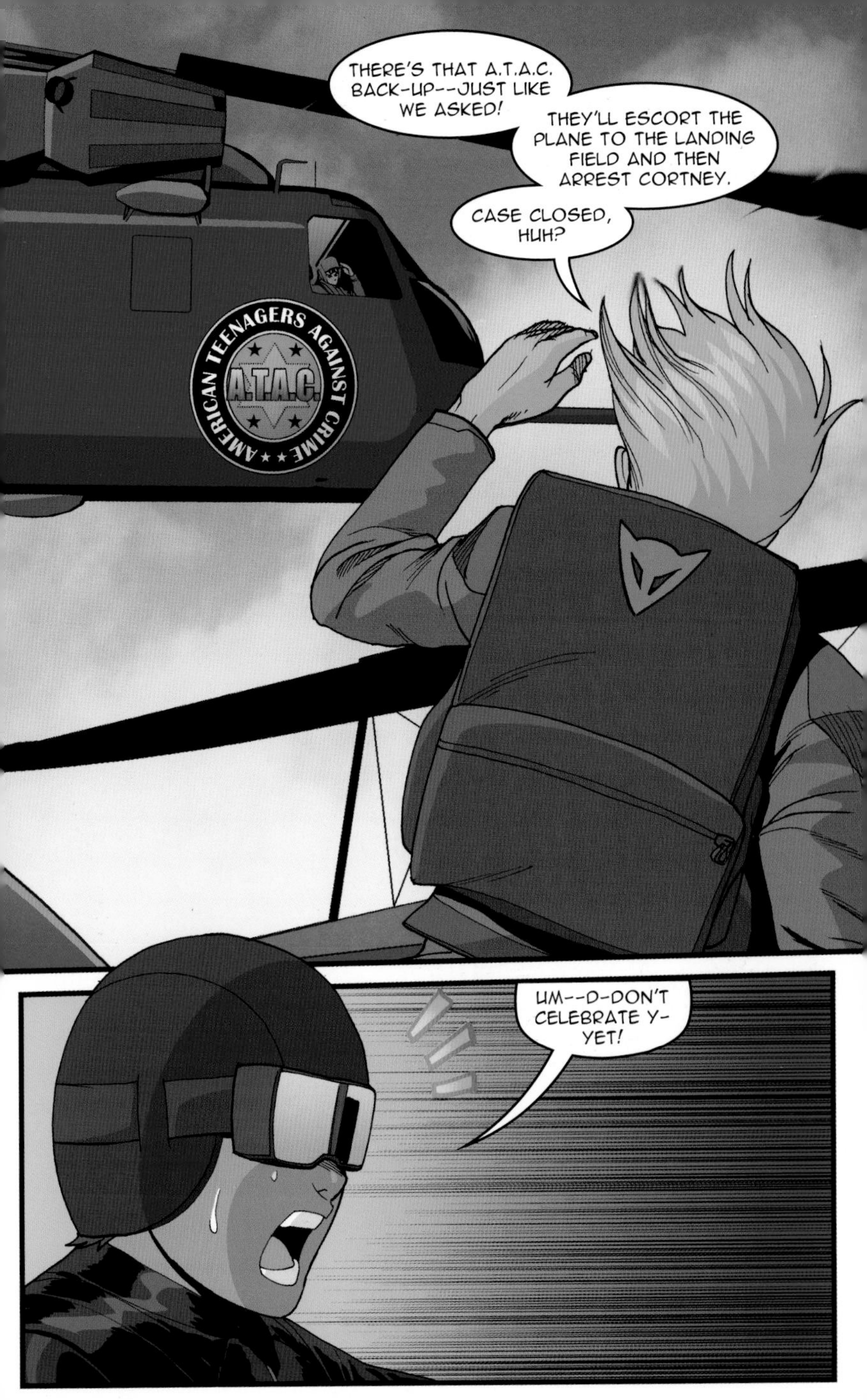
THERE'S THAT A.T.A.C. BACK-UP--JUST LIKE WE ASKED!
THEY'LL ESCORT THE PLANE TO THE LANDING FIELD AND THEN ARREST CORTNEY.
CASE CLOSED, HUH?
AMERICAN TEENAGERS AGAINST CRIME
A.T.A.C.
UM--D-DON'T CELEBRATE Y-YET!

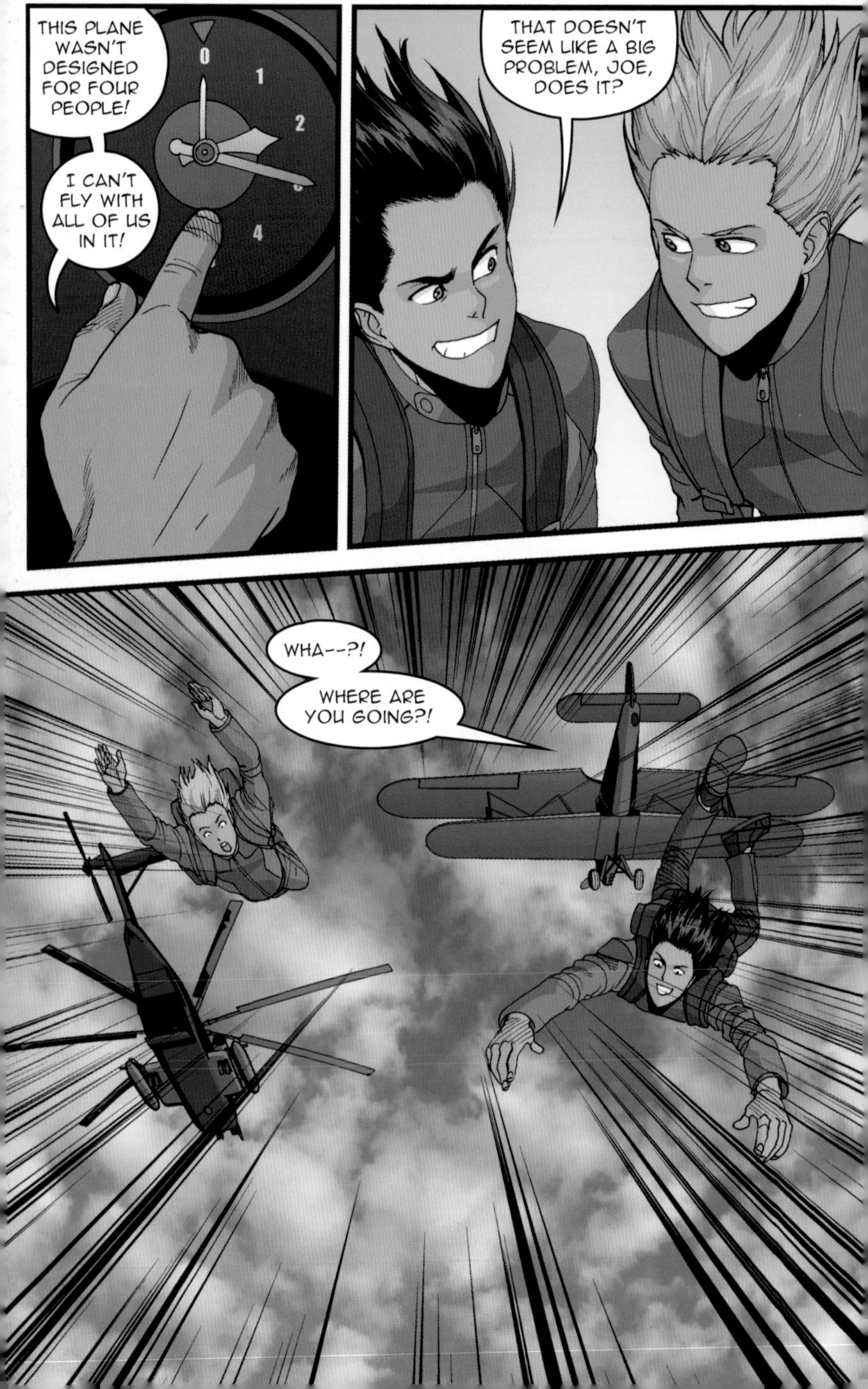
THIS PLANE WASN'T DESIGNED FOR FOUR PEOPLE!
I CAN'T FLY WITH ALL OF US IN IT!
THAT DOESN'T SEEM LIKE A BIG PROBLEM, JOE, DOES IT?
WHA--?!
WHERE ARE YOU GOING?!

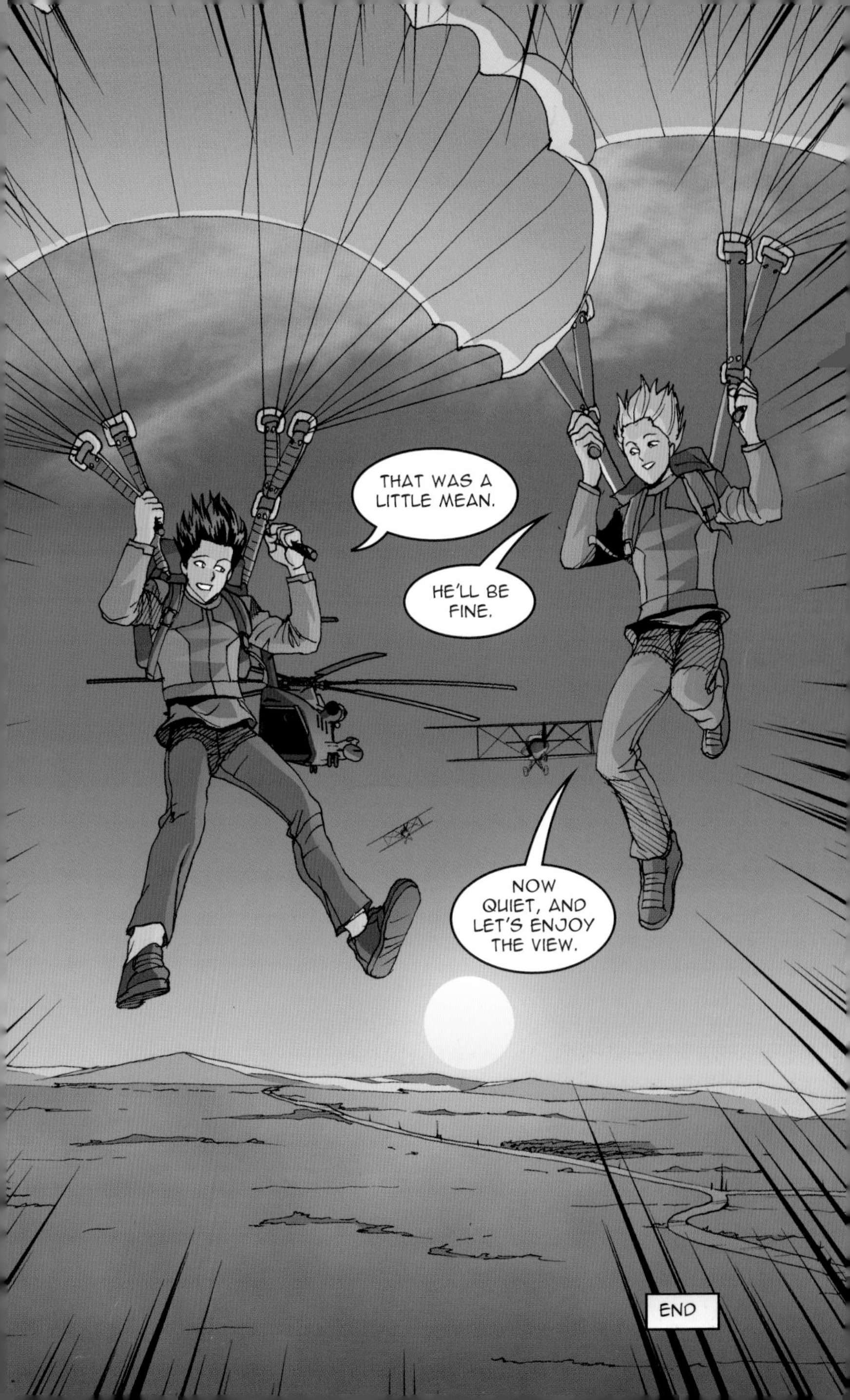
THAT WAS A LITTLE MEAN.
HE'LL BE FINE.
NOW QUIET, AND LET'S ENJOY THE VIEW.
END

SPECIAL PREVIEW OF THE HARDY BOYS GRAPHIC NOVEL #20 – "DEADLY STRATEGY"!

CHAPTER ONE: "DEATH... IN BLACK AND WHITE!"

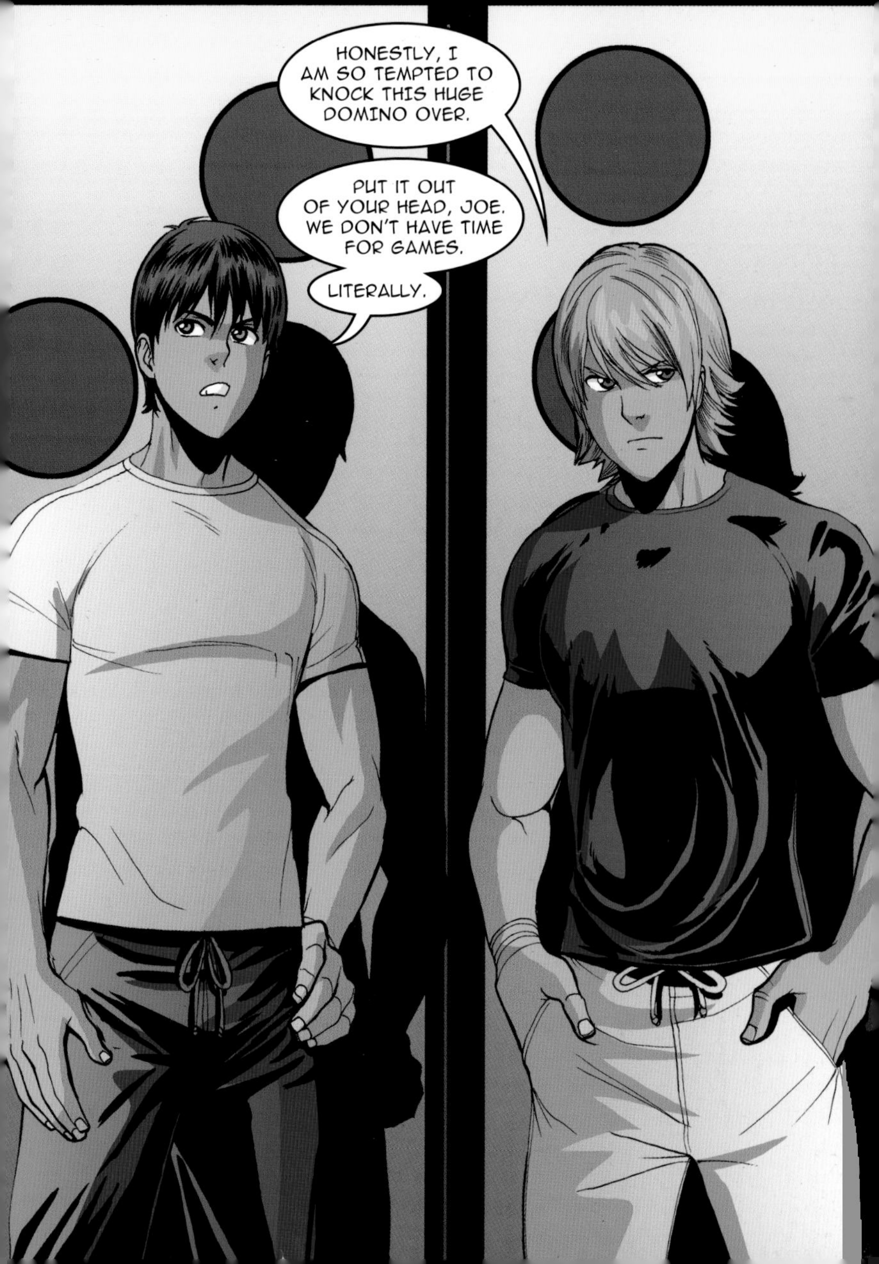
HONESTLY, I AM SO TEMPTED TO KNOCK THIS HUGE DOMINO OVER.
PUT IT OUT OF YOUR HEAD, JOE. WE DON'T HAVE TIME FOR GAMES.
LITERALLY.

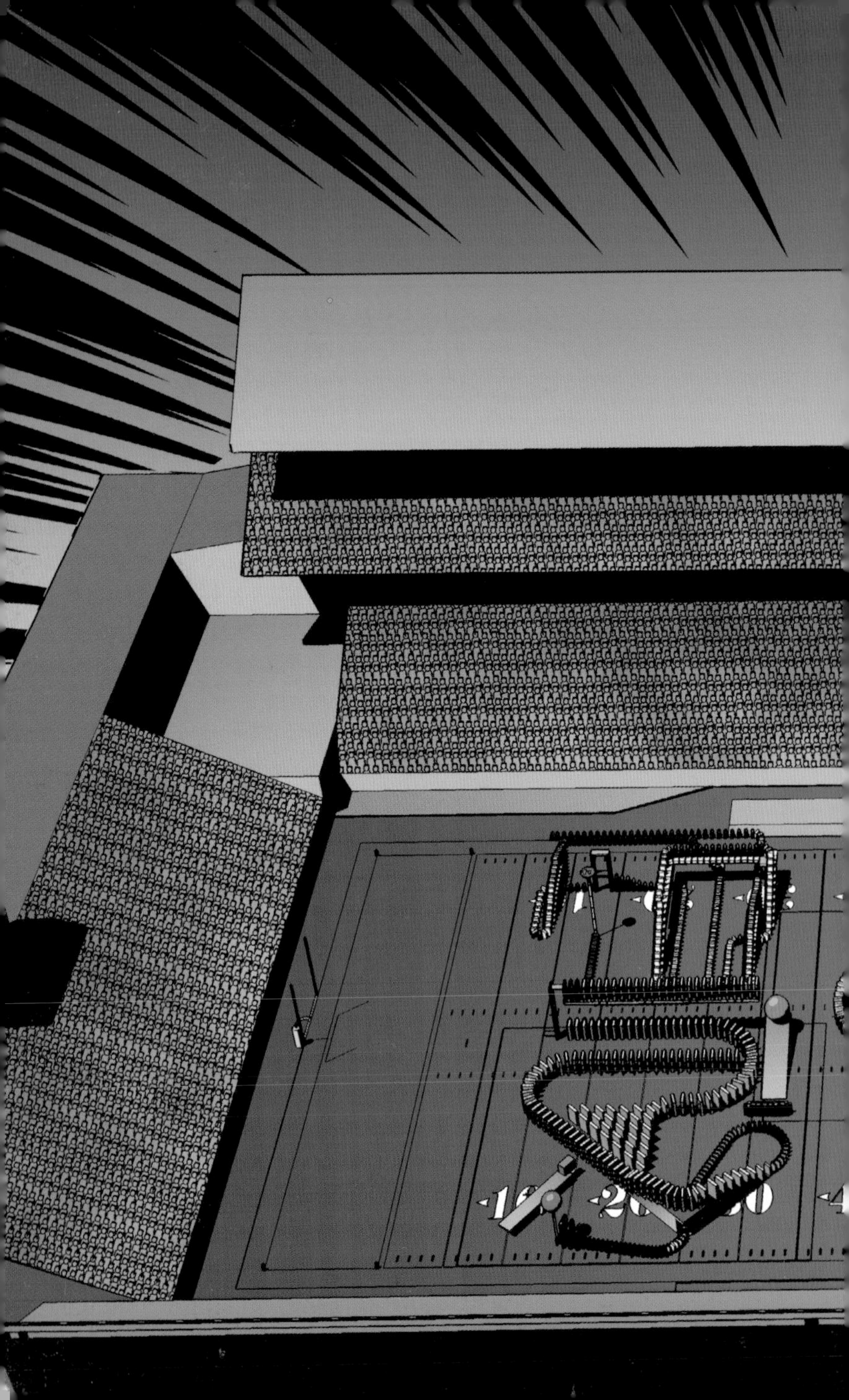

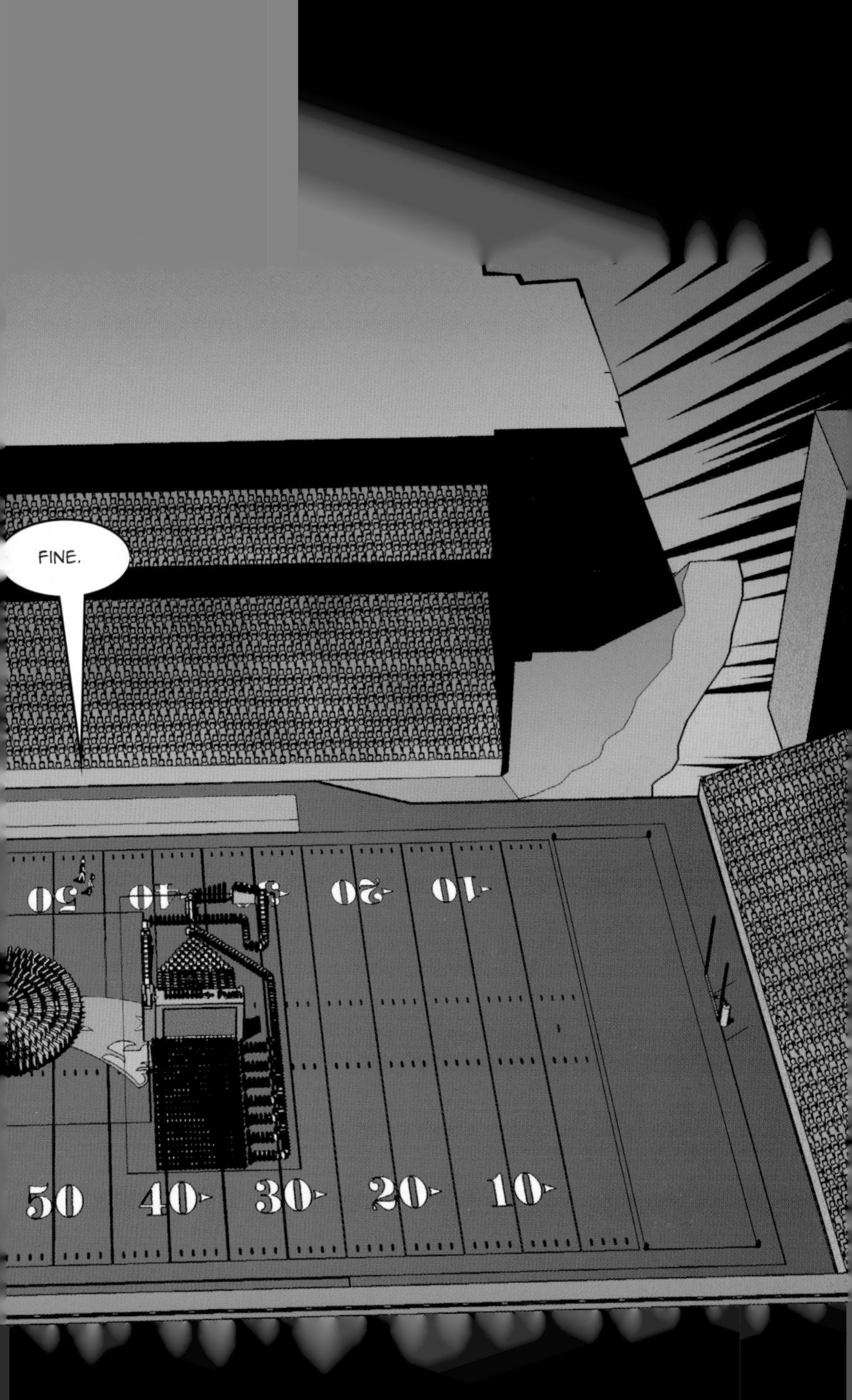
FINE.

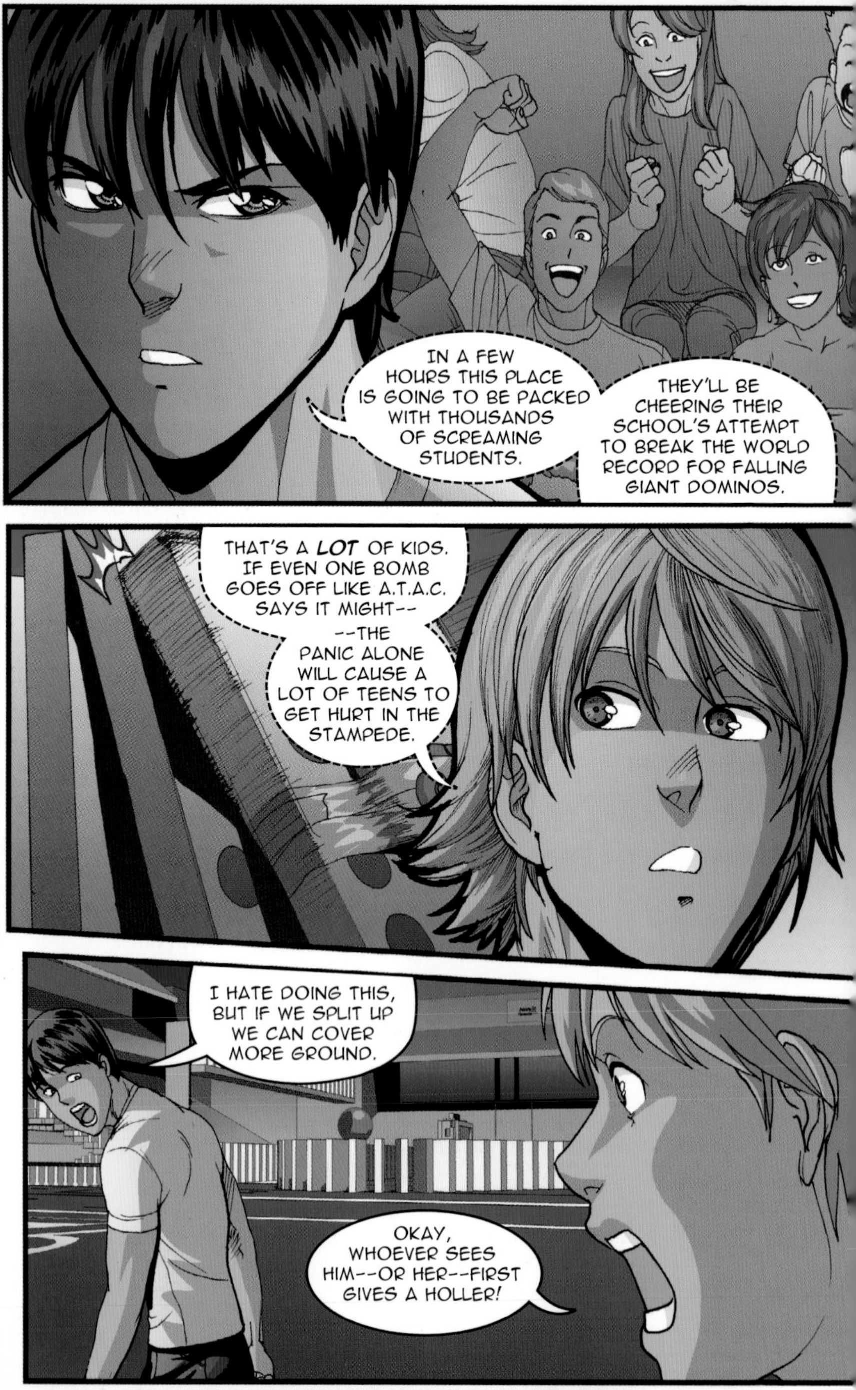
IN A FEW HOURS THIS PLACE IS GOING TO BE PACKED WITH THOUSANDS OF SCREAMING STUDENTS.
THEY'LL BE CHEERING THEIR SCHOOL'S ATTEMPT TO BREAK THE WORLD RECORD FOR FALLING GIANT DOMINOS.
THAT'S A LOT OF KIDS. IF EVEN ONE BOMB GOES OFF LIKE A.T.A.C. SAYS IT MIGHT--
--THE PANIC ALONE WILL CAUSE A LOT OF TEENS TO GET HURT IN THE STAMPEDE.
I HATE DOING THIS, BUT IF WE SPLIT UP WE CAN COVER MORE GROUND.
OKAY, WHOEVER SEES HIM--OR HER--FIRST GIVES A HOLLER!

DON'T MISS THE HARDY BOYS GRAPHIC NOVEL #20– "DEADLY STRATEGY"

WATCH OUT FOR PAPERCUTZ™

There's so much exciting stuff going on at Papercutz right now that my head's spinning! Hi, again, it's me – Jim (Head-Spinnin') Salicrup, your befuddled Editor-in-Chief and world's oldest A.T.A.C. agent!

But before we get to all that, let's take a moment to thank our hard-working HARDY BOYS creative crew! Scott Lobdell, who as we all know, has written each and every one of the nineteen HARDY BOYS graphic novels never fails to find new and exhilarating ways to keep getting Frank and Joe in trouble! And the Boys have never looked more dynamic thanks to the comics artistry of Paulo H! Of course, we must never forget the valuable contributions of letterer Mark Lerer and colorist Laurie E. Smith who add the vital and necessary finishing touches. In fact, everyone on the HB creative team is so darn good it's easy to take them all for granted.

And wait till you see HARDY BOYS Graphic Novel #20 "Deadly Strategy"! In an all-new adventure that involves the mysterious Ocean of Osyria jewels—those jewels are like the Castafiore Emerald or the Pink Panther Diamond!—you'll be seeing the return of many familiar faces—both friends, and mostly foes-- from previous HB adventures! Whatever you do don't miss HB #20— it's the big one!

As for what's going on at Papercutz, just check out some of the new releases out now…

Girl Detective NANCY DREW is up to her pretty neck with an all-new HIGH SCHOOL MUSICAL MYSTERY, in which she meets for the very first time The Dana Girls, the sister sleuths also created by Carolyn Keene! It's all in graphic novels #20 and 21.

Speaking of the Ocean of Osyria and other famous jewels, you don't want to miss CLASSICS ILLUSTRATED DELUXE #5 "Treasure Island" by Robert Louis Stevenson! It's the original pirates and buried treasure story, brilliantly adapted by David Chauvel and Fred Simon. Check out the preview pages for a peek at the stunning artwork! And don't forget CID #4 "The Adventures of Tom Sawyer" by Mark Twain— seeing Tom and Huck in action is like seeing the Hardy Boys go back in time.

And since mere words can't possibly describe the artistry in BIONICLE Graphic Novel #8 "Legends of Bara Magna," we're also including a few preview pages of the great work by Greg Farshtey and Christian Zanier as well!

And if you happen to see a copy of TALES FROM THE CRYPT Graphic Novel #8 "Diary of a Stinky Dead Kid"—grab it! It's been selling out so fast, that we simply can't print the books fast enough! The third printing is almost sold out…!

Well, we're out of room, so be sure to check out www.papercutz. com and the Papercutz Blog for more news. Till next time, be sure to straighten up, and fly rite!

Thanks,

Jim

Special Preview of BIONICLE #8
"Legends of Bara Magna"

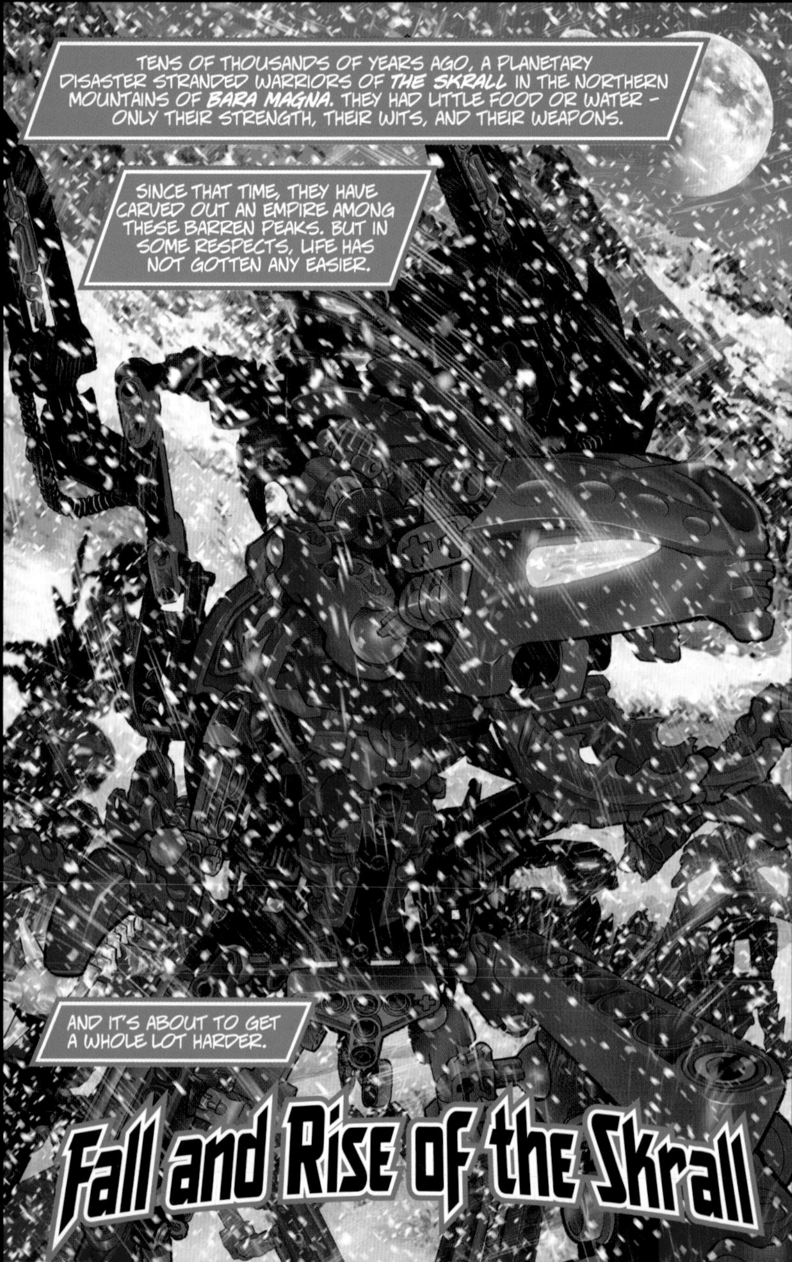
TENS OF THOUSANDS OF YEARS AGO, A PLANETARY DISASTER STRANDED WARRIORS OF THE SKRALL IN THE NORTHERN MOUNTAINS OF BARA MAGNA. THEY HAD LITTLE FOOD OR WATER - ONLY THEIR STRENGTH, THEIR WITS, AND THEIR WEAPONS.
SINCE THAT TIME, THEY HAVE CARVED OUT AN EMPIRE AMONG THESE BARREN PEAKS. BUT IN SOME RESPECTS, LIFE HAS NOT GOTTEN ANY EASIER.
AND IT'S ABOUT TO GET A WHOLE LOT HARDER.
Fall and Rise of the Skrall

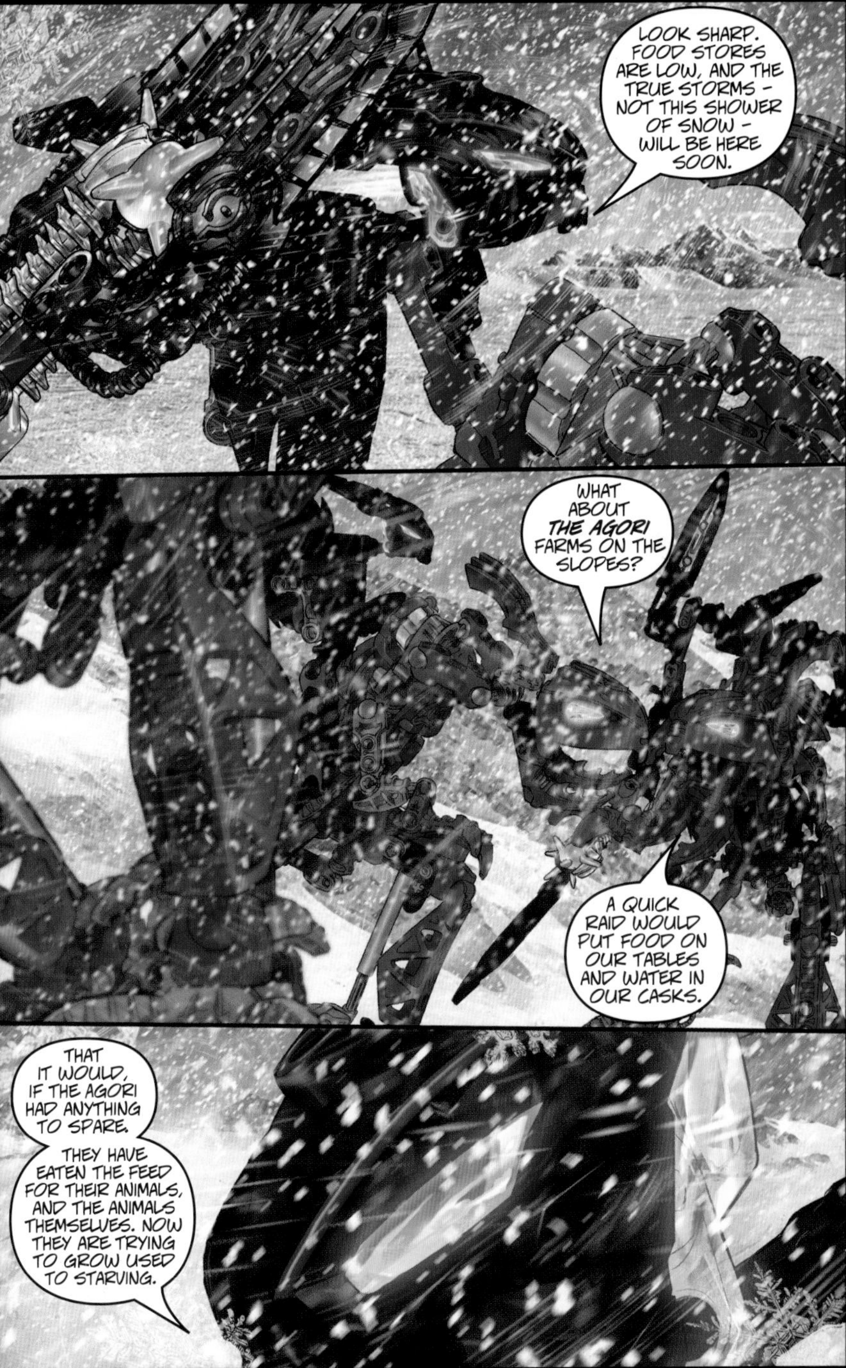
LOOK SHARP. FOOD STORES ARE LOW, AND THE TRUE STORMS - NOT THIS SHOWER OF SNOW - WILL BE HERE SOON.
WHAT ABOUT THE AGORI FARMS ON THE SLOPES?
A QUICK RAID WOULD PUT FOOD ON OUR TABLES AND WATER IN OUR CASKS.
THAT IT WOULD, IF THE AGORI HAD ANYTHING TO SPARE.
THEY HAVE EATEN THE FEED FOR THEIR ANIMALS, AND THE ANIMALS THEMSELVES. NOW THEY ARE TRYING TO GROW USED TO STARVING.

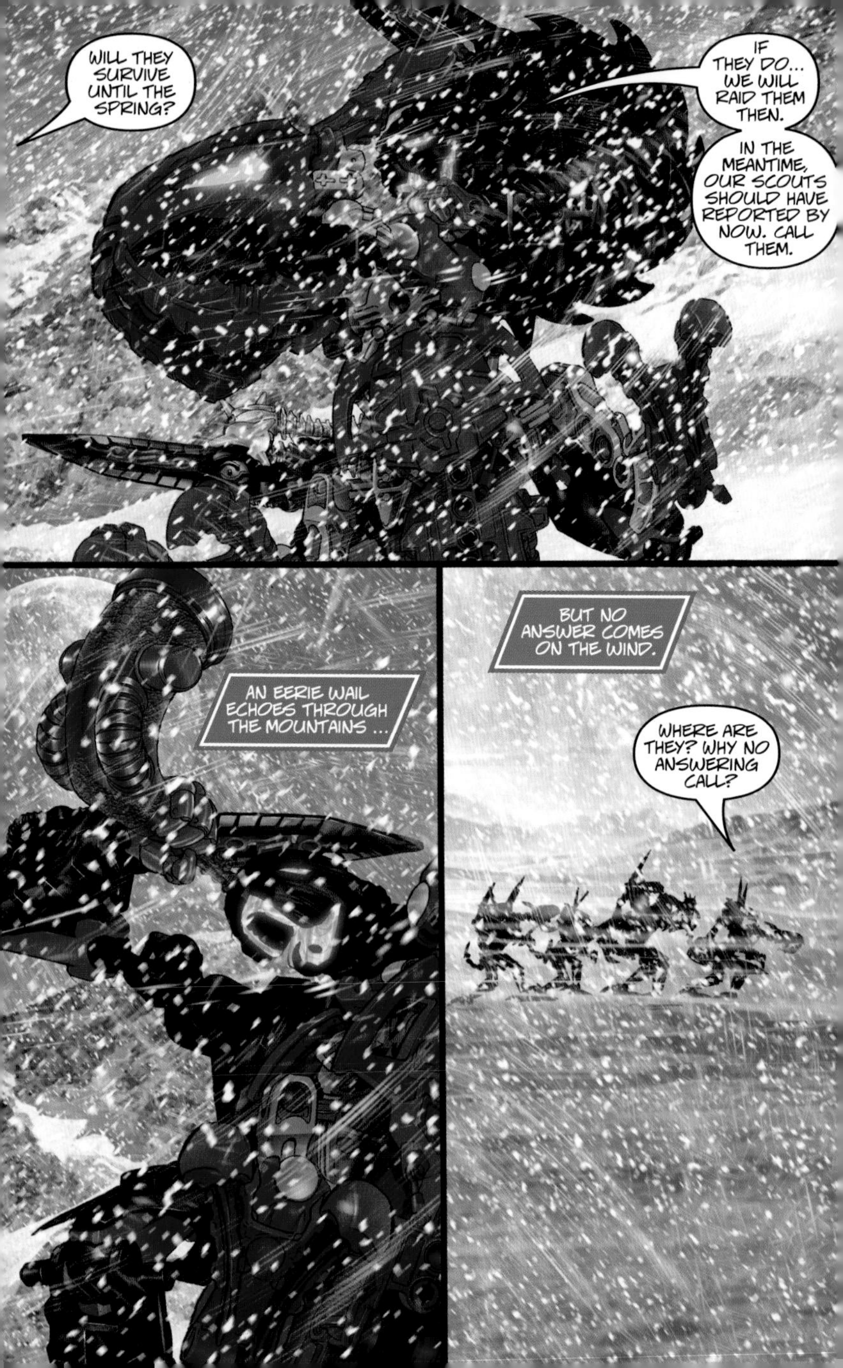
WILL THEY SURVIVE UNTIL THE SPRING?
IF THEY DO... WE WILL RAID THEM THEN.
IN THE MEANTIME, OUR SCOUTS SHOULD HAVE REPORTED BY NOW. CALL THEM.
AN EERIE WAIL ECHOES THROUGH THE MOUNTAINS ...
BUT NO ANSWER COMES ON THE WIND.
WHERE ARE THEY? WHY NO ANSWERING CALL?

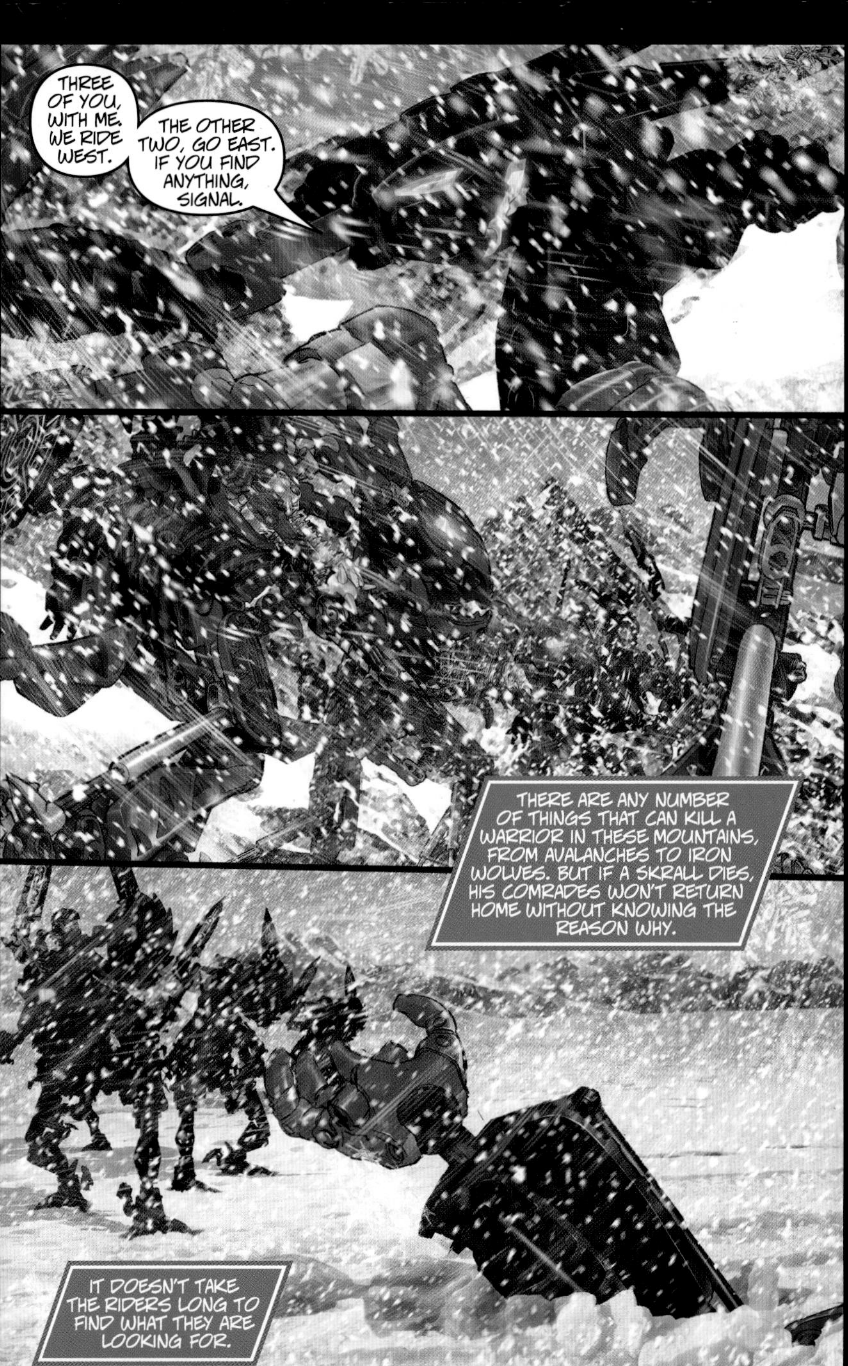
THREE OF YOU, WITH ME. WE RIDE WEST.
THE OTHER TWO, GO EAST. IF YOU FIND ANYTHING, SIGNAL.
THERE ARE ANY NUMBER OF THINGS THAT CAN KILL A WARRIOR IN THESE MOUNTAINS, FROM AVALANCHES TO IRON WOLVES. BUT IF A SKRALL DIES, HIS COMRADES WON'T RETURN HOME WITHOUT KNOWING THE REASON WHY.
IT DOESN'T TAKE THE RIDERS LONG TO FIND WHAT THEY ARE LOOKING FOR.

DON'T MISS BIONICLE GRAPHIC NOVEL #8
"LEGENDS OF BARA MAGNA"

Recover Royal Treasure on the Rails in Europe in

THE HARDY BOYS®
TREASURE ON THE TRACKS

NEARLY A CENTURY AGO, the Russian Royal Family attempted to flee from Russia with their treasure to avoid the impending Revolution, planning to return the following year by train. But the family disappeared, and no one can account for the missing Romanov treasure—until now. Journey on the Royal Express to track down the lost clues and secrets of the Royal Romanov Family in the great cities of Europe!

Order online at www.HerInteractive.com or call 1-800-461-8787. Also in stores!

SPECIAL PREVIEW OF CLASSICS ILLUSTRATED DELUXE #5 "TREASURE ISLAND"...

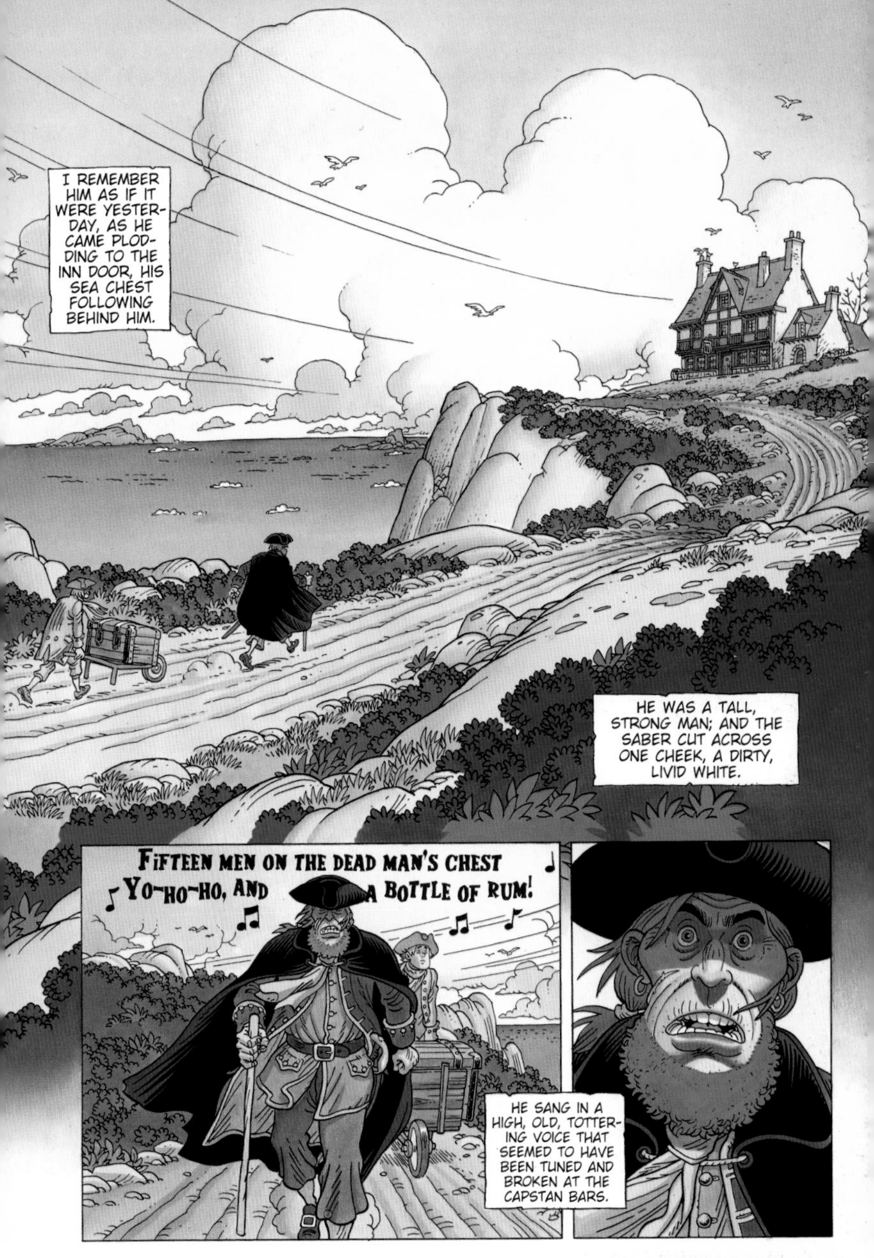
I REMEMBER HIM AS IF IT WERE YESTERDAY, AS HE CAME PLODDING TO THE INN DOOR, HIS SEA CHEST FOLLOWING BEHIND HIM.
HE WAS A TALL, STRONG MAN; AND THE SABER CUT ACROSS ONE CHEEK, A DIRTY, LIVID WHITE.
FIFTEEN MEN ON THE DEAD MAN'S CHEST
YO-HO-HO, AND A BOTTLE OF RUM!
HE SANG IN A HIGH, OLD, TOTTERING VOICE THAT SEEMED TO HAVE BEEN TUNED AND BROKEN AT THE CAPSTAN BARS.

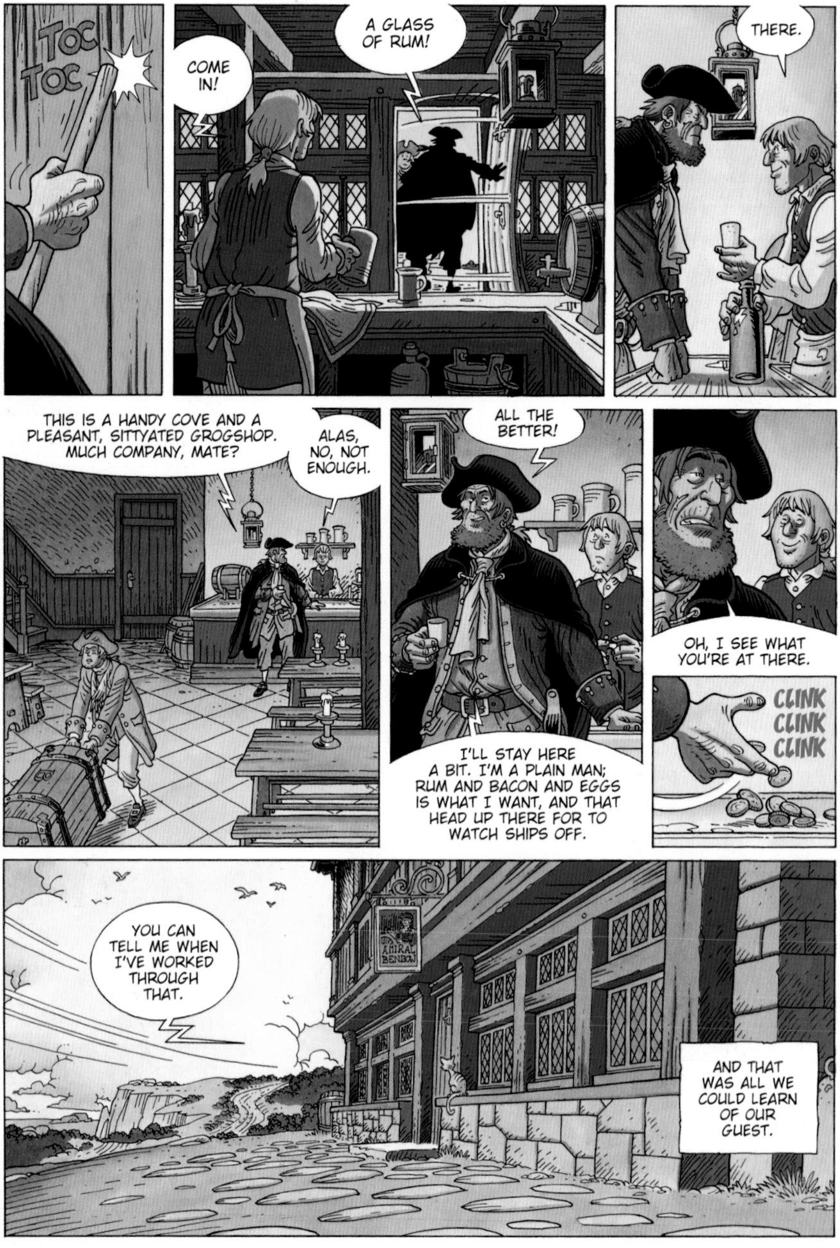
TOC
TOC
COME IN!
A GLASS OF RUM!
THERE.
THIS IS A HANDY COVE AND A PLEASANT, SITTYATED GROGSHOP. MUCH COMPANY, MATE?
ALAS, NO, NOT ENOUGH.
ALL THE BETTER!
I'LL STAY HERE A BIT. I'M A PLAIN MAN; RUM AND BACON AND EGGS IS WHAT I WANT, AND THAT HEAD UP THERE FOR TO WATCH SHIPS OFF.
OH, I SEE WHAT YOU'RE AT THERE.
CLINK
CLINK
CLINK
AMIRAL BENBOW
YOU CAN TELL ME WHEN I'VE WORKED THROUGH THAT.
AND THAT WAS ALL WE COULD LEARN OF OUR GUEST.

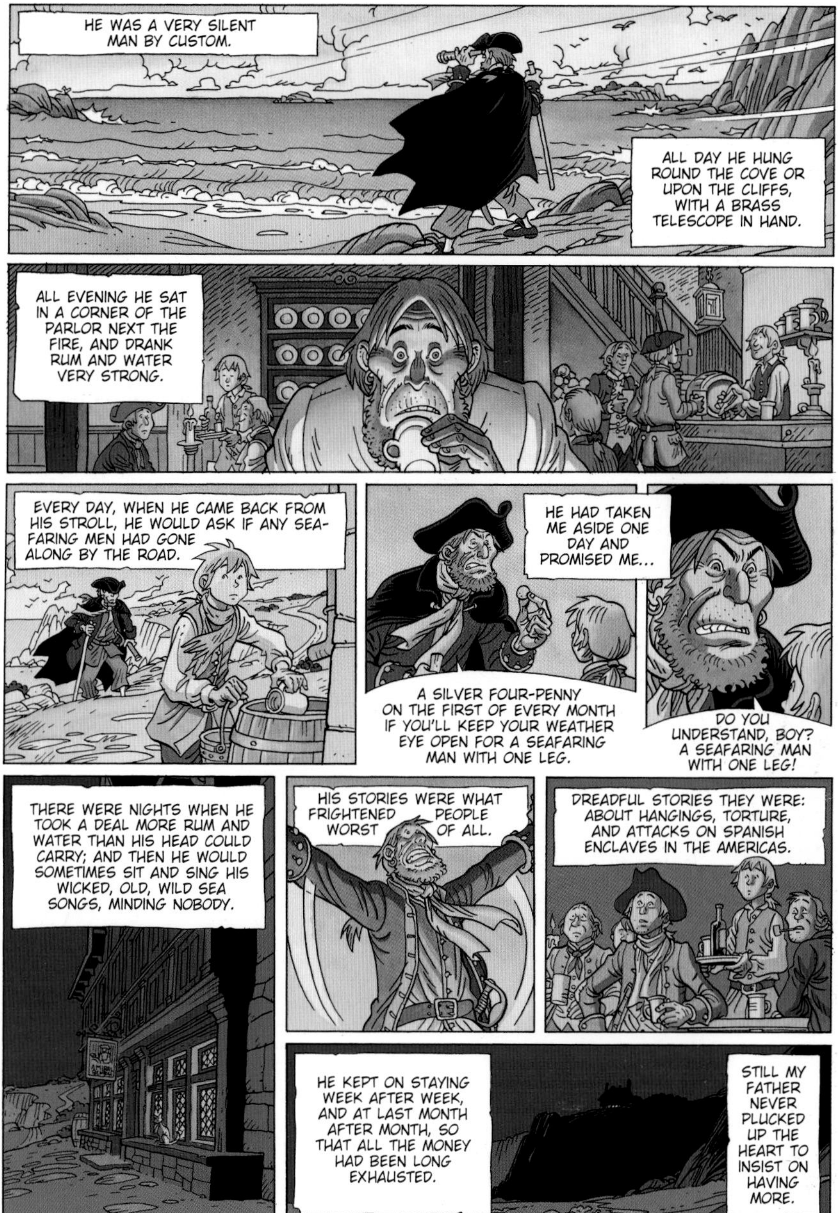
HE WAS A VERY SILENT MAN BY CUSTOM.
ALL DAY HE HUNG ROUND THE COVE OR UPON THE CLIFFS, WITH A BRASS TELESCOPE IN HAND.
ALL EVENING HE SAT IN A CORNER OF THE PARLOR NEXT THE FIRE, AND DRANK RUM AND WATER VERY STRONG.
EVERY DAY, WHEN HE CAME BACK FROM HIS STROLL, HE WOULD ASK IF ANY SEA-FARING MEN HAD GONE ALONG BY THE ROAD.
HE HAD TAKEN ME ASIDE ONE DAY AND PROMISED ME...
A SILVER FOUR-PENNY ON THE FIRST OF EVERY MONTH IF YOU'LL KEEP YOUR WEATHER EYE OPEN FOR A SEAFARING MAN WITH ONE LEG.
DO YOU UNDERSTAND, BOY? A SEAFARING MAN WITH ONE LEG!
THERE WERE NIGHTS WHEN HE TOOK A DEAL MORE RUM AND WATER THAN HIS HEAD COULD CARRY; AND THEN HE WOULD SOMETIMES SIT AND SING HIS WICKED, OLD, WILD SEA SONGS, MINDING NOBODY.
HIS STORIES WERE WHAT FRIGHTENED PEOPLE WORST OF ALL.
DREADFUL STORIES THEY WERE: ABOUT HANGINGS, TORTURE, AND ATTACKS ON SPANISH ENCLAVES IN THE AMERICAS.
HE KEPT ON STAYING WEEK AFTER WEEK, AND AT LAST MONTH AFTER MONTH, SO THAT ALL THE MONEY HAD BEEN LONG EXHAUSTED.
STILL MY FATHER NEVER PLUCKED UP THE HEART TO INSIST ON HAVING MORE.

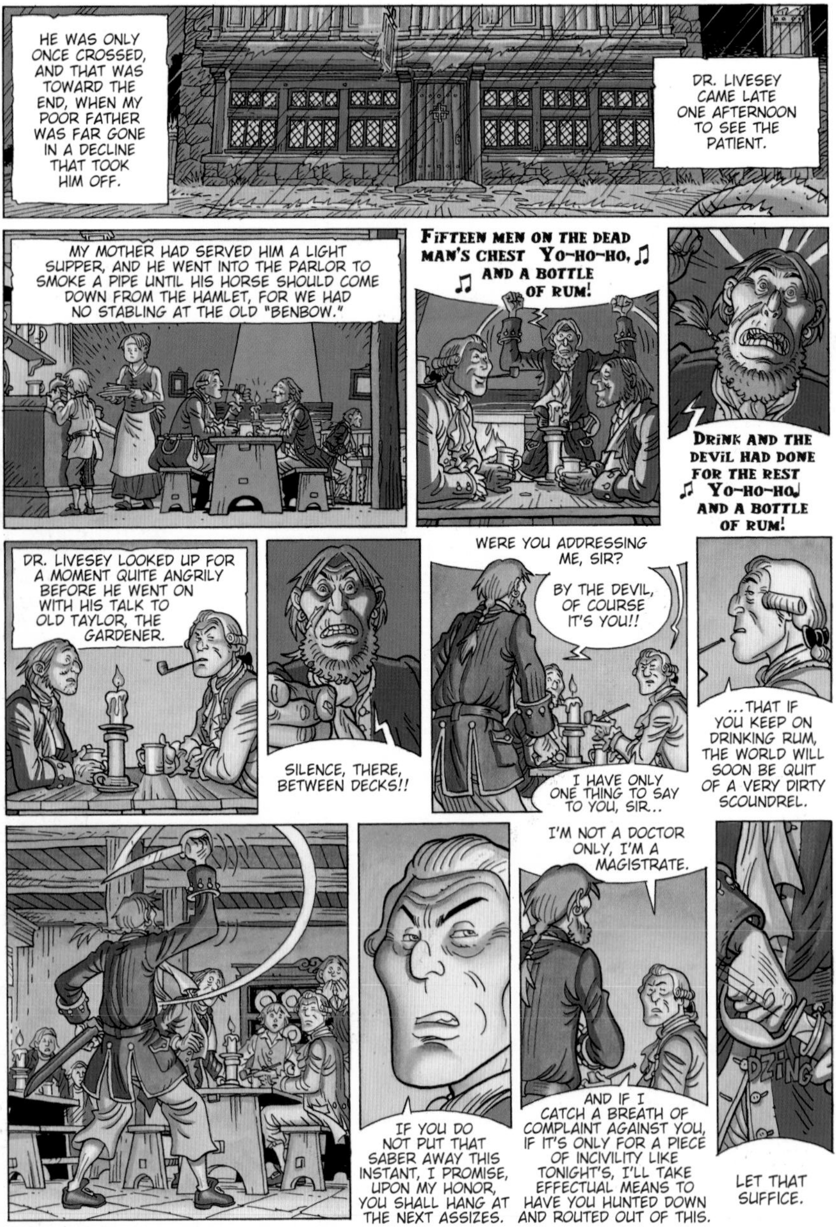
HE WAS ONLY ONCE CROSSED, AND THAT WAS TOWARD THE END, WHEN MY POOR FATHER WAS FAR GONE IN A DECLINE THAT TOOK HIM OFF.
DR. LIVESEY CAME LATE ONE AFTERNOON TO SEE THE PATIENT.
MY MOTHER HAD SERVED HIM A LIGHT SUPPER, AND HE WENT INTO THE PARLOR TO SMOKE A PIPE UNTIL HIS HORSE SHOULD COME DOWN FROM THE HAMLET, FOR WE HAD NO STABLING AT THE OLD "BENBOW."
FIFTEEN MEN ON THE DEAD MAN'S CHEST YO-HO-HO, AND A BOTTLE OF RUM!
DRINK AND THE DEVIL HAD DONE FOR THE REST YO-HO-HO AND A BOTTLE OF RUM!
DR. LIVESEY LOOKED UP FOR A MOMENT QUITE ANGRILY BEFORE HE WENT ON WITH HIS TALK TO OLD TAYLOR, THE GARDENER.
SILENCE, THERE, BETWEEN DECKS!!
WERE YOU ADDRESSING ME, SIR?
BY THE DEVIL, OF COURSE IT'S YOU!!
I HAVE ONLY ONE THING TO SAY TO YOU, SIR...
...THAT IF YOU KEEP ON DRINKING RUM, THE WORLD WILL SOON BE QUIT OF A VERY DIRTY SCOUNDREL.
IF YOU DO NOT PUT THAT SABER AWAY THIS INSTANT, I PROMISE, UPON MY HONOR, YOU SHALL HANG AT THE NEXT ASSIZES.
I'M NOT A DOCTOR ONLY, I'M A MAGISTRATE.
AND IF I CATCH A BREATH OF COMPLAINT AGAINST YOU, IF IT'S ONLY FOR A PIECE OF INCIVILITY LIKE TONIGHT'S, I'LL TAKE EFFECTUAL MEANS TO HAVE YOU HUNTED DOWN AND ROUTED OUT OF THIS.
DZING
LET THAT SUFFICE.

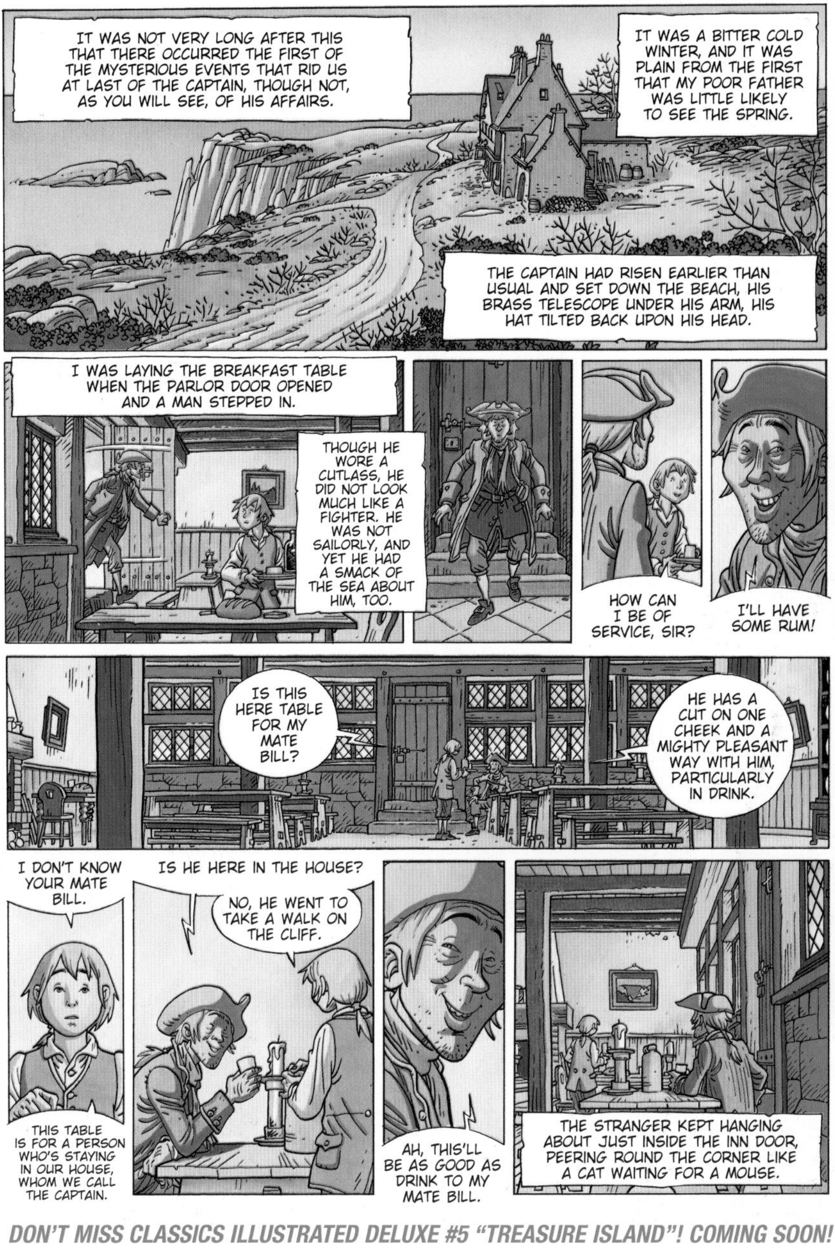
IT WAS NOT VERY LONG AFTER THIS THAT THERE OCCURRED THE FIRST OF THE MYSTERIOUS EVENTS THAT RID US AT LAST OF THE CAPTAIN, THOUGH NOT, AS YOU WILL SEE, OF HIS AFFAIRS.
IT WAS A BITTER COLD WINTER, AND IT WAS PLAIN FROM THE FIRST THAT MY POOR FATHER WAS LITTLE LIKELY TO SEE THE SPRING.
THE CAPTAIN HAD RISEN EARLIER THAN USUAL AND SET DOWN THE BEACH, HIS BRASS TELESCOPE UNDER HIS ARM, HIS HAT TILTED BACK UPON HIS HEAD.
I WAS LAYING THE BREAKFAST TABLE WHEN THE PARLOR DOOR OPENED AND A MAN STEPPED IN.
THOUGH HE WORE A CUTLASS, HE DID NOT LOOK MUCH LIKE A FIGHTER. HE WAS NOT SAILORLY, AND YET HE HAD A SMACK OF THE SEA ABOUT HIM, TOO.
HOW CAN I BE OF SERVICE, SIR?
I'LL HAVE SOME RUM!
IS THIS HERE TABLE FOR MY MATE BILL?
HE HAS A CUT ON ONE CHEEK AND A MIGHTY PLEASANT WAY WITH HIM, PARTICULARLY IN DRINK.
I DON'T KNOW YOUR MATE BILL.
THIS TABLE IS FOR A PERSON WHO'S STAYING IN OUR HOUSE, WHOM WE CALL THE CAPTAIN.
IS HE HERE IN THE HOUSE?
NO, HE WENT TO TAKE A WALK ON THE CLIFF.
AH, THIS'LL BE AS GOOD AS DRINK TO MY MATE BILL.
THE STRANGER KEPT HANGING ABOUT JUST INSIDE THE INN DOOR, PEERING ROUND THE CORNER LIKE A CAT WAITING FOR A MOUSE.

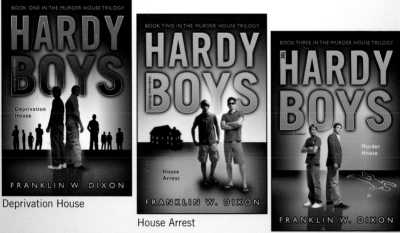